THIEF OF
MAGIC

SHADOWED MINDS BOOK 1

BREE MOORE

INNATE INK
PUBLISHING

Cover design by Moorbooks Design

Ebook ISBN-13: 978-1-956668-04-9

Paperback ISBN-13: 978-1-956668-03-2

Published by Innate Ink Publishing

Salt Lake City, UT 84119

www.authorbreemoore.com

CHAPTER 1

No one would notice when Lee slipped out of this world. She curled her fingers and took a breath of cool night air, the smell of rain on asphalt filling her senses. Pedestrians dodged around the edges of the bus stop shelter she stood beneath, walking with umbrellas held upright and hunched shoulders to guard against the drizzle.

10:46 p.m.

Lee tucked the phone into her pocket and hummed softly to calm herself. Tonight had to go off without a hitch. She didn't have any reason to believe it would go wrong, except for the anxiety building in her chest.

A bus hissed to a stop on the glistening street, and the people who waited under the bus shelter filed up the steps. Lee stayed behind, and the driver stared at her. She waved him on.

As the bus pulled away, tingling started in Lee's fingers and toes. The Liminal Realm had closed in on the now-quiet bus stop, calling her to step through the curtain of space and time and transport herself somewhere else, anywhere else.

Lee eased into it. Her skin itched, turning ashen, and changed to intangible shadow. A red aura glowed around her hands. The traffic light reflections on the road blurred.

She took a single step forward. Earth's fabric of time and space tugged at her skin, sending pins and needles across it, but she took another step and the sensation lessened. Speed was of the essence tonight. Fortunately, there were no crowds or glaring daylight to thicken the air and make Liminal travel more difficult, and she only needed to travel a couple of blocks.

Lee stepped between the cars that crawled on the road at a sluggish pace. She surpassed the speed of traffic in the other realm as she jogged down the wet sidewalk. Nothing else moved around her, the sounds like muffled static. She rounded the block and headed north until she stepped onto the grave-yard-like campus for St. Louis University.

In an alternative reality, one where she wasn't Liminal, but a normal young woman with normal aspirations and interests, she'd be studying art there right now. Studying, maybe even partying, finding a guy to settle down with, selling her art...

But that reality didn't exist. It never would. Lee shoved the sadness away and let the beautiful thoughts exit her mind the way they had come. She had already mourned that life. Now she would settle for a chance to have a future at all. Any future.

In the Liminal Realm, she walked past a campus security guard without pause. The man might have felt a breeze, or heard a single footstep, but by the time he turned around, Lee would be long gone.

Being essentially invisible came in handy as a thief.

She walked the paths between the tall brick buildings with

confidence and came to a stop in front of her destination.

The Samuel Cupples' Mansion. A brick monstrosity with Romanesque architecture dating back over a hundred years. To anyone else, it would look like a museum, dark after hours, nothing remarkable about the exterior. But to Lee, a dozen pinpoints of silver light shone out from the inner walls. One of them was her mark, the brightest, shining from beneath a window on the second floor.

Lee walked up to the ornate wooden door on the front porch. Safe in the dark alcove, she shook her hands and felt intuitively for the access point back to Earth's realm. For this next part, she had to be physical. She wasn't a ghost that could go through doors and walls, and there weren't any ley points inside the house.

Stepping out of the Liminal Realm made her break out in a light sweat, and her hands trembled. Lee adjusted the slouchy beanie on her head, tugged on her jacket, and pulled a worn black leather case from her pocket. She traced the 'S' scratched sloppily into the leather surface, then flipped the case open. The metal lock picks gleamed back at her.

"You should wear a less recognizable hat. What if someone noticed you loitering around here? It's the first thing they'd see."

Lee jumped. Risa walked up the steps behind her, dressed like she was ready for a steampunk convention, down to the goggles on her head.

Lee snorted, trying to cover up how startled she'd been. "You're one to talk."

"Hey, eccentric is my brand. People don't remember what I'm doing when they see me. There's a fine line between an invisible style like mine and a blaring alarm like that hat."

Lee fingered the pick in her hand, the anxiety she felt

earlier creeping back. "You're not supposed to be here."

"Neither are you. Look, I'll cut straight to it. Sam said you were doing something tonight and you might need help."

"Of course he did." Lee rubbed a hand on her cargo pants. Sam, the crew's tech guy, had tracked her movements to an obsessive point lately. Had Silas put him up to it? Or did he have his own reasons for tracking her?

Risa ignored Lee and kept talking. "He didn't have many details, but he found your searches for this place on the computer and guessed this was where you were headed when you snuck out after dinner. What kind of trouble are you getting yourself into, kid?"

Lee's eyes narrowed. She hadn't been a kid for quite a few years now, but the nickname stuck. "I don't need help."

"Well, I'm here. And judging by the aura of this house, you're going to need me. Just because you're a Traveler doesn't mean you can deal with ghosts." Risa crossed her arms and adopted a stubborn expression that Lee knew meant she wasn't budging.

Risa raised her eyebrows. "You going to pick that lock or not?"

Lee turned to the lock and inserted the first pick. She was stuck with the tag-along, it seemed.

With some maneuvering, the lock clicked open. The museum had modernized the locks. What they hadn't done was maintain a reliable security system. Something about paranormal activity setting it off and causing too many false alarms. So they had the regular bolts and locks in place, and kept some of the valuable items in special alarmed cases, but otherwise it was a laughably easy target. And Lee knew for a fact that the item she sought wasn't in any safe. She would stroll in and carry it out without anyone raising a fuss.

Lee slipped through the door and Risa followed. The door clicked shut, and Lee pocketed the leather pick case. Dim light from outside illuminated a large painting in a frame. The subject was a woman with pale clothes and a pale face, dark hair barely visible above her head. Her beakish, disapproving look seemed to be aimed specifically at the two thieves standing in her hallway.

The nape of Lee's neck prickled. She wasn't here to steal a painting. She pivoted away from the painting and speed-walked down the hall. More than ever, she wanted to get the item and get out of that creepy place.

"Not so fast. We don't want to disturb the spirits of the house," Risa stage-whispered from behind. Just like a Speaker to be worried about disturbing the dead with too much noise.

"The spirits don't have to worry about getting caught," Lee shot back. "We don't have a Screener to cover our signature. And there aren't any ley lines here, so if someone catches us, we'll have to make it out on foot or risk getting trapped."

Lee's spine crawled with a bug-like sensation. Lee wasn't supposed to be on this job, and the longer they took, the more suspicious their crew leader would get. Silas didn't like it when anyone did their own jobs. According to him, it took money from the crew and risked valuable resources. But this job was worth every risk. After this, she wouldn't need the crew anymore.

"You can't go Liminal here?" Risa's voice wobbled.

"I can enter the Liminal realm. That doesn't have much to do with ley lines. But if a ley line doesn't exist, I can't travel on it."

"Makes sense," Risa said.

Lee passed the first set of rooms, headed for the stairs at

the center of the house. Going Liminal would be harder if any security showed up. Having other people around made the Liminal realm more distant and difficult to reach. If only she had a ley point she could use to jump to safety! Walking the Liminal realm was like having a secret passage to follow. Jumping ley lines was like having a magical elevator that could get her almost anywhere.

But this house had no ley line. She'd just have to not stick around long enough to get caught, like any normal burglar.

Lee glanced over her shoulder. Risa had halted at a room that might have been a kitchen once. Now, it was lined with locked glass cases filled with blueprint ceramics and other assorted dishes and cutlery.

"What about these items? I can't believe there's nothing in here," Risa said.

"Nothing we want. Come on." Lee put her hands in her pockets.

The ornate rugs padded their steps as the room opened up. A banister arched grandly above them. Lee took the stairs two at a time. No time to stop and admire the architecture.

"Lee!"

She ignored Risa's hissed whisper, passing another painting of an austere woman with pale, curled hair. What was with all the cranky women? Why not draw someone with a smile for once?

Lee paused, staring into the dark first floor. The silence had closed in, and she felt watched, like she did in every church she had ever entered. Risa caught up to her, contraptions on her waist clinking. She held one in her hand, a brass and glass compass-like instrument that whirred when she held it up.

"Lee, what do you know about this house?"

Lee shrugged. "The tour guide said the owner had a couple of wives—one died young, and their child. He had another wife and kids that all lived. He hated dancing, apparently." But none of that was relevant to their job.

Risa turned, brow creasing as she stared at the arms of her instrument. "I'm picking up a strong spirit presence," she muttered.

"Aren't you supposed to talk to them? Calm them and such?" Lee turned a corner and a doorway opened into a sitting room. She wanted a bedroom.

Risa hurried to catch up with Lee. "Did you bring an offering?" she hissed.

"Why would I do that?" Lee asked, walking further down the hall. She poked her head into the next room. A four-poster bed stood sentinel against the left wall.

"You knew the house was haunted, and you didn't bring anything to appease the ghosts? Damn, kid. You're lucky I'm here." Risa pulled a palm-sized glass disc out of her pocket and set it on the floor outside.

Lee glanced at it. "What's that?"

"A bauble. Ghosts love them. Did you find it yet?" Risa asked.

Lee scanned the room, passing over a glass case holding an angelic sculpture and a broad wooden chest until she found the dresser. She stepped into the room.

"This looks like the place," Lee said.

"I do not have a good feeling about this," Risa muttered, exchanging the first instrument for a second one with a handle and a protruding metal end. She waved it over her head, the metal arm making a low thrumming sound.

Lee breathed deeply, putting her fingers against her temples. She felt for the tingling curtain of the Liminal realm, leaving Risa frozen in the Earth realm. A silver light shot out from beneath the dresser, glowing through its wooden surface. Lee looked at Risa and saw her mouth open mid-word, still holding that instrument. Her hand reached slowly toward Lee, as if to stop her.

Lee pulled herself back to Earth and fell to her knees, groping beneath the dresser.

"—of here!" Risa hissed.

Lee cursed. She scrabbled against the wooden surface, searching for a panel, a false bottom. "Just...a moment."

She gripped the lip that caught her fingers and shoved in two directions. It moved on the second, thrusting to the right. An item clunked to the floor, and Lee snatched it up. Now that she had the bracelet, she had all the luck she could need. The bracelet was a Way Mary, and it drew luck from the wearer's surroundings, storing it to be used later. According to Lee's intel, each bead could be filled and used one time. An item like that was rare and valuable. Valuable enough to be sold in exchange for information that would lead Lee to the cure for the magic that ate at her like cancer.

Risa tapped her shoulder, startling her.

"What?" Lee snapped, jamming the Way Mary into the front pocket of her jacket. Her fingers brushed a second bracelet that waited inside, a fake that would fool just about anyone at a glance. It would come in handy if Silas figured out what she'd been doing tonight.

The lights flickered on. She glanced back at Risa, whose eyes widened in fright. The woman wasn't standing anywhere near the light switch.

Lee stood, glancing around the room. The lights flickered again, turning off, then on, then off. Lee didn't see anything, but the hair on her arms rose and a screech sounded from a radiator in the corner, long and low. It shouldn't have been running, but it hissed and rattled like it was possessed.

"I don't think it likes your offering," Lee said. She grabbed Risa's arm, shoving the item in her pocket with her other hand. "That light will draw attention. Let's go."

Risa stumbled after her, gabbling some Latin words. The room went dark as they left, and ahead of them another set of lamps started to strobe.

"Banish it, or whatever you do!" Lee shouted, ducking as several books flew up from a shelf on the first floor. A hailstorm of literature.

"Spirit, hear me!" Risa called, skidding to a halt. Lee stood with her, panting. Risa raised her arms, and her hair rose as if filled with static. The books fell to the floor.

"Do you object to our presence or to our theft?" Risa swayed in place, eyes shut tight.

Nothing moved, but the lights stopped flickering.

"What is it saying?" Lee asked, speaking from the corner of her mouth. Something was out there, whatever she believed.

"Do you mean us harm?" Risa asked. The lights flipped off, plunging them into darkness again.

"Was that a yes or a no?" Lee asked.

"The spirit is giving us obscured passage from the house. It means us well," Risa replied.

"Then why all the—" Lee was cut off by a thudding sound downstairs, and then the front door of the mansion slammed open. Flashlights sliced through the darkness of the hall.

A bold female voice cracked like a whip through the room. "Stop right there!"

Shit.

CHAPTER 2

Flashlights sliced through the darkness of the front hall, and Lee froze on the stairs. Most likely, these were campus security. They didn't stand a chance against a Traveler and a Speaker.

"Grab my arm and don't let go," Lee murmured to Risa. She would have killed to have her ear wire in so Sam could tell her the Intention of the security guards, or whether more help was on the way, but it wouldn't do her any good to mourn it now.

Risa gripped Lee's arm, squeezing like a boa constrictor. A ley line would have enabled Lee to travel a distance in the blink of an eye and escape, but there weren't any here. Perhaps due to the conflicting energies of the ghosts? It didn't make sense. But without a ley line, the only option was Liminal travel on their own two legs. If Lee was having a bad day, she wouldn't be able to carry Risa out with her Liminally.

Lee mustered her energy, gritting her teeth as she tore through the fabric of space and time. She peeled it back layer by layer. Stepping forward was like moving through thick mud with the flashing lights and the shouting of the security guards. And she'd brought a whole extra person with her.

The familiar prickles danced over her skin like pinpoints of fire, and Lee slid her foot forward, then another. Her legs became shadow, then her waist and hands. Risa whimpered as she became immaterial. Lee's head was last to vanish, as a beam of light swept over her.

She breathed a sigh of relief as the four guards on the first floor froze, caught in Earth's sluggish time stream while Lee slid below and between the normal laws of physics. She moved achingly slow down the stairs, encumbered by Risa, who shuffled forward giving off tiny squeaks of fear. She probably felt the maelstrom between worlds whipping at her. To Lee, it was a pins and needles prickle. Shane was the only other person she'd taken into the Liminal Realm, and he'd said it felt like being clawed by a tiger.

Lee inched off the last step and moved across the floor at a crawling pace. The agents' faces blurred and smeared as they moved in a different layer of time. A fifth form moved among them. She must have missed one.

"FBI!"

Lee turned without thinking. A man in a blue FBI uniform stood about ten feet away, face shadowed by the visor of his hat, but most notably he wasn't blurred like the others. His outline was crisp, the part of his face that she could see—his chin—clearly defined. He moved toward her, then froze, staring at his hands.

"What the hell?" He muttered, proving that he was just as shocked as Lee to find himself inside the Liminal Realm with her.

Lee's heart rate pulsed, and her breath caught. Where had

the FBI come from? How had they found her? Lee's entire body trembled with effort and adrenaline. She'd never been followed into the Liminal realm before. Unless...could he be Liminal, like her?

Lee picked up her pace, straining as she hauled Risa along beside her. Sweat broke out on her brow. They still weren't moving fast enough. The agent gained on them, only a few steps away.

A glistening white being materialized between the agent and Lee. A wall of smoke shifted and changed until it settled in the shape of a man. It had to be one of Risa's ghosts.

The agent hollered and swiped at the being, distracted as it lunged and shrieked at him.

Beside Lee, Risa grinned. "Mr. Cupples is rather pleasant to talk to."

"How'd you get him on our side?"

Risa tapped her chest. "It took a moment for him to learn how to communicate with me. Hence the hullabaloo earlier. Just a misunderstanding. Let's get the hell out of here."

Lee booked it, barely moving at a full-paced walk, but pulling away from the FBI agent. She made it through the maze of frozen agents, breath hitching in her chest. She walked down the dark hall, stretching for the door hanging open ahead.

"Stop!" the agent called.

The word snagged at Lee, catching her somewhere near her navel. Her stomach flip-flopped as she pulled against the force that held her back, as if the single word somehow had power over her.

"Why aren't we moving?" Risa whispered.

Lee grunted and braced herself, exerting every effort to move towards the doorway. "I—don't—know."

She stopped, panting. Risa's hand still gripped Lee's arm, and she tapped it, getting Risa's attention. "We're going to have to break for it. I wanted to put more space between the agents and us, but only one of them knows where we went. By the time they reorient themselves, we'll be half a mile away. Split off, meet back at the house, okay?"

Risa nodded firmly, eyes widening a bit.

"Ready, one...two...three." Lee dragged herself and Risa through the curtain between realms and emerged, gasping, skin burning, back to Earth. They sprinted through the front door and leapt off the porch of the old mansion.

Risa split right. Lee veered left. Shouting echoed behind Lee, a flashlight strobed on the lawn. She turned between buildings on the university campus. Another turn. Another. She stopped pumping her arms and legs, slowing to a walk. Her heart beat thrummed through her body, but she didn't have time to panic. If she entered the Liminal realm this close to the museum without a Screener to scramble her signature, she might draw the attention of that agent who had somehow followed her into the Liminal realm. Only time would tell if the FBI had someone who could track her through the Liminal realm or if the recent incident was a fluke. For now, she had to get invisible in a more traditional way.

Lee dug into her front pocket for the Way Mary. Touching the other bracelet she had planted there, she took it out and analyzed them for a brief moment.

The fake meant to fool Silas in case she got caught was practically flawless, but it weighed slightly less and had the maker's signature stamped on one of the stone beads. She moved the real Way Mary into her jeans front pocket for safe keeping, then swiped the orange beanie off her head and took off her jacket. She rolled the clothes into a ball and shoved them into a garbage can just off the sidewalk.

She pulled her hair back into a ponytail and tucked a casual hand in her back pocket, resisting the urge to scratch her still-burning skin. She took on a confident, bouncing stride. She'd have to circle back for her clothes—she liked that hat. The FBI agent had glimpsed her face, if not gotten a full view, but she didn't have any fancier disguises with her to change that.

Her access to the Liminal realm was reduced in certain areas and stronger in others. She called areas with easy access 'Liminal zones'. They had to have a particular sort of energy about them. Abandoned buildings, certain places after dark like schools and museums and parks, things like that. It took more out of her to attempt going Liminal in wide open places where anyone could walk up at any moment, like outdoors on a university campus.

The time of the day mattered, too. She had a higher chance of success entering the Liminal realm when everything was dark and quiet. She conserved her magical energy so when situations grew extreme, she could enter the Liminal realm just about anywhere without draining herself too much.

Anxiety over being caught cut through any relief she might have felt at the successful heist. She headed for the edge of campus to avoid security. It wasn't far. She passed a few buildings, and gradually, her heart rate slowed. She jumped at every flash of light from cars on the road ahead, but the campus remained silent.

Lee crossed the busy road and entered a gas station, pretending to browse through the meal replacement bars and energy drinks. At the register, she dug through her pocket for some cash. She made a couple purchases, including a ball cap, and pulled it over her ponytail. Outside the gas station, she leaned against the wall and watched the dark buildings across the street.

There, a lone guard walked around a building near where she had stowed her stuff. He was too far away to tell if he was the agent who had gone into the Liminal Realm with her. How had that happened? Could she have accidentally pulled him in somehow? She'd always had to be touching someone before.

The thoughts pricked her mind, making her feel like she was wearing an itchy sweater. She finished her drink and pocketed the meal bar for later, adrenaline still buzzing too high to stay still any longer.

The FBI agent had disappeared. Lee crossed the street and entered the campus again to retrieve the jacket and hat, which she tucked under her arm.

A shuffling sound to her right brought her out of her thoughts and into the present. A narrow, short alley between a rundown laundromat and a closed convenience store drew her attention; it was the perfect place for someone to hide.

Lee flexed her hands and took a few steps. The shuffling followed, as if someone was trying to mask the sound of their steps in the sound of her own. Was this the same agent as before? The last thing she needed was a street showdown right now. Lee reached internally for the veil between realms. She broke into a run, passing into the circle of the green-tinged streetlight outside the laundromat. Her would-be assailant cussed as Lee phased into the Liminal Realm.

A dozen red threads spun out around her. Ley lines. The laundromat was a hotspot for them. They didn't exist every-where, but they gave her ability to go Liminal a long-range boost. To travel in the blink of an eye. Essentially instantaneous transportation. All she had to do was reach out and touch one...

Lee's finger contacted a thread, which hummed excitedly beneath her touch. She extended herself along the ley line, her soul stretching until it was so taut it might snap. There was a spark and a sound like a fuse breaking, and she stood in the center of a children's playground at what appeared to be a school. Lee breathed in deeply and braced for the pins and needles feeling as she went Liminal again, selecting another ley line that seemed familiar.

She startled a feral dog behind some dumpsters at a restaurant, then nearly woke a sleeping man in the silent wing of a hospital. A few miles at a time, Lee skipped across St. Louis, headed east in a convoluted zig-zag pattern, until she landed on a street corner, heart racing, breath coming fast and short, with the oddest sensation of her fingertips going numb.

Lee walked across the street toward a dingy brick house, shaking her hands to get rid of the numbness. A grey cat scurried out of her path. She adjusted the jacket under her arm, the grocery bag from the gas station crinkling in her other hand.

Walking up the broken sidewalk that led to the front porch, she rapped on the brown, peeling paint of the front door, using the pattern the crew had agreed on two weeks ago. Bolts clicked as they unlocked, and the door squeaked open.

"Hey, Sam," Lee said, moving to enter.

Sam's bulk blocked the way. His round, Polynesian face creased with suspicion. "Anyone follow you?"

Lee pursed her lips, ignoring the flutter of her nerves from the FBI agent following her into the Liminal realm earlier. She didn't want Sam to see her anxiety.

"Do you think anyone could follow me? Let me in." She

ducked under his arm, squeezing through the narrow space between him and the door.

Sam shut the door, and they moved through the hall together. The way he loomed behind Lee with his massive frame filling the hallway gave her chills. He wasn't his usual warm and jovial self. Sam was never this grim, unless he had a damn good reason. Which meant she had to be on guard for whatever scene waited for her in the common area.

Lee strode into the open living room with her chin cocked and a blank expression on her face.

Risa sat in an armchair, hands gripping the arms so hard her knuckles whitened. Sam entered behind Lee and scooted around the wall until he found a place to stand. They both fidgeted. No one moved.

Silas, the crew boss, stood in the middle of the room. He stared deadpan at Lee and raised his robotic arm. The mechanism in his forearm disassembled to reveal a gun, which pointed without hesitation straight between Lee's eyes.

CHAPTER 3

Agent Adam Finley lifted his binoculars to get a closer look at the woman wearing the orange hat over her indigo hair. She passed as just another person on the street, shoulders hunched against the chill of the damp afternoon, scowling at the sidewalk like it had done her wrong. The clicking sensation near his heart told him there was more to her. He'd learned to trust that feeling; it had led to apprehending some of the biggest names in thaumaturgic crime in the past five years. Now, he believed, he was looking at a rising star in the industry.

Name: Leana Mitchell
  Age: 24
  Height: 5'4"
  Weight: 143 lbs.

Dropped out of high school at Roosevelt. No listed jobs, no college education, no family still living. The trail stopped cold. Until Adam had picked it back up two weeks ago and crashed the two-person party at the Cupples' mansion.

The security guards being briefed still didn't remember what had happened, or how the targets had gotten away, but Adam had seen this woman go Liminal. Somehow she'd moved through his thaumaturgic block and dragged her friend out of that house like the hounds of hell chased her. Her Liminal ability was the strongest he'd seen; it had to be, otherwise he would have her in custody at headquarters right now.

He dropped the binoculars as the target ducked into the doorway of a local coffee shop. She was just getting coffee for now, but if he watched her long enough, she'd tip him off to whatever job her crew was planning next, and Adam intended to be there to arrest the Liminal.

The static of his radio crackled, startling him. He set the binoculars down.

"We've got a 4-1-1. Repeat, a 4-1-1." A large-scale thaumaturgic event. Adam cursed. They would need back-up, but he didn't want to lose this chance to discover where Leana Mitchell called home.

"Agent Finley, do you copy?"

Finley picked up the radio and pressed the talk button. "Copy, Agent Zarrow. What's the nature of the attack?"

"Flamethrower at the half flounder on Keokuk. We've got the fire department, but we need you."

We need you. Because he was apparently the most capable law enforcement officer in St. Louis with the ability to cut the power of a thaumaturgic on a rampage. Call it a blessing, call it a curse, it was his duty. Adam pulled the car out of park and turned on his white and green lights. The siren whirred with a different pitch than typical law enforcement, so people would know this was no ordinary cop. This was an agent with the Thaumaturgic Division of the FBI for managing and apprehending magical disruptions to society.

When he pulled up on a street adjacent to the half flounder house, there was smoke billowing from the building. The fire department was working overtime on the hoses, but every time they got a section managed, a new flare would go up.

It was a shame. He'd often passed the quirky little building that looked like a house chopped in half, an architecture unique to the area from a century past. He had wondered if it would ever get restored, but watching the flames licking the edges now, he doubted it.

Adam jogged over to Zarrow. "You can't get a lock on him?"

Zarrow shook his head. "He's been cooking too long. The bullets are melting before they reach his skin."

Adam eyed the building. A section of roof on the far side crumbled, sending a thicker column of smoke into the sky. "No people inside?"

"Just the flamethrower."

"Tell the fire department to clear me a path." Adam took off toward the building.

"Get a helmet on," Zarrow yelled.

Adam gestured to a firefighter, who hesitated, then tossed him the helmet from his own head. Adam strapped it on.

"Get the firefighters to focus the hoses on the south side. I need to get within his radius." Adam didn't wait for an answer, but strode purposely for the doorway on the south side, away from the area that had collapsed. It seemed safest, with the least amount of smoke coming out.

His senses clicked inside his chest, ticking like a clock against his heart. Heat poured off the building, lessening when the high-pressured jets of water shot through the doorway and the nearby windows.

Adam stepped through the dripping doorframe. Inside, smoke wafted off of timbers, and tiny sparks sprang to life like seeds of fire. He walked through the burned-out hallway, skirting the trail of spontaneous flames that grew larger as he got closer to the elemental. The building was dark with the smoke, the only light coming from the fires. Smoke billowed through a doorway ahead. Crackling filled the air, and faint shouts from outside.

Adam turned a corner. In the middle of the room, a figure stood outlined in red with bright orange cracks flashing through the coal-black form. The form was definitely feminine. She raised a hand and a knee-high spout of flame shot out of the floor near Adam.

He jumped, then brought his own hand up and clenched the fist, turning it upside down in a smooth motion.

The flamethrower lifted both of her hands. The fire remained small, crackling hungrily at Adam's feet without spreading. She raised her arms again with more energy.

"I neutralized you," Adam said. "Leave your elemental form and come without a fight."

The figure cocked her head. Elementals, like this flamethrower, couldn't talk in their thaumaturgic forms. She would have to shift into human form to tell him anything.

To Adam's surprise, the elemental didn't shift forms or speak. She pointed wordlessly to a spot above his head. He looked up just in time to see the beam overhead give way. He dove to the ashy ground, shielding his head from the shower of sparks. When he glanced back up, a billowy column of smoke stood where the flamethrower had.

As soon as he was outside of the building, Adam jerked

the helmet off, then handed it to the nearest firefighter and ran his hands through his hair. He put his hands on his hips and approached Zarrow.

"No one saw her leave?"

Zarrow laughed. "We saw her leave all right. Got a few shots off, but she vaporized. Did you know fire elementals could do that?"

Adam spat onto the pavement. "Only powerful elementals can do that. Experienced ones. But experienced ones don't commit mindless arson; they're hired. Tell the firefighters to go easy on the water. There may be evidence in that building of a larger crime that's being covered up."

Zarrow nodded and turned, shouting for the fire chief's attention. Adam watched the building burn until an EMT reached him and requested to do an exam. Adam submitted, putting on a breathing mask for show, but when his cell phone started buzzing, he took it off and left the medical area.

"Finley, report." The familiar bark of the director of operations in the Thaumaturgic Department came crackling through the line, and it almost made Adam smile. He would have smiled if the elemental hadn't gotten away.

"Director Hatcher. Nice to hear your voice."

"Cut the shit, Finley."

Adam chuckled, then swallowed another urge to spit. He ran his hand through his hair again and turned to view the surrounding scene. "Building's a loss. No casualties, but the subject got away."

"Damnit, Finley. I thought you could stop them?"

"I can temporarily and within certain circumstances stop their magic, sir. Their bodies can move like anyone else's. She dropped a flaming beam on my head and vaporized."

Hatcher made an interested sound. "Vaporized, eh? So this wasn't a bright burning idiot riding the arson high."

"Someone hired her. Someone is setting these fires on purpose." This was their sixth warehouse arson in two months. "I suspect some sort of illegal trafficking ring."

"A lot of trouble to go through for a drug," Hatcher said.

Zarrow ran up to Adam, wide-eyed and panting slightly. Adam held up a hand before he spoke. "If they're getting paid enough to deal it, they'll go to any length. What else do we have on this?"

"While you were off spying on your pretty, dying girls, I followed up with a few leads. I need you back here in half an hour to go over them."

"The Liminals could be part of this, boss. I'll make the connection, eventually."

"If you can keep one of them alive long enough, maybe. Half an hour." Director Hatcher's line went dead.

Adam pocketed his phone and Zarrow launched into his report.

"We've been going around asking the onlookers if they saw anything prior to the fires, including the one who reported it. Miles Neal saw the flames when he got off for lunch. He works nearby. The place looked normal this morning when he came in to work."

Adam shook his head. "That's not much to go off of. We need to see if we can find any evidence of illicit activity inside. We won't know if we're looking at a prank gone wrong or a murder scene until we do. Get evidence in there. I've got a meeting with Hatcher, but if you find anything, call."

Zarrow nodded. "Will do."

Adam sped off in his car, making it to the department

building in record time. He found Director Hatcher in his office.

"You wanted to brief me on the leads for the flamethrower case?" Adam leaned against the doorway.

"That can wait. We've got a council room filled with government officials, and they're all asking to talk to you." Hatcher stood, straightening a stack of papers and sticking them into a file folder that he tucked into a binder and then placed under his arm. "You're coming with me."

"Sir," Adam said, alarm making his forehead breakout in sweat. "Am I in trouble?"

"You're either in trouble, or you're about to be," Hatcher said, expression grim.

Adam followed him from the room, steeling himself for a meeting that could determine whether he walked out of the building still employed by the FBI.

CHAPTER 4

"Well, well, well. The prodigal daughter returns." The gun in Silas's cybertronic arm cocked itself.

Lee rolled her eyes. "This is unnecessary."

"I heard you got made." Silas's robotic red eye targeted its sighting laser on Lee while the human one stared coldly at her. A slight whirring sound caused Lee's muscles to tense reflexively.

Lee glared across the room at Risa, who shrugged. Boss needed to know. Lee understood, but she didn't have to like it. She would never enjoy having to answer to Silas.

"Put the gun down, Silas. No one followed me. You know no one could ever keep up with my abilities," Lee said. She tossed the grocery sack onto a nearby empty chair.

"With our Screener gone, someone will. Someday. Can't be too careful."

"When you point guns at your own crew members without cause, you're being too careful," Lee said.

"Mistakes are how people end up dead." His metal arm

didn't flex, and his mechanical eye didn't blink or give Lee any sign of what he might be thinking. Stupid cyborgs and their stupid, emotionless faces.

The fleshy side of Silas's face twisted in a strange expression, and he lowered the weapon, joints and gears clicking as the gun flipped back into its holder inside his forearm and the skin reassembled.

Silas rarely talked about how he'd become half-man, half-machine, but everyone knew about the state-of-the-art medical procedures being offered to thaumaturgics now. Have your magic cut out of you through surgery, like a cancer that could simply be removed. Surgery was for the lucky ones. Even if Lee could afford the surgery, Liminality riddled her body too deeply for modern medical means to cure.

Lee tried not to look too closely at the mechanical workings, her empty stomach churning with mild nausea already. Instead, she unrolled her jacket, shaking it out and retrieving her beanie. The soft wool hat went back on her head, giving her a boost of confidence, as if the hat held some aspect of her essence that could help her stand up to the scrutiny of her crew boss.

Tomorrow she would contact the Speller who had promised her coordinates to the Ceteri, and she would get her cure. Then she could leave. She would find her own place and new people that didn't constantly remind her of Shane and everything that could never be.

Silas had always made them out to be a family. The kind meant to look out for each other. If the Gadai was a family, it was a majorly dysfunctional one, and it had taken Lee far too long to build up the guts to leave. The promise of a family and the lure of the security of being in a group had kept her there for far too long already. She'd been planning to leave when

Shane showed up, and he'd convinced her to stay. Convinced her they could make the crew into the family they had both always wanted.

"What did you find?" Silas crossed his arms. "After the risks you took, it had better be good."

Lee had been caught, but she had outsmarted Silas this time. She just had to pull this next con off without a hitch, and she'd be in the home stretch, or as good as.

After tugging the jacket sleeves over her arms and straightening her collar as if nervous, Lee then reached into her pocket. She pulled out the fake bracelet, its milky green stones gleaming in the dim light.

Lee swung the bracelet around and clasped it in her palm. "Ever heard of a Way Mary?"

Silas scrunched up his face.

Sam's quiet voice responded from the back of the room. "Waimari. It means Luck Finder."

Silas grunted. "That Japanese, or what?" He held out his hand, and Lee reluctantly moved forward and handed over the bracelet. If she didn't, he'd shoot her. He might have taken her in when she was just a skinny little street rat, but she didn't have any delusions about him caring for her. He ran a thieving crew. It was a business, nothing personal about it.

Sam pointed at the Way Mary in Silas's hand. "When activated, it's got the ability to absorb luck from people nearby. It takes time to charge, and each bead is one use, but a piece like that could get you ten grand. Easy."

Silas whistled, then looked sideways at Lee. "Ten grand is a lot of money to hoard to yourself when your crew is scrambling to make a dollar. You planning to leave the family, Lee?"

Lee's chest went cold, her fingers numb and tingling as

guilt pricked her heart. She licked her lips, looking at all three of the crew members facing her. Time to direct this attention away from herself and onto the real problem.

"We're only scrambling because you take our money and do who-knows-what with it," Lee blurted. "None of us have seen our share of a score since Shane died."

"When Shane died, we lost our Screener. You know how much it costs to hire one of those to obscure a Liminal's thaumaturgic traces?" Silas held up the Way Mary. "This will cover us for a while. Maybe we can finally get ahead, and I can start paying y'all again. You get paid after expenses."

His mechanical eye glowed as he spoke. "If we're going to keep this family of ours together, those expenses are higher. If you were to split and take your cash, you'd be buying food, paying utilities, and finding Screeners of your own or dealing with the cops knocking on your door. Instead, I handle all of that. To keep you safe. To keep you comfortable."

Lee's confidence wavered. Sam's and Risa's gazes seemed accusatory. From their standpoint, this had to look like a betrayal. And since she'd brought Shane into it, Silas had used that to remind everyone that Lee was the reason they were short a Screener.

Silas thumbed his nose and leaned back, then gestured to the others. "Sam, Risa, you have anything to say about this?" He raised the Way Mary.

Sam shook his head. "No," he muttered, shuffling his feet.

Risa's stare bored holes into Lee's skull. Was she mad? She'd followed Lee and agreed to do the Way Mary heist. Maybe she was just mad that Silas had somehow caught on and squeezed it out of her. Or maybe she thought Lee was selfish, too.

Risa looked to Silas. "I think you've said enough."

"That's what I like to hear. Now, Lee, don't make me ground you. Stay here, don't make trouble, don't go out on your own." Silas looked at Risa, who twirled a pocket watch chain around her fingers. "And Risa, don't let her talk you into that again. We'll chalk this up to restlessness and call it good."

A compartment opened in Silas's mechanical shoulder and he placed the Way Mary inside, sealing it with a definitive click. He sat down in his armchair, heaving a sigh.

It was the perfect opportunity to make them believe Silas had bested her. Lee took it, pivoting on her heel and fleeing into the kitchen. She kept one ear to the chatter in the other room, listening for anything that might be about her, but for now, the conversation had moved on.

Staring into the fridge at the sparse ingredients, Lee dug her other hand into her pocket, fingering the cool metal of the bracelet there. She allowed herself a small smile at the victory she'd already won in getting Silas to accept the fake Way Mary.

Reality squashed her celebration. When would Silas realize he had a fake? If he tried to sell it, she'd be screwed.

Lee yanked two slices of bread out of the package and slapped on pickles and cheese to make herself a sandwich. She went back for lunch meat, but they were out. Shane had preferred turkey to ham. He always kept the crew fridge stocked. He'd lean on the counter, hop up and talk too loud with his mouth full. Lee straightened and glanced at the empty counter, as if staring could make him appear.

Grief spiked through Lee, freezing her in the harsh light from the fridge.

Shane was gone. Dead in a heist gone wrong, all because Lee's powers had glitched at the wrong moment, and she couldn't take him with her into the Liminal realm. Cold spread through her from the inside out, and her hands trembled. Moments like this, she wished the Fade would take her sooner rather than later. At least then she'd have peace from these thoughts.

CHAPTER 5

"Lee!" Risa's voice pulled Lee back from the thoughts of Shane that had threatened to pull her under like quicksand.

"Coming!" Lee shut the fridge, wiped her face dry, and steeled herself. She carried her plate back to the living area. Silas didn't even glance her way. She flopped on the couch, chewing past the knot in her stomach.

"What about the drop Lee witnessed at the bank two months ago? The one rumored to have those rings imbued with strength?" Risa asked.

Silas grunted. "The Yeggry crew got it a couple of weeks back. Derrick was pimping it in the market yesterday."

Lee took another bite, the sharp scent of dill pickles filling her nostrils. "There's always the Jewel Box."

"You always bring that up, and Silas always says no," Sam complained as he wandered out of the room toward the kitchen.

Silas muttered to himself, then stopped short. "We need more manpower. This was a simple job, and they nearly caught Lee and Risa. Our next job needs to be smaller and better planned. Take more time casing it out, have escape routes that don't rely on anything Liminal, since that's not a guarantee."

"We need to take more of the right risks, Silas, not fewer," Lee argued, brushing off her hands and sitting up. "Our accounts and our fridge are nearly empty. Rent is due. We'll get kicked out of here and put on the streets if we don't pull more in."

Silas wiped his non-robotic hand across his mouth and paced from the armchair where Risa sat to the window on the opposite wall. His mechanical arm whirred and shifted between several of its uses as he stared at it."The Jewel Box is too risky. We'll do the Children's museum job."

Sam walked back into the room, munching on a slice of cheese. He had a stack of them in one hand. "Why do they call it a museum? It's more of a playground."

"Didn't they lock the museum down hard after the last theft?" Risa adjusted the tinted goggles on her head. "Rumor has it they hired a chimera. It lives in the basement."

Silas snorted. "There's no such thing as a true chimera. There's a treasure trove hidden in those exhibits. We'll hire ourselves a new Screener and give them a trial run. It'll be a nice, predictable job."

"Unless there is a chimera," Sam said.

Lee laughed hollowly. "You're going to hire someone? With what money? We're broke. If we wait until we can afford a Screener, the museum will get cleaned out behind our backs."

"A buddy owes me a favor. Time to cash in," Silas said. The way his cyborg eye roved wildly in its socket made Lee's eyes narrow in suspicion.

"If you can get us a Screener, why go for a dinky job that

will get us nowhere? Shane would have done the Jewel Box," Lee argued.

"Shane is dead!" Silas spat. A terrible silence filled the room, except for Silas's angered breathing. "Not all of us are on death row like you, Lee. We don't have lives we can throw away."

Lee tensed her arm. Punching that smug metal jaw would hurt like hell, but it would be worth it if she could loosen a few of his bolts and send him to the shop.

Out of the corner of her eye, Lee noticed Risa making a slicing motion over her throat and mouthing, "Don't."

Lee shook out her arm. She didn't feel like bruising her knuckles today. Besides, Silas was full of it. They needed her more than ever, with her ability to slip through time and space. But she had grown tired of taking Silas's crap. She'd been taking it for six years. Now she had the real Way Mary hidden away in her jacket pocket, burning a hole in her common sense. If she couldn't punch sense into the overblown cyborg, she would shake him up a little.

Lee straightened her shoulders. "If that's how you feel about it, I don't see a need for me to be here any longer." Her skin prickled as she reached for the Liminal realm, and she vanished.

Under cover of the alternate time-stream in the Liminal realm, Lee walked toward the end of the hallway, watching Silas's face slowly morph into panic.

She made it nearly to her bedroom doorway when a sharp pain pierced her abdomen.

What was that? Indigestion?

Lee held her stomach until the pain subsided. The prickling started up again, like she was phasing back through realms, only she wasn't doing anything.

She took another step and her chest split with lancing agony. A sound like wind howled in her ears.

"Lee!" Risa's voice, shouting. Lee shouldn't have been able to hear her. Her powers were failing, like they had the night Shane had died. Her vision flickered between the dull colors and sounds of the Liminal Realm and the bright reality of Earth.

It shouldn't have been happening, but it was. Was it the end?

Risa reached her first, her movements appearing to flinch and jerk. Lee moved her shoulder away from Risa's hovering hand.

"Don't touch me," Lee warned through gritted teeth. Pain swallowed her. Her hands became shadow, then flesh, then shadow again. The red glow outlining her body gleamed even when she phased back to Earth's space and time. She knelt on all fours, gasping until the pain faded, and her hands became solid and flesh-colored again. A red haze shone at the edges of her vision.

"It's the Fade." Sam whispered from behind Risa.

"Don't be stupid," Lee panted. "Just tired, is all." Her vision flashed and spun, and panic consumed her. She would never get out, never be free of this house, these people, this life. Shane had been wrong. She couldn't change her fate after all.

No one spoke.

"Where were you going?" Silas asked. Glancing over her shoulder, Lee could see his electric yellow eye adjusting, its tiny gears grinding.

"On a walk," Lee snapped. She was tired. Exhausted, and she'd barely made it down the hall. Lip curled, she pushed herself up onto one knee, then used her hand on her thigh to balance and stand. She leaned against the wall, feeling like she'd traveled ley lines for a hundred miles instead of walking a few feet. Forget her stuff. She still wanted out of there. Away from Silas, away from all of them. She shuffled towards the exit.

Silas let out a metallic-sounding groan. "Lee, this is pathetic. You can't leave like this."

"I can," she spat. "And I will. You don't care about the crew; you just care about your bottom line."

Silas scoffed. "I can't believe you're giving me that line after you took off and did a job by yourself, recruiting Risa. You think you are more deserving, that you need the money more than the rest of us."

"That's not true!" Lee said, resisting the urge to turn and look at him.

"Because Sam's depraved family and Risa's dreams don't matter a bit to special, diseased Lee. You turn the tables so neatly trying to distract us from your real motives, but I'm not fooled. You know, after all this time, I thought we mattered to you. That we'd become like a family. But you arrived a selfish teenager, and you haven't grown up one bit."

The words scrambled in Lee's brain and she ran through all the things she could say, how she could prove that she hadn't done this out of selfishness or spite, but desperation. She wasn't making money on their jobs because Silas kept putting her money towards their supposed bills and investments, but they had nothing to show for his efforts. And she had no proof.

"You can walk away, Lee. But if you do, I'm calling in every debt we have and pointing the collectors at you. You're the reason we are failing. Your condition has deteriorated ever since Shane left."

Lee pushed against the wall and turned herself around, leaning back on the solid surface for support. "Oh, I'm sorry, maybe I'm grieving my best friend's death."

"You don't think I'm grieving?" Silas said. "We're all grieving. You're the only one who seems to think that it's okay to go behind her crew's back and take advantage of them while they're down."

The accusation hit far too close to Lee's heart. She put her hand over her mouth, hiding her quivering lip.

Risa stepped in. "Silas, maybe that's enough. Lee's just been through an ordeal. She was sick before Shane died; it isn't fair to put that on her."

Lee expected Silas to turn on Risa, to yell at her and twist her words and make her feel like crap.

Instead, he took a deep breath, jutted out his bottom lip, and nodded. "Maybe you're right there. My hurt ran away with me again." He sighed, rubbing his flesh hand down his face and glanced at Lee. "I'm sorry. Let me make it up to you. To all of you. I'll get pizza for us tonight, and we can take another look at the Jewel Box if it's that important to you, Lee."

Lee searched his eyes, glancing between the blue human pupil and the glowing yellow cyborg one. Not a trace of malice remained. All the ugly things he'd said, erased from his expression like they never happened.

"Do you mean that?" she asked hesitantly.

Silas bobbed his head. "I do, I really do. You're right, it's what Shane would have wanted. Far be it from me to ignore that. No more trinkets, no more pocket change. We'll find the biggest and best that they've got on display and it'll make us so rich we can retire."

Sam laughed, a rich, hearty laugh that healed the lingering

tension in the room. Lee slumped against the wall, still feeling exhausted, though the red tinge at the edge of her vision had vanished, and her hands had stopped trembling.

"Let's case out the museum job first," Lee said. "We'll need some cash flow for the Jewel Box job." She would still go find the Speller and use the real Way Mary to get the coordinates to the Ceteri to find a cure for Liminality. Right now, she said what Silas wanted to hear, so he wouldn't suspect her intentions to leave.

"That's what I like to hear." Silas paused. "Do you think you'll be able to do both? After…" He gestured at her, showing he meant what had just happened.

"I can do it," Lee said. Though she wasn't sure she believed herself. Silas grinned at her and rubbed his hands together. "Things are finally looking up."

Lee pressed into the wall harder, steadying herself in its solidness. She had almost died, and Silas didn't seem to care. But what else was new? As soon as she traded the Way Mary, she was done. Done wasting the rest of her life stuck in this place.

Sam watched her, his eyes heavy with the same accusation she'd seen in them before.

Lee pressed down the guilt and pushed herself away from the wall, walking with measured steps towards her room without glancing back. She couldn't afford to get sidetracked; she had to focus on surviving long enough to get out of there.

CHAPTER 6

Adam stopped in his tracks when he saw the people who waited in the meeting room ahead of him.

He grabbed Director Hatcher's arm. "That's the Thaumaturgic Council!"

Hatcher patted Adam's arm. "Lucky you. Time to make some friends."

What did the Council want with a run-of-the-mill FBI agent? True, Adam had some unique passions regarding thaumaturgy, and he had been on the original team that was now part of the Thaumaturgic Department of the FBI, but that shouldn't single him out. Adam really wished Hatcher would fill him in before he threw Adam to the wolves.

Hatcher opened the door and strode through, taking his place at one end of the table and tossing the binder down.

"Welcome to the FBI, ladies and gentlemen. Can I introduce Agent Adam Finley?" Hatcher gestured towards Adam, who tried not to look like a startled deer as all eyes turned on him.

"Uh, hi. Thanks for...having me." Adam swallowed. Public speaking wasn't his strong suit.

Marcia Cruz, Head of the Thaumaturgic Council, smiled, tucking her chin-length white hair behind one ear and then clasping her hands in front of her. "We're glad you could meet us on such short notice, Agent Finley. Please, have a seat."

Hatcher motioned to the chair beside him, and Adam took it.

Adam scanned the individuals in the room. He knew Bob Hawkins, the Vice Head of the Thaumaturgic Council. He was the skinny man with a beakish nose sitting next to Mrs. Cruz, leaned back in his chair and twirling a pencil as he stared back at Adam.

Adam moved on. He nodded at Gwen Padilla, a red-head in the position of secretary, and Jon Baldwin, a balding man in a plaid shirt who served as the Thaumaturgic Council Medical Advisor.

Marcia smiled. "You likely haven't met Edina Morgan yet. She's a recent addition to our Council."

The short woman had dark hair and brown skin with a red dot in the center of her forehead.

Adam stood and extended his hand across the table to Edina. "Nice to meet you."

Marcia continued. "Edina is our International Relations expert."

Edina took Adam's hand. "Nice to meet you." She spoke with a New York accent.

Adam sat back down, rubbing his hands on his thighs under the table. All the faces looking at him were calm or smiling, but the tension in the room was palpable.

"So...why am I here?" Adam asked.

Marcia adjusted her glasses and glanced at the paper in

front of her. "Yes. Well, the Council has determined that your department will receive reduced funding. Fewer than half of all cases get solved, and the ones that get solved use up an inordinate amount of resources. Your statistics haven't improved in six months, and have, in fact, gone down."

Adam gaped. "There isn't another team like ours in the country. A reduction in funding would put an unnecessary strain on teams that don't specialize in thaumaturgy. Who is going to respond to those calls?"

Bob Hawkins sat up. "Did you know scientists estimate that at the rate that thaumaturgy gets passed down through genetics, within twenty years, nearly a third of the human population will have some magical ability or another? A single department in the FBI will not solve the thaumaturgic crime issue. The CSI has put in a serious bid for establishing their own team, and they are also asking for government funding. If their team proves more successful at curbing thaumaturgic crime, your department will receive reduced funding."

"If the problem is evolving, funding needs to be increased, not reduced," Adam argued, glancing from Mr. Hawkins to Mrs. Cruz and back again.

"That's what I said." Hatcher tugged a sheet out of his file. "This shows the crime rates, our hiring rates, the funding amounts offered by the government and the cost of running our department."

His eyebrows raised, and he tapped the paper before sending it around the table, passing it to Adam, who immediately passed it on. He'd already seen the numbers.

"The numbers have never matched the need. Allowing another organization to receive funding that was inadequate from the beginning isn't the answer. You'll spread the funds too thin," Adam said. He still didn't see why he was in this meeting. Hatcher knew all of this. He could argue these points just as well.

"Then I think it's obvious," Mr. Hawkins said, adjusting his position in his seat. "Only one department can exist. The government won't give us any more money right now. We're lobbying, but bills take time to pass through all the checkpoints. What we need from you is a guarantee that you can improve performance or make an offer that the CSI can't. If you can deliver that, we will reinstate your funding and reject the proposal from the CSI."

"If you want improved performance, we need more funding. We need to hire and train more agents with abilities like Finley's." Hatcher gestured to Adam.

Ah. That was why he was here.

"What, exactly, are agent Finley's abilities?" Mrs. Cruz asked, looking at Adam over her glasses.

"I am a Neutralizer," Adam said. He looked to Hatcher, who nodded, encouraging him to tell them more. "I'm also an Enhancer. And the intersection of the two somehow allows me to sense when thaumaturgy is about to be activated."

"You can stop magic and increase its effects? Interesting," Mr. Baldwin, the Medical Advisor, mused, pushing his glasses up his nose. "That is a rare combination indeed. How would you find more with your abilities?"

"We don't need his exact combination. Mainly, we need more Neutralizers and agents who can detect magical use. These criminals are getting away because we're up against proverbial dragons with only toothpicks to fight with. Guns don't bother elementals in their pure forms. We can't see invisible criminals. Where's the tech to back us up? It's stuck in developmental or approval stages. I know we're

THIEF OF MAGIC   45

new to combatting Thaumaturgy, but it's about to get ugly. They know we can't do anything to them," Hatcher explained.

The Council members shuffled uneasily.

"We would approve the use of technology more quickly if it weren't for funding. It's all tied up, and as we mentioned, your department is the biggest drain," Mr. Hawkins explained.

"Our department is the only one using the funding!" Adam said, his voice rising. "Unless you've already started funding the CSI, there's no reason the money can't be used to purchase relevant tech or hire new people for the FBI."

The long pause after he spoke was all the evidence Adam needed that what he'd said was exactly what had happened.

Adam kept his clenched fists hidden from view under the table. "How long do we have?"

"How long?" Mr. Hawkins asked.

"Until you shut us down." Adam nearly snapped, but he contained his anger, letting it fume just beneath the surface.

"Once we receive the initial quarterly report from Director Causey at the CSI, we'll know all we need to know."

"So, three months?" Adam asked.

Mr. Hawkins looked at Mrs. Cruz, who glanced at Ms. Padilla, the secretary.

Ms. Padilla produced a paper from the stack in front of her. "Three weeks."

Director Hatcher harrumphed. "Guess that proves that theory. You approved Causey's proposal months ago."

Mrs. Cruz seemed unflustered. Hatcher looked at Adam, something in his gaze. He wanted Adam in this meeting for a reason. What did Adam have that no one else in the department did?

"What if I told you I could get you a Liminal by then?

Alive and well, ready to help you decipher the secrets to finding the Ceteri?" Adam's words hung in the air.

Director Hatcher's eyebrows raised, and then he recovered, steepling his fingers together. "Working with a Liminal could enable you to negotiate with the Ceteri to erase their magic from humanity. You could be responsible for returning all of our lives to normal."

"We can't speak for the people, Director Hatcher. And who's to say that they want to be normal?" Mr. Baldwin used air quotes around the word 'normal'.

Mrs. Cruz shot him a glance.

Ms. Padilla jotted notes furiously, her pen scribbling filling the room. Then she passed a paper to Mrs. Cruz.

The Head of the Thaumaturgic council scanned the paper, then set it on the table facedown.

"There are those within the government who would be highly interested in your proposal, agent Finley. They may sponsor a bill to increase funding for the FBI. But I would need assurances. What makes you think you can land a Liminal, much less one who will help us?"

"I'm tracking one right now. She has a criminal record. I'm sure if I bring her in, she'll be willing to cut a deal. Her help in exchange for her freedom." Adam licked his lips, wishing he had a glass of water. His throat was dry as a desert.

Mrs. Cruz considered him, then exchanged looks with Mr. Hawkins. Her fingers tapped the table, and then she sat upright. "I admit I am intrigued. You don't seem like one to exaggerate. So I will make you this promise: bring in a Liminal, and we can renegotiate the future of your department. You have three weeks to bring her in."

Adam nodded. "Yes. Of course. You got it." He didn't know if he could do it. Cornering a Liminal was hard work.

Keeping them alive even more so. Leanna Mitchell seemed more stable than the last Liminal he'd tracked, but he had to go about it differently this time. More subtle.

Could he find a position on her crew? Get close enough to convince her that helping the FBI was the right thing to do?

"This has been a productive meeting. I'm glad we could have this discussion," Mrs. Cruz smiled, but it didn't reach her eyes.

The other council members gathered their papers, all except for Mr. Baldwin, who stared at Adam, rubbing his chin.

"Do you have something to add, Mr. Baldwin?" Adam asked, an uncomfortable feeling rising in his chest.

"As Medical Advisor of the Thaumaturgic Council, I have special interest in Liminals. I agree we need to use her abilities to find the Ceteri, but if that avenue fails, I would like to study her."

Adam stiffened. The way the man said "study," and the eagerness in his eyes, set Adam's nerves on edge.

"Part of her plea deal would include her freedom, Mr. Baldwin. I can't guarantee you'd get unlimited access to her, or any access. But if she agreed to some testing, I'm sure we could work something out," Adam said.

"Of course," Mr. Baldwin conceded. He looked disappointed, and Adam had the feeling he'd have to navigate this deal carefully and make sure that they respected the Liminal's rights.

The Council members filed out of the room without further comment, leaving Adam behind with Hatcher.

"I sure hope you can live up to your promise, Finley."

Adam snapped his fingers. "Right. Speaking of, I've got a meeting with an informer about that. I'm getting close."

"You said that last time." Hatcher grimaced.

"If I fail, you can fire me," Adam said, grinning at the joke.

"If you fail, you won't have a job to be fired from. We're counting on you."

Adam sobered up. "I know."

Hatcher gathered his things and left Adam sitting alone in the meeting room.

A few hours later, Adam changed into civilian clothes, turned his radio off and put his gun in its holster, then drove to the east side. Crumbling brick facade and overgrown, patchy lawns decorated each property. He pulled into a vacant parking lot behind a specific set of rusted blue dumpsters and waited.

A rapping on his back window made him glance, but no one was there. The rap came from the other side. Adam knew better than to look. He rolled down his window, and when a man appeared out of thin air just outside it, Adam didn't jump like he had the first time he met the man who could make himself invisible.

"Suarez." Adam squinted in the daylight. The Hispanic man grinned and rubbed his bristly mustache, brushing off his leafy green Hawaiian-style shirt before sticking his hands in his pockets and bouncing on his heels.

"Hey! How'd you know it was me, eh?" Suarez chuckled, rocking back on his heels.

"Old dog, old tricks."

Suarez sucked air through his teeth. "That stings, man. You know I got arthritis. These tricks make it worse. I did it just for you, eh? For your amusement."

"What do you have today?" Adam slowly slipped a white envelope from the bag on the passenger seat.

Suarez eyed it, rubbed his nose and sniffed. He shifted his stance. "I got something big today, boss. Maybe we could…?"

"Make up for last week when you gave me nothing? Sounds good." Adam gave Suarez a mocking smile.

Suarez pasted a smile on his face. "Of course, of course!" He rubbed his hands together and leaned in closer to the car window, his cigar-breath sour in Adam's face. "I've caught words on the wind that the Gadai are looking for fresh blood to bulk up their team."

Adam's mind jumped to a paper he had tucked away in the folder in his bag. Suarez was the one who had given him the name of the thieving crew that this Liminal belonged to.

"And how does one…apply, exactly?"

Suarez only hesitated a moment before he coughed and rested his hand on the car. "There's this coffee shop, Black Aroma, right? Be there at opening tomorrow. You're looking for a tall black man with a mechanical arm. He'll ask if he's seen you around, and you'll tell him it's been a while. The code phrase is 'Economics with Professor Gadai'."

"That's it?" Adam asked. Seemed simplistic.

"He'll invite you to chat. What his requirements are, I don't know. Supposedly, the crew is short a Screener. Other than that, you're on your own." Suarez rubbed his hands.

Adam considered the short man. A Screener. He could pull off pretending to be one of those as long as the crew didn't have the equipment to test for thaumaturgic traces to test his "ability." He could get in, get the Liminal, and get out before anyone was the wiser.

Adam held out the envelope, but just before Suarez

grabbed it, he held it back. Suarez made a protesting sound, and Adam wagged the envelope of cash.

"You know if this is a trap, or if my cover gets blown and I trace it back to you, our deal is done." He let the hardened tone he saved for arrests seep into his tone.

Suarez swallowed, and a choked sound came from his throat, but he nodded.

"Oh yeah, you got it, boss. I'll be across town, no need to worry about me." He shuffled his feet and stuck his hands in his pockets."What business do you have with the Gadai, anyway?"

"It's no business of yours." Adam slid a pair of shades onto his face and started the car. Suarez jumped back and his color faded until he became transparent, waving cheekily at Adam, who pulled out of the parking lot before the informant became fully invisible.

As he drove away, Adam tapped the wheel. This was his chance to get close to a Liminal. He couldn't afford to blow it.

CHAPTER 7

No one was dead, but the day wasn't over yet. Amidst the giggles and gleeful shouts of the children flooding the warehouse-turned-playground that was the City Museum, Lee glared at the woman snapping subtle pictures across the room. It was Risa, late as usual. She had agreed to meet Lee there an hour ago.

Risa sauntered over, casually dodging a pack of kids, her goggles glinting in the multi-colored lights of the museum's second floor. As soon as the older woman reached her, Lee swiped out with a knife, stopping just before Risa's throat.

Risa calmly pushed Lee's hand away. "Museum security won't like you having that. Especially with the wee biddies running around." She waved vaguely as a string of waist-high children darted past, shrieking.

"Oh, but it's yours. It's the knife you stuck in my back." The tiny knife flashed silver as Lee palmed it. She glanced around, making sure no one had seen. Kids ran and screamed. Parents trailed behind. College students made fools of themselves.

Risa blinked. "You had to know Silas would wring it out of me. We were gone too long for him to not be suspicious. And you've been sulking around."

"So come up with another story, Risa. You're good at play-acting, or whatever this costume is to you." Lee gestured at the steampunk getup.

"Cosplay. Simple lies don't get past Silas. You know that. He's on to you. He's noticed your focus shifting since Shane died. What I want to know is why you didn't tell anyone you were planning to leave." Risa crossed her arms.

She appeared nonchalant, but Lee could see the tremor in her eyes. An inner quaking. Lee and Risa had always gotten along. Not close, but no bones to pick. Until now.

"I'm—"

Risa held up a hand. "Don't say it unless it's true. I'm surprised you're even here. Why not take off while you can?"

Lee swallowed and lifted the slim camera, snapping a useless picture. The truth was, she'd thought about just biting the bullet and leaving all night, tossing and turning. She had the real Way Mary in her pocket. But her appointment with the man who had the ability to guide her to the Ceteri was tomorrow. Some sources said he was certifiably insane. What if he wouldn't help her? She had to keep her options open, and for now, that meant not burning all the bridges with her crew.

Lee breathed in and lowered the camera. "It's probably because I'm an idiot."

Risa snorted. "I believe that." Her tone jested, but her expression was drawn and serious. "We both look stupid standing here."

A few wary parents eyed them, so Lee walked away swiftly to another part of the floor, dodging a kid running at breakneck speed. Two haggard-looking adults followed behind him.

"What held you up?" Lee said at last.

"Silas. He met someone in a coffee shop. I was tailing him until he caught me and sent me after you." Risa grinned when Lee looked back. Lee felt a smile grow on her own face, suddenly not so mad at Risa anymore.

Risa looked around, then gestured with her head towards the artificial cave system that led to the second floor. Lee adjusted the tiny camera on her jacket collar. Sam had given it to her. It would give him a first-person view of the museum, and he would be better prepared to manage the tech end of things on the night of the heist.

"You know, if you need money for something, you could just ask Silas. He's helped me out of a tight spot before." Risa halted and looked into a hole in the ceiling of the dark cave tunnel. She reached up, grabbing a pair of rebar monkey bars above her head and pulled herself up with a groan.

Lee had to jump higher to grab the bars, but she exerted less effort getting her five-foot-four frame up into the iron tunnel. She followed Risa, both women crawling up the fabricated shaft.

"You really think he'd understand after the conversation last night? The man is impossible to reason with," Lee said.

"Being part robot would make anyone cranky."

"Don't justify what he does." Lee paused to catch her breath before continuing her climb. Someone was panting as they hightailed it behind her. Lee doubled her efforts to catch up to Risa and get out of earshot of the newcomer. When her head peaked through the hole in the floor, a hand stuck out towards her.

"Okay, so he's an asshole," Risa acknowledged. "Still a

damn good crew leader. He's got a tactical mind. I think he's military."

"Duh, he's military," Lee said, grabbing Risa's hand and letting herself be pulled up.

The two women walked past a giant Egyptian statue as they headed toward the hall of mirrors.

"What kind of nut thought up this place? It's insane." Risa wrinkled her nose at the wall-to-wall, hodge-podge architecture that made up the second floor of the museum.

"Speak for yourself," Lee muttered, eyeing the goggles askew on Risa's head.

They rounded a corner, and a flash of silver blinded Lee. She blinked it away and caught sight of herself in the floor-to-ceiling mirror panels that marked the entrance to the hall of mirrors. She adjusted her orange beanie, noticing the purple shadows under her eyes that seemed permanent, no matter how much sleep she got. Her face had become gaunt, too. She looked like the spectres she could sometimes see in the Liminal Realm.

Thinking about that place made her palms sweat. Lee rubbed them and entered the tunnel of fractured light reflecting broken images of herself. Ahead, Risa walked with a confident stride through the short hallway, headed for the wide, bronze vault door hanging open.

There was no vault behind it. The door was a design element, an interesting feature, no longer a keeper of riches. But the wall of gunmetal grey lockboxes beside it held far more secrets than anyone knew.

Lee sucked in a breath. Risa didn't look at her, just ran her fingers along the lockboxes.

"Which one?" Risa whispered.

Lee embraced the fire and stepped through the veil

between realms. The screams and shouts of joy from the children in the museum faded into an inaudible murmur. A red light blossomed around her hand, flickering in the grey light of the Liminal Realm. Lee frowned, shaking her hand as if it were a flashlight with a low battery. The outline didn't change. Her breathing hitched, and she was taken back to the day before when the atmosphere of the Liminal realm seemed to crush her and paralyze her lungs, squeezing her between worlds...

No. She was fully here, fully Liminal. She looked at the wall of lockboxes.

Silver lights beamed out of a third of the designated spaces. Oh crap. She phased quickly back to the Earth realm, gasping like coming out of water from the quick trip between realms.

"Which one is it?" Risa asked again.

"It's not going to be that easy. Apparently, these lockboxes aren't empty. And most of the items are imbued with magic."

Risa whistled, then her gaze darted around. She nudged Lee and hissed, "Move. Act like we're headed to the ramps over there."

Lee tried to spot whatever—or whoever—had Risa worried. A figure moved near the stairs. A ten-year-old boy darted up ahead of a breathless adult. The figure was gone.

"Liminal?" Lee murmured from the corner of her lips.

Risa drew her lips into a thin line. "Muvengi." Risa hated the Muvengi. She often left the room whenever the rival crew was brought up. She'd been on a crew before finding Silas and founding the Gadai. Did she have history with the Muvengi crew?

Risa spat to one side. "It's that scrawny rat, Kellan. His twin won't be far behind."

Lee wanted to ask how she knew a Muvengi crew member by name, much less that he had a twin, but a low-hanging iron contraption nearly hit her in the face and she had to duck, inching through the tunnel-like area.

Ahead, Risa scooted to the entrance of a steep, dark slide. She grabbed the bar over the top, then glanced back at Lee.

"We'll need to move before the Muvengi do, or we're going to be battling them for burglar's rights."

"Right. Where are you headed next?" Lee asked.

"I'm going to scope out the northeast side. You take the southwest? Check for planted cameras as you go, and try to sabotage them. We don't want them to have any advantages. Meet back at the hideout."

Then, she was gone, shrieking in the tunnel like any person just there to have fun. Lee turned and went in another direction, until she got outside and found the white cage-like tunnel made of rebar that she could climb to the top of the museum, where she found the rooftop Ferris wheel. The Ferris wheel stood alone on a platform at the highest point of the unusual funhouse, looking over the haphazard construction of the rest of the building and out across the city.

Lee climbed into the bucket seat, and as she rose, she caught sight of a man on the sidewalk below holding a large object under his arm. He was so far away it was impossible to see what was inside, but Lee watched him kneel by the fence surrounding the museum and open the container.

After a moment where nothing apparently came out of the container, the man sealed the case again and rose, walking off without another glance at the place he'd knelt.

Lee got off the Ferris wheel the next time it stopped and made her way through the maze of play structures on the various floors to the entrance, coming out near where the man had been with his container.

She waded through bushes, careful not to step on any flowers, scanning the ground for any sign of what the man had left behind. Or perhaps he'd picked something up? Nothing was visible to her naked eye, and she was wary of going Liminal. It took more effort in the daylight with a bustling tourist attraction nearby. She'd have to come back after dark and see if there was anything to see. Most likely it was nothing, but she had a hunch that the man with the case wasn't a lunatic. He had a purpose. The question was, would it interfere with the heist?

Darkness hugged the space between buildings when Lee finally headed to the hideout. She was a regular pedestrian tonight, swaying on a bus and walking the remaining blocks to the brick house that stood sentinel on the corner. She needed to rest, she told herself, but deep down she recognized the rising tide of fear. Fear that if she travelled through the Liminal Realm for any length of time, she would feel her soul disintegrating.

Silas was right; the crew relied on her ability too much. And before too long, she would be gone, fragmented into a permanent part of the Liminal realm. Unless she did something about it.

Lee fingered the real Waimari bracelet through the secret lining of her jacket. Tomorrow she would go talk to that Speller, the one her contact said had a way to reach the Ceteri.

Lee's hand was on the doorknob before she realized the door was cracked open, and the house was dark inside. Her skin prickled with a premonition-like feeling—too bad she didn't have the gift of Sight, even if it did make one go blind or mad.

She took a breath and nudged the door. It swung open with a slight creak, and Lee stepped into the hall. She moved forward, flexing her hands and reaching slowly for the larger knife at her back. Her fingers curled around the hilt beneath her shirt.

The floor creaked, and Lee jerked, pulling out the knife. A figure hurtled towards her. Lee swiped with her knife, and the intruder ducked, then knocked her legs out from under her. The knife clattered to the floor, and Lee grunted, trying to find her attacker's eyeballs with her thumbs.

A masculine grunt came from the figure as she scrambled on top of him. He grabbed her elbow and twisted it. Lee shrieked, hand chopping at his face. She struck his nose and he groaned, then pulled his arm up and locked it around her middle, flipping her as he rotated. Lee gritted her teeth as his weight settled on her. Paralysis or not, she had to chance it, had to use her abilities to get away and find the others, to warn them they were compromised.

The light flicked on, blinding her momentarily, and a slow clap echoed down the hall.

"Well done, both of you. Though I thought Lee would end up on top," Silas's voice carried through the air.

Lee cussed, staring up into a stranger's face. The man had curly, reddish-brown hair, and the kind of smile that could woo a drunk woman in an instant, but Lee was neither drunk nor in the mood for wooing. She glared into his green eyes.

"Get off," she snapped. "Before I remove you with force."

The man raised one of his eyebrows. "I'm curious how you would achieve that. Maybe I'll stick around and see if you're good on your word."

"I wouldn't mess with the Liminal," Silas said, walking closer to them. He reached his mechanical arm out to the man.

Wisely, the man took the hint and slowly got off of Lee, who immediately rolled over and stood up.

She retrieved her knife and inspected the blade, hoping to see blood but knowing she wouldn't find any. She scowled and sheathed it between her shoulder blades.

"You didn't say she would have a knife." The man ran a hand through his ridiculous curls. "Hardly what I call a fair fight."

Life's not fair. Had to see how you'd handle yourself against one of our own." Silas glanced at Lee and chuckled. "You did better than I thought. You're in."

"You're in?" Lee echoed, stepping forward and getting into Silas's face. "You can't audition people without the rest of the crew knowing. You said you were looking for a Screener, not that you had started interviews."

"Those vaults are going to be empty by the end of the week, whether or not we get to them first. In times of crisis, a leader is expected to step up and take care of his crew."

"Without skipping crucial steps that keep the crew safe," Lee shouted and gestured where Risa leaned against a doorway and Sam had peeked his head out. "I thought that was what this job was all about. Something small and safe. If we're going to take risks like letting a stranger in with no vetting, then we might as well storm the Jewel Box tonight."

Silas's gaze hardened, his mechanical eye telescoping in and out and flashing from blue to red to yellow. His mouth twitched, and it looked more like anger than a glitch. Lee braced herself for the yell, but it never came. Instead, he took a deep breath and patted the man on the shoulder.

"Eventually, you'll come to accept that what I do, I do for the good of the crew," Silas said. "Finn, meet Lee. Lee, Finn.

You'll be working and living under one roof for the foreseeable future, so you'd better get used to each other."

Lee scanned from the top of Finn's curly hair to his worn tennis shoes. She held her expression clear of any outward judgement, but her insides squirmed.

Finn held out a hand.

Lee ignored the gesture and clenched her hands into fists. "My trust has to be earned. I'm no dog to give it out for every stranger that walks through the door."

Lee brushed past Finn's extended arm, ignoring Sam's wide eyes and Risa's smirk as she marched to the room she shared with Risa. She slammed the door behind her, then leaned against it, breathing hard to keep the tears at bay.

Lee clenched her fists. If Silas thought she would lie down and accept this without question, he had another thing coming.

CHAPTER 8

Lee snuck out of the crew's hideout at a quarter past 11 p.m. Hunching into the warmth of her jacket, she wished she'd put on more than just leggings, but it would be warmer at her destination. She would hop from the gas station on the corner to the alley next to a particular bar in downtown St. Louis, where the Speller she needed to see resided.

A shuffle behind Lee put her on high alert. She turned her head slightly, as if looking down the street next to her, glancing out of her peripheral vision to try to identify her follower. They'd gotten out of her line of sight too fast, and the sidewalk stood empty behind her. Lee hurried forward, listening for the sound of pursuit.

There it was, a quiet shushing noise, like the fabric of pant legs moving against each other. This one was good, but Lee was better. She sped up slightly, not enough to let them know she was on to them, but enough to get them to work to follow her. She crossed a street. A footstep slapped on the pavement and she stopped to give them a scare, but didn't look. She turned onto another road, pretending business as usual.

As she passed beneath the streetlight on the corner,, the tingle in her fingertips indicated the veil between realms had thinned, and with a single step she phased away from Earth. A strong red line shone around her hands and up her arms. The harsh fluorescent lighting in the gas station parking lot dimmed, as if she looked at it through a transparent black curtain.

Lee turned and ran towards the figure frozen in a crouch behind a bush half a block away, the shadow barely visible on the grass in the light of the Liminal realm. She shook off the remaining pinpricks in her hands and slipped the knife out from between her shoulder blades.

There was no need to be quiet in the Liminal realm. Her footsteps were swallowed up. The figure in the bush shifted slightly, still moving, just at a slower speed than Lee could achieve in the Liminal realm. She approached from behind, placing her knife sideways against the man's chest, so if he jerked, she wouldn't kill him instantly.

Lee took a deep, calming breath and phased back into the Earth realm.

The man pushed against her knife, then froze, likely realizing he could no longer see her ahead and that someone had him from behind. His curly hair pushed into her face.

Finn. The new guy.

"Did you think you could sneak up on me?" Lee kept her voice lowered. Her legs trembled as if from exertion, and it took some effort to keep herself from shaking them out. She focused on Finn, who breathed raggedly.

"Silas assigned me to keep an eye on you."

She pushed the knife into his shirt a bit further to scare him before pulling it away and re-sheathing it.

"First Risa, and now you? Silas can shove it," she hissed. "Go back to bed."

Without waiting for a response, Lee jogged off the lawn and across the street. She could have gone straight to downtown instead of confronting her pursuer. Damn her curiosity.

"Lee!"

Lee closed her eyes, but didn't turn around. She raised her hand, ready to phase out, feeling the pulse of the ley lines that crossed here. It thrummed through her chest, filling every corner of her body. In the beginning, it had felt like power. Now, it felt like disease. Invisible, penetrating her cells. She didn't have time for this.

"Let me come with you. Silas will have my hide if—"

"Let's get three things straight." Lee whirled around, finger jutting into Finn's face. "I don't care about your hide, and I don't care what Silas thinks. And I don't need a babysitter."

She growled the last part, then held out her hand and stepped forward into the Liminal realm, her skin glowing like a burner on a stove.

Finn grabbed her hand, and Lee's essence jerked back to Earth. She gasped at the tearing sensation through the center of her body, blinking back tears. How had he done that? It shouldn't have been possible.

No one had ever prevented her from going Liminal before. Except there was that FBI agent from the Cupples' Mansion that had weirdly followed her into the Liminal realm. Lee squinted at Finn, trying to remember the agent's face. But the agent had worn a hat that made it impossible to make out his likeness. How would an undercover agent act?

She'd known him for less than 24 hours and so far, except

for attacking her in her own hideout, he'd been nice. Maybe too nice.

Lee glared up into Finn's eyes, trying and failing to decipher what was going on behind them. He looked concerned, but not for his own well-being. He should have been.

"Let go." Lee growled and tugged at her hand. Her mouth felt dry. "Damnit, let go!"

"How long do you think you have left?" Finn asked quietly.

"What kind of shitty question is that?" Lee spat, tugging on her wrist.

He let her go, stepping back quickly. "Silas is concerned about you."

"Silas is only concerned about losing his moneymaker." Lee turned away, hiding the trembling in her hands by shoving them in her pockets.

He shouldn't have been able to stop her from going Liminal. She hadn't asked if he had thaumaturgic abilities.

"You can tell him I'm working on a way to cure this," she said. "If it succeeds, maybe I'll be around for a bit longer."

"And if it doesn't?"

"Why do you care?" Lee's voice rose, and a dog barked in the distance. A screen door slammed. Lee backed toward the edge of the street lamp's circle of light, bouncing on her heels and getting ready to run if trouble headed their way.

Finn stood under the light, head bowed. He scuffed the ground with his shoe.

Lee snorted. She couldn't help it. Acting submissively wasn't earning him any respect.

He looked up, eyes blazing with an emotion Lee couldn't read, but it was anything but submissive.

"It's my job," he said simply.

It gave her a weird feeling. Silas had assigned him to her for some unknown purpose. Probably asset protection. But the way Finn crossed his arms, guarding himself, made her think something else was going on, something deeper, something more personal. She watched him from the corner of her eye, a dozen questions swimming through her mind.

A vibration from her phone alerted her to the time. She had fifteen minutes to get to her appointment.

"If you're good, I'll bring you next time," she said with a smirk. She moved into the Liminal realm, appreciating the look of surprise on Finn's face perhaps a little too much.

She jumped from ley point to ley point, stretching herself farther and faster than she had in a while, skipping stopping points and not resting halfway like she normally would have. Sweat broke out on her skin, and her breath came heavy, as if she had run a half marathon in the minutes it took her to cross St. Louis and land on a specific street in the Energia District.

The cool evening air touched her skin as she emerged from the Liminal realm. She straightened her beanie, shoved her hands in her jacket and headed for the neon pink and blue sign in the middle of the block.

The Witch's Brew. Regular humans just saw a run-down bar. Most avoided this street, thanks to redirection lines drawn by those with spelling ability. It gave thaumaturgics like Lee a place to call their own. A place where they could be themselves without drawing the attention of gawking normies.

A sudden tap on Lee's shoulder made her swing around, reaching for her knife.

"You! How did you follow me?" she hissed.

Finn looked nonchalant, hands in his pockets, appearing deceptively laid back. He shrugged. "I have sources."

It dawned on Lee. "Silas gave you the teketeli, didn't he?"

It was an object she'd stolen for the crew a few months ago, one that gave the user the ability to "hook" into a person and track their magical signature. They'd chosen to keep it rather than sell it, a decision Lee hadn't regretted until now.

Finn pulled a large medallion out of his pocket. "He did indeed. I told you he gave me a job, right? Well, he also gave me the tools to finish it. An efficient leader, if you ask me. And rather concerned about your well-being." He rocked on his heels and gave her a pointed look.

"You can't tell him what I'm doing here. Tell him I came, but don't tell him why. I'll make it worth your while."

"Bribing a fellow crew member? Lee, are you planning a coup?"

Those damned green eyes probed her. Lee shook off the discomfort. Silas and the others would be fine. The fake Way Mary would likely sell without issue, and they'd forgive her for disappearing.

"No, of course not. But this doesn't concern the crew, and Silas needs to butt out."

Finn considered her, clearly drawing out his answer to make her antsy. "What does it have to do with, then?"

Damn. Why couldn't this guy be more like Risa? She had taken the promise of extra cash without question. Then again, Lee didn't know the new guy's angle yet.

She turned away and got across the threshold before Finn's hand on her arm halted her.

Lee glanced from his hand to his eyes.

He nodded once. "I'll do it. You'll have to explain a few things, though, and help me come up with a story. You know what he'll buy."

She was going to regret this. The fear trembling through her limbs told her to stab him and run, but Silas would kick her out of the crew for sure, no matter how long she'd been part of it.

She didn't give Finn an answer, but walked down the short blacklight-lit hall to the door and opened it. A cheerful chime announced her presence, and a few of the occupants turned. One raised a glass to her, and Lee waved. That was Harlin, a good source for vetting sellers for some of the stuff the crew needed to move fast. He took a hefty percentage, but he was good at what he did when he wasn't drunk.

Lee wove between the chairs. It was full tonight.

A woman with pinned-up purple hair wiped glasses at the bar, eyeing customers and sending the twin waiters out with food and drinks any time someone looked low. She looked at Lee and set down her glass.

"You have a barnacle." The bartender gestured at Finn with her eyes, the question obvious in her gaze even without the telepathy that threaded its way into Lee's mind. *You want me to get rid of him?*

"Hey, Chloe. He's with me. Tonight only." Lee glared at Finn.

"Gotcha. What'll it be?"

"The usual." Lee patted the counter and Chloe smiled, turning to pull out the gin and one of her special mixes. You couldn't get a drink just like Choe's anywhere in town. As a telepath, she'd spent a lot of time in peoples' heads figuring out what combinations they liked best and created new blends using emotions as her foundation. Chloe was a brilliant bartender, but she had no filter, and the longer she used her abilities, the more it altered her mind. She'd revealed to Lee that she meditated and took lots of drugs to hold the insanity at bay.

"Black Drop," Finn said as Chloe finished pouring Lee's drink, yellow liquid bouncing in blue like a lava lamp.

Chloe eyed him. "Less rum. More cock."

"Excuse me?" Finn sputtered.

Lee laughed.

"Cock: to make ready. Like a gun. It'll put you on edge a bit, but not enough to feel paranoid," Chloe explained, pouring the red-hued rum into a short glass and pulling out a tiny dropper bottle without a label. She carefully measured three drops. They sank to the bottom of the glass and spread out, then slowly rose.

Lee didn't like the Black Drop. She found it a tad sour. Chloe told her it was because Lee was ready to go all the time. She'd only put one drop of the black liquid in when Lee had tried the drink.

Lee swirled her glass and tried to relax. Her gaze drifted toward Finn, who sniffed his drink.

"It's not poisoned," Lee said.

"I know, it's just...odd." He swirled the drink one last time before taking a sip. His eyes widened. "Wow."

"Why did you join the crew?" Lee hoped to catch him off guard. She saw him pause before downing a large swallow of the Black Drop.

Finn turned his glass, watching the liquid slosh. He smacked his lips with satisfaction. "You know, I never understood thieves who stuck with one crew. I'm a drifter, myself. I want to see new people, experience the thrill of a good hit. You know?" He raised his eyebrows at her and drank again.

"You aren't like most thugs I know," Lee said.

"Who said I'm a thug?" He flashed a charming smile at her, his curly hair flopping across one eye.

The back of Lee's arm itched, but she resisted scratching it and shifted in her seat. "Why did Silas hire you?"

"He likes me. Thinks I'm good looking."

Lee snorted and made a face into her drink, trailing her finger on the rim of the glass.

Finn brushed his hair back. "You needed a speller. You know, he tries pretty hard to take care of you guys. You've been through a lot together."

"There's a difference between caring about someone and protecting an asset."

One of the black-haired twins approached. Lee was never sure if they were male, female, or one of each, and she could never keep them straight. Their names didn't help with their gender. Morgan and Val could go either way.

The twin whispered in Chloe's ear, and Chloe looked at Lee.

"The Speller is ready for you." Chloe leaned in, lowering her voice. "Are you certain you want to see him? He's unstable on the best days, and his worst days are getting… well, worse." Chloe grimaced.

"I have to see him," Lee insisted. She'd take an unstable Speller over an awkward conversation with the man in the seat next to her.

She knocked back a swig of her drink. A slow burn ignited in her gut, a liquid resolve that strengthened what she already had inside. There was no turning back now. She would see the Speller tonight, and she wouldn't leave without the location for the Ceteri.

Chloe clasped Lee's hand and gave it a quick squeeze. "Hope he's in a good mood for you. Good luck."

Lee nodded and thanked Chloe for the drink, then squared her shoulders and left the bar. One of the twins waited for her, face half-hidden behind a curtain of hair. This twin looked feminine to Lee, but perhaps that was just the liberal amount of blue eyeshadow they had applied. They widened their raccoon-eyes and put out a hand to stop Finn, who had followed Lee from the bar.

"Her only."

"I'm with her," Finn insisted.

The twin shook their head. "The Speller will see only the one."

Lee glanced over her shoulder, grinning broadly. Finn's expression was a beautiful mix of disbelief and exasperation; his eyes bulged and his eyebrows shot up past his curly hairline. He shook his head. Most likely, he didn't think she should go alone.

"I'll be fine. Get your next drink on me." She winked, just to be annoying, and followed the twin through the beaded curtain over the doorway.

The hallway darkened to pitch black as she walked, and a sensation like spider legs crawled up her arms. She rubbed them through her jacket and listened for the twin's footsteps to reassure her. Nothing. She stopped, listening. Silence ricocheted around her.

A chill brushed the back of Lee's neck and trickled down her spine while a cold laugh echoed around her. The laugh trailed off in a raspy cough.

When the voice spoke, it pried its way into her mind like an undead hand opening a coffin lid.

At last, you're mine!

CHAPTER 9

The invisible, icy grip clenched Lee's throat, strangling her cries for help. No one from the bar could hear her. She grasped for the Liminal realm, but it seemed beyond her, the thin veil moving away as she reached. There was no escape there. She couldn't see her attacker, and even as her hand closed on the hilt of the knife strapped against her back, she knew she didn't stand a chance against this ethereal thing.

She thrashed about in a desperate attempt to free herself, pain flashing in her hand as it struck the wall.

A flare of blue flashed from far off, illuminating a hallway-like space for an instant. The frigid touch in her throat and lungs fled.

Soft purple-red light flooded Lee's vision. She blinked back tears, rubbing the warmth back into the skin of her throat and the muscles beneath.

Ahead, a man straightened his grey waistcoat, adjusted the chain in his pocket and straightened his glasses, then cleared his throat.

"So sorry about that," he said. "They're getting smarter."

The Speller, Lee supposed. She'd hoped to approach him confidently, to prove the urban legends were wrong, but she couldn't control the trembling in her legs and had to sit down. She sank to the floor, putting her head between her knees.

"What exactly are 'they'?" Lee asked once she could talk.

"The manifestations of my increasing madness." His smile was crooked, and one eye twitched violently. He smoothed his expression. "When we allow the extraordinary to inhabit our bodies, we also bear the curse that comes with it. Humans weren't made to hold magic."

"I'm not interested in paying that price. Hence why I'm here." Lee closed her hands into fists. One felt bruised where it had struck the wall during her encounter with the Speller's... manifestations.

"I want you to guide me to the Ceteri."

"Even if you reached them, you think you could reason with beings so high on the spiritual plane?" The Speller turned as she met him and walked swiftly towards a door at the end of the hall. When it opened, green light spilled into the purple and Lee found herself staring into a room drooping with nets.

No, not nets. Plants.

Plants of all shapes and sizes sat on shelves that went to the ceiling. The ceiling itself was draped in a canopy of vines, and beyond, Lee could make out glass panels. The floor held dozens of pots containing small trees and flowers.

Lee whistled. "Like plants much?"

"I've found that they focus my abilities." The man straightened his glasses again, and cleared his throat. "I'm Nathaniel, by the way."

She reached out her hand. "Lee."

Nathaniel eyed it, but didn't extend his own, instead

rubbing them together. "No offense, I don't shake hands. It makes *them* restless."

Lee squirmed at the mention of the beings that had attacked her. The consequence of the Speller using his abilities. Her own risk of death seemed preferable to a life of madness. Lee looked where Nathaniel pointed, at the white shadows peeking out from the vines above. Glancing around the room, she saw that there were some of them in every pot.

Her eyes widened. "Are those..."

"The manifestations? Yes. Cute right now, aren't they? As you know, they can become quite terrifying. You're here for a reading, then?" Nathaniel pulled out a probe device attached to an electric monitor. The monitor was like an old-time cassette player. He held the metal probe end out toward Lee and fiddled with a dial, pushing several buttons at once.

"Er. No. I came for directions. Someone told me you knew how to get to the Ceteri."

Nathaniel chuckled and nudged his glasses, a motion Lee recognized as entirely unconscious on the man's part. Almost a tic.

"That is very expensive information. Mostly because everyone who has ever attempted has died. The cost is to dissuade hot-headed idiots, you see. And it requires a Liminal guide." He squinted at the numbers on the screen, too small for Lee to see. "Although, judging by these numbers, you *are* a Liminal guide."

"I'm Liminal at least." Lee crossed her arms, nodding towards the device. "How can that read anything without me touching it?"

"It picks up on your personal atmosphere. Some might say aura. But the numbers are far more accurate if you hold it."

Nathaniel gestured with the probe again. "You just need to grab the metal part. It won't hurt."

Lee hesitantly took hold. The machine whirred, like it was working overtime.

Nathaniel bobbed his head as his expression turned to amazement. "These are high numbers. Which is good. But…" He tapped the screen. "This one is concerning. Have you experienced any paralytic episodes? Moments you couldn't move realms when you tried? Like a glitch?"

"Yes! But what does this have to do with the Ceteri?" She felt like she was at a doctor's office waiting for a diagnosis.

Nathaniel pushed against the bridge of his glasses. "Nothing. And everything. Most people come in here for a reading, to determine how advanced their deterioration is."

Lee hadn't cared to know, but now that she had some measure of it, she felt like she needed to know more. "I know I'm going to die. Just…when?"

Her arm brushed against a soft-leafed plant on a shoulder-high shelf. The surface felt like velvet. She rubbed the leaf between her fingers.

"Oh, there's no way to tell that specifically." He made a show of arranging his equipment on the desk, as if trying to figure out how to say what he didn't want to. "I know you came for information on the Ceteri, but I can't help but make sure you know that there is a way to cure the Fade. Or postpone it, at least. I've seen a few successful pairings."

"Pairings?" Lee echoed. She dropped the leaf, glancing at Nathaniel.

"Yes. We call them Anchors. They keep your soul tied strongly enough to Earth that you don't fragment when you travel. It's a deep bond."

"Like a soulmate," Lee said flatly. She shook her head. "It's a fairy story. I can't believe you promote it."

Nathaniel raised his hands defensively. "I wouldn't if I hadn't seen it. Terminal clients, like yourself, flickering and fading and glitching, healed." He snapped his fingers. "Just like that."

Lee turned back to the fuzzy plant. "What's this called?"

"*Stachys byzantina*. Lamb's ear. Look, it's an alternative to the suicide of attempting to travel to the Ceteri's realm. Join some speed dates, see what you find."

"I had a soulmate once. He died," Lee snapped.

"I've heard of one person bonding with a cat," Nathaniel said hopefully.

"Are you a matchmaker or a Speller?"

Nathaniel managed to look decently offended. "Are you sure this is what you want?" His warm tone had dropped several degrees.

Lee set her jaw and nodded, sliding a hand into her pocket and closing it around the Way Mary.

"Very well. How will you pay?"

Lee dangled the jade bracelet on her finger in front of her, then tossed it at the Speller. He caught it and turned it over in his hand.

"This is real?"

"Of course," Lee said indignantly. She'd double and triple-checked to be sure that Silas had the fake.

Nathaniel made eye contact with her as he pulled the probe back out, turning the machine on. It whirred quietly as the metal touched the bracelet. The stones glowed a soft white color.

He jutted his bottom lip out, his eyes widening like he was impressed. But then he tossed the bracelet back to Lee.

Lee barely caught it against her stomach. "I was told this would be enough."

"It would be. If my prices hadn't gone up."

Lee's shoulders shook with her rage. She clenched her teeth. "When, exactly, did the price go up?"

"The price is always higher for hopeless cases." Nathanial examined his fingernails while leaning against the desk with the other hand. "I told you. It's a filter. I won't risk my own madness for your failed venture."

"This ends in death no matter how you look at it!" Lee shouted. The white manifestations grew in size, their color darkening..

Nathaniel's eyes narrowed. "I recommend you remove yourself from the premises. I can contain them only for so long once they feel I've been threatened."

His eyes flashed orange beneath his brow, and Lee drew back, stumbling towards the door. She hadn't gotten what she'd come for. None of this had gone the way she'd expected.

"Please, I just need directions."

"Death comes to us all. You are not exempt from meeting the fate intended for you, and I can See that nothing I do will change your course for the better. Leave!" He bellowed the last word with eyes burning like coals, and Lee fled through the wooden door and down the purple-hued hall. The lights flickered as ghost-like figures crossed in front of her. The chill swept past, reminding her of what had happened before.

Mine. Mine. Mine!

The voice chanted in her mind, the cold fingers sinking deep again. Gasping, Lee burst through the beaded curtain into the barroom that didn't feel warm and inviting anymore. She glanced around frantically, finding Finn sitting at the bar, leaning on one hand and talking to Chloe. He sat up as she came in, taking in her disheveled appearance and standing up.

He seemed to walk in slow motion, thanking Chloe for his drink and dropping a tip, striding toward Lee with his red-brown curls waving in a sudden breeze.

It came from behind her–that reaching, icy touch accompanied by angry whispers followed her from the tunnel. She bolted away from the door, stumbling and running into a chair. Hands reached to help her, and she brushed them away, her eyes fixed on the front door of the bar. A new energy entered the room, rushing over Lee and overwhelming her senses.

From *there*.

The door chimed, and a man walked in. An impossibly tall and skinny man with sunken cheeks, clicking his tongue at the massive black dog on a leash in front of him. A dog with the body of a purebred Great Dane.

A dog with three heads. *The dog had three heads.*

There was only one three-headed dog Lee had ever heard of. She blinked. Was she hallucinating?

"Chloe!" Lee ran for the bar and leapt over it. The other customers scattered.

Finn ran after her, crouching down with her beside a shelf of bottles. "Lee, who is this?"

"I don't know," she panted. "But I don't want to stick around to find out."

The man had seen her. Everything about him reeked of death. And death meant the Reaper was involved.

"There's no need to hide. I came in for a drink. The dog belongs to a friend." The man's voice dripped, sickly-sweet.

Above Lee, Chloe gave the man her best forced smile, but her hand hovered over a button beneath the counter.

"What will you have tonight?"

"Well, I believe it's sitting just under your bar."

Sweat chilled on Lee's neck. Blood rushed in her ears.

Finn nudged her, mouthing something she couldn't read in her panic.

Why would the Reaper send one of his minions after *her*?

CHAPTER 10

Agent Adam Finley had seen a lot of things in the short time he'd spent working the Thaumaturgic Department with the FBI, but a three-headed dog wasn't one of them. What had Chloe put in his drink?

The magical sensor in Adam's chest ticked so fast that his breath caught and his head pounded and pulsed. His hand went to his gun, but what could that do against a creature from Greek mythology?

Lee's hands glowed faintly red. Tingling warmth flooded Adam's body, and a tugging sensation dragged at his abdomen. Lee glanced at him just before she faded, a wry smile on her face.

"Sorry about this." And then she disappeared.

Adam tried to catch her a split second before her face vanished, and he brushed the skin on her arm as it went incorporeal. The hook sensation in his stomach jerked, and then he was gone too, spinning through a dim world with muffled sounds and flashing lights.

We've gone Liminal. Adam thought, in utter awe. When

he'd followed her through before it had been so different. A muffling of everything. This, this was an entirely new experience. He had suspected for a long time that Liminals could travel in more ways than one. This confirmed itl It was like he was flying, and he couldn't see Lee or make out details of the world around him.

The hook in his belly jerked, and he landed on a sidewalk, stumbling until he came across a wall. His breath gasped in and out.

"What are you doing here?" Lee shouted. Her voice sounded loud in the small space.

When Adam's vision cleared, he took in several rows of industrial washing machines, chipped greenish tile beneath his feet, and the distinct smell of musty laundry soap.

"Did you bring us to a laundromat?"

"Us? I didn't bring *us* anywhere. You aren't supposed to be here." Lee's straight hair was exposed; the orange hat she usually wore held in her hands. Even with the flyaways, she had a beauty to her in that moment, standing bathed in the early dawn light that streamed through the glass windows, her olive-toned cheeks flushed with exertion. Or anger—Adam couldn't tell.

Best send those thoughts packing and focus on the job .He rubbed at the sleeve of tattoos on his forearm. He had to get the Liminal to the station. But first, he needed her to trust him.

He cleared his throat. "So, you planned to leave me behind with that...that..."

She brushed off her sleeves like she hadn't just seen a creature of legend. After all, if the three-headed dog existed, did the gods? Adam's hands still trembled. One of them clutched at his gun in its holster. He released it, shaking out his hands and rolling his shoulders.

"Agent of the devil, hellion, whatever it was? Yes, yes I did. Every newbie needs a chance to prove themselves."

"Who said I was a newbie?" He put on a grin. "New to the crew, maybe. But I've been around the block a few times."

Lee's eyebrows raised. "You've met a hellion before?"

"Well, not that block, maybe. But you definitely underestimate me." He gave her his best cocky smile.

That arched brow disappeared as she rolled her eyes. She folded her arms over her chest, and scuffed her shoe on the linoleum.

Adam glanced around again. "Don't these places open pretty early?"

Lee shook her head. "Not this one. It's been closed for years."

Now that she mentioned it, Adam noticed the layer of dust on the row of machines in the center of the room.

How did her abilities work? Other Liminals he'd followed also seemed to teleport to strange, abandoned places.

"Is that how it always works? The traveling? You can take people with you?"

Lee frowned. "Not usually. It's...difficult. Like dragging a heavy object. I hardly noticed your weight, though..." She trailed off, her voice no more than a murmur, then shook her head. "It doesn't matter. That mad Speller wouldn't guide me to the Ceteri, so I'm back at square one."

Adam's chest constricted, as adrenaline increased his heart rate.. "You were trying to get to their realm. For a cure."

This was the side project Director Hatcher had him working on for the past year. Find the Ceteri and convince them to remove thaumaturgy from the human race. Everything could go back to normal.

Lee's eyes narrowed. "You promised you wouldn't tell Silas."

"Sure, but why not? Wouldn't he support you finding a cure?"

"He wouldn't support me stealing from the crew to pay for it. Stupid Speller changing his stupid prices." She jammed the beanie back on her head.

Adam took in a breath. "Maybe...maybe I could talk to him? The Speller?"

She froze, adjusting the hat. "Why would you do that?"

Adam shrugged and kept his expression carefully composed. "It doesn't seem like he treated you fairly." And if he talked to the Speller and got the location of the Ceteri, building up trust with Lee so she would take him there, then he had a chance at regaining normalcy for himself and thousands of others.

Lee dropped her hands from the hat on her head. "It's the business we're in. Sometimes people change their minds. He didn't want to help me. I'll find another way."

"But I could..."

"Leave it, okay? I don't need your pity, and I don't need your help. And keep Silas out of it. Damnit." She kept muttering and walked away from him, pointing at the different machines as if counting them.

Adam thought he heard something about "the damn bleeding heart that Silas hired". He did sound pretty soft. Did she suspect him? His sources had told him that the Gadai, the crew Lee was part of, didn't kill during their jobs, and they prided themselves in that fact. He'd created a persona that would fit the goals of their crew. Make money, don't harm anyone. They weren't violent, hardened criminals.

In fact, in all of his interactions with the crew members,

they seemed like decent people trying to earn a living, most of them supporting family in addition to themselves. Lee and her Liminality. Risa and her clairvoyant abilities. Silas and his mechanical parts. Sam…Well, Adam hadn't figured out Sam yet. The big man was disproportionately quiet. He moved like a shadow through the house, but his thaumaturgic ability, if he had one, was a mystery.

Lee exclaimed at the end of the row and swung open one of the washing machine doors. She rubbed her hand around the inside rim and triumphantly pulled out a key.

"Is that for the front door?"

Lee nodded.

"How did you find it?"

"I swiped it off the owner when I found out they were closing. Figured it would come in handy. I can come to this place any time without issues."

"But why not just use your abilities?" Adam scratched his head.

Lee cocked her head at him. "How much do you know about Liminals?"

"Everyone knows you can teleport. And it's more… terminal than most abilities."

"It's not teleportation. I've met people who can do that. They stay within Earth's realm and move a few feet, maybe a few miles if they push themselves. Liminals can move between realms. It takes a lot more out of the human body and mind to travel through an alternate dimension. Doing it in certain places makes it easier."

He knew that. But his persona didn't, and it was a good way to gauge her trust of him.

Lee brushed past him, walking swiftly without making eye

contact. She jangled the keys and inserted one into the front door. The lock clicked, and Lee opened the door.

"Are you staying there all night?" she asked.

"Nah. I've got some buddies I wanted to meet." He shrugged his way past her, hands deep in his leather jacket pockets, rubbing the cell phone there. If he didn't check in soon, Hatcher would call.

Lee raised her eyebrows. "You have buddies? Do they know about your new job?"

"Course not. Just some friends. You know how it goes."

Judging by the way she looked away from him, the crew was all she had. Adam felt for her. A lonely woman with a terminal illness, turned to thievery to buy the chance to talk to the ones responsible for the magic that burned in her veins. Not everyone was as lucky as he was in keeping their regular jobs and being only mildly affected by their ability. Eventually, it might stop his heart, but his doctor thought it was more likely his line of work would kill him, and Adam agreed.

Lee stood on the sidewalk, rocking on her heels, then waved. "See you around, Finn."

Adam waved back and watched her walk away. This was one of the hardest parts of his job. Pretending to be someone he wasn't. Connecting with people he would later turn in, and in many cases, flat out betray. For the good of the masses. To keep criminals off the streets. He would always be Finn to Lee, until the day she learned who he was, and once that happened, she would hate him irreparably. His stomach clenched. He hadn't eaten for a while. He should pick something up before...

His phone rang, buzzing in his hand with a life of its own.

Adam picked up the phone, expecting the FBI director asking for a report. "Hey."

"Meet me at the river side of the West Lake Landfill in an hour."

Adam's skin prickled at the sound of the gruff voice. It was the cyborg, his new "boss". He probably wanted an update on Lee's activities. What could Adam tell him?

"Sure, boss. How will I find you? That's a big place."

"I'll find you." The line on the other end clicked, indicating the end of the call.

Was there a secret to talking with that guy, or did he act that way with everyone? Adam would have to ask the others. For now, he got on the next bus towards the Mississippi river and the massive waste site Silas had indicated.

Adam had to hike up to the river. As the brown water ran past, the thaumaturgic signature from the dump surrounded him. They had built it near an illegal radioactive dump site from the seventies, and a subterranean fire had burned there for nearly two decades.

When thaumaturgy hit the Earth, the radioactive waste went magical. Official reports stated the waste had turned into a well of magic they had yet to figure out how to harvest or use, but Adam suspected those reports were a cover-up. Either it wasn't what they claimed, or they had figured out how to use it but weren't telling anyone.

It wasn't his jurisdiction. Yet. Once he succeeded on this Liminals case, he might be able to get put on the dump site as a new case. But not until he had more answers about Liminals. The more he found out about Lee and other Liminals, the more he could help his daughter with her thaumaturgic abilities.

Gears whirred behind Adam, and he whirled around.

"Do you have a stealth mode or what? I'm not easy to sneak up on," Adam said.

Silas chuckled, raising and flexing his robotic arm. "I'm not heard unless I want to be."

"Why are we here?" Adam asked.

"Come with me," Silas said. The cyborg led Adam back the way they had come, then split off to a dirt road leading toward the thaumaturgic well, guarded by a fence covered in signs noting the dangers and consequences of crossing.

Adam stopped once he realized where they were headed. "This is a restricted area."

"Yeah, so?" The cyborg scoffed. "You a thief with a conscience?"

"Just no desire for a death sentence," Adam replied.

"It's safe if you stick with me. I'm not that eager to get rid of you. I have a job for you." Silas walked right up to the gate and shifted his robotic arm, producing a probe-like device that he stuck into the electric box controlling the gate motor. It beeped three times, then a light on the keypad flashed green and the gate opened.

Silas grinned at Adam. "Comes in handy."

"I'll bet," Adam said, trying to shove away his misgivings about entering the site. He leveled his breathing and walked at a controlled, casual pace, passing Silas.

Silas clapped an arm around his shoulders. "Let me show you around."

There was a single, nondescript cement building in this section of the waste site. Silas hacked the keypad at the door to the building as well, letting them inside.

"Won't there be guards?" Adam asked, ducking cautiously into the cool, quiet building. They were in a white hallway with two rows of doors branching off either side.

Silas switched the fixture on his arm to a lockpick and headed straight for the door he wanted.

"It's only staffed three days a week. They have an offsite location where they analyze the research for safety reasons. The thaumaturgic fallout has started to have...unanticipated consequences for long-term employees here."

"Makes sense." Adam sniffed and followed Silas into the room, where panels and screens flashed in the dark.

Silas ignored all of them and unlocked another door beside the wall filled with monitors. Adam caught a few words here and there. *Critical thaumaturgic mass. Isolated particles. Essential drafts.* He didn't have much context for them, but all of the red lights did seem concerning. How bad was the fallout here? Was it leaking into the rest of the city?

The next room was enormous, taking up most of the building from the appearance. The main feature was a suspended pathway around the perimeter of the room, and as Adam walked out onto the metal rungs, energy washed over him, coming in waves off of a giant, swirling hole in the ground hundreds of feet down. The thrum of it filled Adam's ears, like a giant wind turbine.

"This is the thaumaturgic well. The government claims to have it contained, but a bit of steel and concrete isn't keeping that from contaminating the air and water," Silas yelled over the sound, then grinned maniacally. "We're going to get a bit closer."

Adam's heart pounded as Silas took him down a staircase, and then through a tunnel that sloped downward. They walked in silence for a long stretch.

"Do you know why I hired you, Finn?" Silas asked.

"Because you need a Screener?"

"Yes, that. But there were a half dozen who applied. Your passion about thaumaturgy set you apart. Liminality in particular. It caught my attention when you said you had experience with others who had it. I was intrigued. Because I have a problem, as you can see after your last assignment."

"Lee," Adam said.

"Yes. She is important to me. And the crew. And I don't want her lost because of her unwillingness to see that frivolous use of her ability is bringing her ultimate demise closer. If she only used her abilities for the crew's heists, I'm certain she could extend her life, maybe live to see a cure."

Adam nodded. "I can stop her with my ability, but only if I stay at her side constantly. And only if I catch her starting to go Liminal." Even without her abilities, Lee was formidable to keep track of.

The tunnel took them to a hard left, then right, and then they walked out onto a platform, the thaumaturgic well only a hundred feet away.

Here, giant tubes led up the walls, filled with a blue substance being drawn out of the well below.

"What is all this?" Adam asked.

"The government's attempt to mine magic for military purposes."

"You were military?" Adam had known. Silas's PTSD could be seen from a mile away.

"I was in special ops before I gained my metal parts, before thaumaturgy plagued the Earth. Do you know what ability inflicted me?" Silas pulled a coil of tubing out of his arm. He went to the wall, where a fixture was hiding in a crevice of the rock. Piping, too small to be part of the tubing system the government had placed.

"I've heard rumors, but nothing has been confirmed," Adam said.

Silas plugged his tubing into the fixture and attached a wire plug from his arm into a small box on the tubing. He pushed some buttons on a panel in his arm and waited. The blue substance pumped directly into his machinery hydraulics.

The cyborg powered himself with magical fallout from an unstable and potentially dangerous thaumaturgic access point? The man was a walking contradiction.

Silas settled back against the wall, his arm attached to the piping that fed directly into the pulsing well of magic below. "I caused others pain. Simply by looking at them, I could torture them. Enemy soldiers, to gain confessions. Other prisoners. Disobedient officers. My superiors. Friends. Family members. The magic didn't differentiate. I wore sunglasses, and that helped most of the time. But the ability grew stronger."

Silas flexed his human hand and gazed at Adam. "Would you want such an ability?"

"You could control a lot of people with the threat of pain," Adam said carefully. He didn't know what answers this man expected.

"Lose a lot of people, too. I met with doctors, with scientists. The military gave me access to every expert they had, and they all resulted in dead ends except for one. One doctor in Berlin who took a risk and performed exploratory surgery. Thirteen hours, in the first one, and then seven repeat surgeries over the next year to complete the job. He cut the thaumaturgy out of my body, leaving me like this." Silas gestured to the robotic side of his face.

"And yet you're powered by magic. I would think you wouldn't want anything to do with it after all of that."

"It runs through the tubing implanted in my body. I control the input and output. It's a tool I use. When the magic ran through my veins, it controlled me." Silas waved a hand,

and Adam had to admit he could see the point the cyborg made.

"Why are you telling me this?" Adam asked.

"So that, when I tell you that keeping Lee alive is my main goal, you will understand that I will do whatever it takes to do that, even if she doesn't like it." Silas unplugged the tubing and wound it back into his arm, fixing the end in its place. He pointed at Adam. "This is your sole responsibility here. Track Lee, keep her from wandering off on her own until I figure out a way to keep her under control. And cover her magical signature to keep her from detection. For her own safety."

"Sure, boss," Adam said. What else could he say at the edge of a thaumaturgic well facing a huge cyborg freshly fueled by the unstable magic from said well? Silas said all the words to imply that he truly cared about Lee and about the crew, but to Adam he sounded like a man who had to have control over all the elements of his life. Control and care weren't the same thing.

"Good man," Silas said. "Now, where did she go today?"

Adam froze. He hadn't come up with a story yet, but it was best to stick close to the truth. "She, uh, went to a bar in the Energia district. Met a woman named Chloe. Chatted her up. Talked with some other friends. Then we left."

He left out the reaper-guy sent to take Lee out, or capture her, or whatever. Adam still had questions himself about what had almost happened there, like why someone from the realm of the dead would want Lee.

"Believable enough. Nice woman, Chloe. Sounds like you were made early on and Lee changed her plans so you wouldn't see anything you could report to me." Silas raised his eyebrows.

Adam let out a nervous laugh. "I wouldn't lie to you, boss. But you're right. Lee's a tricky one to tail. You know, an interesting thing did happen, though. This guy came into the bar looking for Lee, and she made us run without talking to him." Adam hoped the information would be enough to satisfy Silas, at least for now.

"What did this man look like?"

Adam crossed his arms. "Extremely tall. Thin. Kind of sunken eyes. He had a dog with him." He left out the detail of it having three heads.

Silas's brow creased. "That doesn't sound like anyone I know. I want you to find out more about this man. Who he is, what bone he has to pick with Lee, and make sure that Lee doesn't contact him on her own. She might be trying to jump crews."

"Why would she do that?" Adam asked.

Silas narrowed his eyes at Adam. "Because they tell convincing lies. Give her false hope and promises that they can fix her Liminality, in exchange for the use of her abilities. There's nothing that can be done, but her life could be extended if proper care is taken."

Adam kept his mouth shut. He didn't like this man's overbearance or his desire to keep Lee 'safe' from other crews at the cost of her freedom. He would have to keep an eye on Silas. If Lee ever did find a cure and suddenly didn't need the crew anymore, there was no telling what the cyborg would do.

Lee found Silas waiting for her in the otherwise empty house. Either that or Sam and Risa were hiding in the back rooms, and Lee didn't blame them. Silas was full-bot, his mechanical arm switching between numerous firearms and knives as he inspected and cleaned them. Should she back out quietly? No doubt Silas had already heard her open the door, and she didn't need to burn the last bridge she had left. If only she'd succeeded in going to the Ceteri tonight, she wouldn't be facing down with her cyborg crew boss for what felt like the hundredth time.

Lee adjusted her beanie so it fit more snugly over her head, like a security blanket. She tried to tell herself that the trembling in her hands was left over from encountering the hellion and going Liminal with that oaf, Finn, in tow.

Silas looked up and a smile slid across his lips. A warning flashed in Lee's mind. When he was pleased, Lee had learned to be wary.

She cleared her throat. Silas hadn't spoken, just stared at

her with a lopsided grin. Was he drunk? Hard to tell. His machinery seemed to give him a higher alcohol tolerance.

"Sit down, Lee." He patted the seat on the couch beside him.

Lee crossed the room and sat, perching on the edge of the couch. She tried to even out her breathing.

Silas tightened a screw on a fixture in his arm, then flexed all of the fixtures at once, making Lee jump. He chuckled, gesturing at her with the arm, the fixtures still extended.

"You've gone to places you shouldn't, done things you shouldn't," he said. "What's so important you'd risk your life and the crew?"

How did he know about what happened at the Witch's Brew already? Maybe Finn had called him before she got back, but he'd promised not to share details. She clenched her hands. The bastard had probably lied.

"There's nothing life-threatening about visiting a bar in my downtime," Lee said. She didn't know what Finn had told Silas. Being vague might get Silas to give her some more details to work with so she didn't blow the whole thing open. Because if Silas knew she was planning to find the Ceteri and convince them to heal her so she didn't have to thieve anymore, well, it wouldn't be pretty. She could avoid the whole mess if she could keep it under wraps.

Silas held up his mechanical hand with its metal bars and twisting wires moving together like muscles and bone. "You haven't been totally honest with me for some time. Taking Risa on an unapproved heist was one thing. Giving me fake goods is another entirely."

A compartment on his arm opened and the fake *Waimari* lifted into the air on a thin metal bar.

Silas examined the bracelet. "A man at the market was

THIEF OF MAGIC   95

kind enough to inform me that this is worthless. A good replica, though, he complimented that. Where's the real one, Lee?"

Lee's heart skipped a beat and her breathing grew shallow. She hadn't thought much past this point. She never expected the Speller to not accept her payment, she hadn't planned on coming back here, and in the shock of fleeing from the denizen of the Lord of Death and his stupid dog, she hadn't had a moment to make a new plan.

"What would a simple burglar like yourself want with a ten-thousand-dollar enchanted bracelet? Has someone offered you more for it?" Silas spread his hands, then leaned forward and clasped them, eyes fixed on Lee. "Are you working with another crew?"

His robotic eye flashed red. Lee froze, unable to get her mind to work, like a frightened animal in a hole.

The fake bracelet vanished back into Silas's arm, and he shook his head. "You disappoint me. Betraying the crew like this. Have we not taken you in? Treated you like family? Given you a place when you had nothing? Shane would be disappointed."

Silas tsked, crossing his arms over his chest. He looked big, twice her size with five times the muscle. His steady breathing only threw Lee more off balance. He was so calm it was scary. She could go Liminal, but where would she go?

Run, her body said. He hadn't threatened her life, hadn't made any indication that she was in trouble beyond the questions. And he was understandably upset about being duped. Could Lee turn this conversation around? If she told a half-truth, maybe he would forgive her.

Lee swallowed. "I needed a cure."

"A cure, Lee?" Silas straightened, somehow rising several more inches. "There's no cure for what you have."

"I was told there could be." Lee didn't have to fake her tension. Did she sound desperate enough?

"You saw what happened the other day. I was paralyzed. I-I went for an analysis. To see how far...how soon..." She stammered, real emotion rising in her chest as she remembered the prognosis she'd received.

"And...?" Silas raised his eyebrows. "Was it worth undermining my authority and stealing from the crew?"

Lee bit her lip, then immediately stopped. "I know our numbers. We are barely making enough to keep this place. Convincing you to do bigger jobs wasn't working."

She didn't need to feel guilty for taking care of herself. She'd stolen the Way Mary on her own time. Risa had helped a bit, but she had intended to pay Risa back. Then Silas had claimed it for the crew. For himself.

She curled her fingers over her palms. "It doesn't matter anyway. The Speller couldn't tell me what I needed."

"Did he take the payment?" Silas growled, and danger flashed in his eyes.

Lee started to say no, to tell the truth. Then Silas would know that the Way Mary was still on her, or that she knew where it was. The bracelet seemed to burn in the upper chest pocket of her jacket.

It was hers. Silas had no right to it.

He seemed to take her silence as guilt. His expression lifted, and the light in his eye flickered off, returning it to an ice-blue. "I just want to pay for groceries, cover the rent, and tide us over until our next big hit. I understand how it must feel to deal with this alone. But that's been your big mistake,

Lee. You're not alone—you have us. And that's why I insist that you give the real Way Mary over to the crew's coffers."

His kind words, the concerned crease of his brow, those were real, right? Her fingers twitched, but she held them down.

"The Speller took the payment in advance," Lee said. She tried to look remorseful. She touched the edge of her beanie, leaning her head in her hands.

"You let yourself get duped?" Silas bellowed. The unexpected blow of his shout filled Lee's ears, and she clapped her hands over her ears. "Listen when I talk to you!"

Her hands muffled the volume, but they couldn't muffle his anger. She dropped them. "I didn't 'let' myself do anything! I offered to pay fairly for information. He refused and sent his lackeys after me."

Sweat gathered at Lee's brow, hidden beneath the rim of her beanie. She adjusted it, hoping her sweat wouldn't drip and give away her anxiety. She had *lied* to Silas. If he bought it, that disproved Sam's built-in lie detector theory.

"Your lack of consideration for the crew is a concern. Not just a concern, a hazard. To yourself and others." Silas walked back toward Lee. "When you joined this crew, I promised you protection. I'm a man of my word. Even if it means protecting you from yourself. As such, I've set up some extra magical protections around the hideout. You won't be able to leave here by way of Liminal travel, and I've given Finn and Sam the job of making sure you don't leave the premises without permission."

"What?" Lee said, aghast.

"It's all to keep you safe," Silas said in a soothing tone. "You push yourself far too much. Forty-eight hours minimum, complete house arrest. We'll readdress your commitment to the crew and the protections then."

"No, Silas, you *can't* do that." Lee swallowed before she said anything else.

His gaze hardened. "I can. I did." He pivoted and marched out of the room. The front door slammed, adding finality to Lee's sentence.

"Boss says we get to hang out."

Lee tilted her head to see Sam's bulk filling the doorway. She smiled a mostly genuine smile at him. "That's what the man said."

"He's hard on you." Sam's gentle brown eyes watched Lee with concern.

She shrugged, looking across the room at the boarded-up fireplace. "He's hard on everyone."

But the others weren't on house arrest.

Lee slapped her thighs and stood up. "At least I have the best company." She forced a grin on her face.

Sam rubbed his hands. "I'll make us sandwiches."

"I'm going to grab my laundry," Lee said as Sam moved into the kitchen. She walked to her room, not bothering to turn on the light. She grabbed her laundry from her bed. Risa wasn't inside from what Lee could see. The woman must have gone out.

Sam sang quietly from the kitchen in his native tongue of Samoan, the song following Lee as she jogged down the basement stairs to the laundry area.

Exposed pipes and grey cement decorated the walls in a style some would call modern. Lee called it lazy. No one had ever bothered to finish this part of the house. It had its appeal, being a secure place to discuss jobs and plans, but it was too cold in the winter, and you could hear every toilet flush that came from upstairs.

There were a few obvious reasons Silas had paired Lee with Sam during her house arrest. For one, Sam never left the house. Ever. For two, it was impossible to catch him off guard and escape, due to his thaumaturgic ability.

Sam could See intention. In words, in actions, even in thoughts when he was focused enough. Luckily, his abilities worked over technology, so all crew members wore cameras during a heist. Sam manned the different screens from the hideout, giving them hints about who or what might be coming next. The tech filtered out some of the interference from surrounding intentions, but it also dampened the amount of information Sam could interpret. It was still golden. Sam was golden. And he made the best food.

The sandwich he brought Lee when he met up with her in the basement was no exception. Thinly sliced pork, dill pickles, and gooey Swiss cheese on grilled bread melted in Lee's mouth as she took a bite. She inhaled and chewed, catching a dill juice drip with her tongue.

"Sam, you've outdone yourself. Where'd you get the ingredients? We were out of everything the other day."

Sam grunted and held up a finger, still chewing. He swallowed. "Risa went shopping for me. A man can't live on mayo alone."

Lee tried not to think about the bracelet still tucked away in her jacket pocket, a bracelet that could fetch a price worth thousands of sandwiches. She reluctantly set the sandwich down after a couple more bites, brushed off her hands and set to work, tossing one of her loads into the wash.

"You should wash that hat," Sam commented.

"I never wash my hat."

"It looks alive." Sam waggled his eyebrows, and Lee just laughed.

The beanie *was* getting filthy. But she hadn't washed it since Shane had died. Wearing it, she could be close to him again every day. She added soap to the load and sat back on the dilapidated leather couch, grabbing the sandwich with both hands.

Sam looked at the wall where the washer and dryer sat. He stared as if his eyes could bore holes in the walls. They couldn't. At least not that Lee knew of.

"You sense something?"

Sam shook his head and slowly rotated his body, turning his attention back to the sandwich. He chewed much more slowly and kept his head tilted.

"A flicker," he finally said. "Usually it's neighbors out walking dogs, deciding on a different route, mundane things."

"It comes as words?"

"And images, sometimes. Depending on how the person in question primarily thinks, or so I've gathered."

Lee frowned at her sandwich. She paused before taking another bite. "Do you have any other symptoms? Besides crowds being hard?"

"Crowds aren't just hard. They're impossible. Imagine thousands of words and images bombarding you every second. I hyperventilate, get panic attacks."

"What about here? With us?" Lee's voice distorted through the pickle that slid out of the bread instead of biting all the way through.

"I've gotten used to most of the signatures here. Our intentions are usually pretty aligned, but..." He trailed off, and Lee caught him glancing at her, then looking away.

"But what?"

"It's harder with you. Your abilities are so much less predictable, and you constantly think about leaving, so I see a dozen images of you splitting off in different ways. I only see a few moments, mind you, so it's not like I can see your future. Just a few seconds."

"Oh." Lee put the sandwich down, suddenly not hungry. She'd never considered what it might be like for Sam in tight quarters with several other human beings.

Sam shifted, making the couch creak. "Why do you want to leave so bad? Is it because of Shane?"

"That's part of it," Lee mumbled. "You can't sense why?"

"I sense intention, not motivation," Sam pointed out, his mouth full of pork.

Lee didn't know what to say to that. She let silence fall between them, chewing thoughtfully.

"It's harder with him gone," Sam said suddenly. "Shane, I mean. I know he was only here for a few months, but he seemed to balance us out. The new guy isn't like that. He's not around much."

"Yeah, I'm still not convinced we can trust this Finn guy," Lee said.

"His intentions are good. He's really focused on you, though, and it's kind of odd."

Lee must have looked shocked, because he rushed to add, "Not romantically!" He brushed off his shirt, as if to avoid Lee's gaze.

Lee tried to calm her thoughts. If Finn was thinking about her, she wanted to know why. "What have you sensed?"

Sam's voice dropped to a mumble. "He hasn't been around much. And when he's around, you haven't been around, so it's hard to interpret. But I catch glimpses of this girl. Maybe someone he knows is like you?"

Lee snorted. "Unlikely."

"There are more people like you than you think," Sam insisted. "You should meet some of them. Maybe it would be easier."

"Sure. What's easier than making friends with a bunch of people who are going to die?" Lee couldn't help the bitterness. It spilled out of her in a wave.

"Sorry," Sam said after a moment.

She needed to stop taking her frustration out on people who didn't deserve it. Sam had only been trying to help her not feel so alone. He knew how much Shane meant to her, and what she lost when he died. She took a shaky breath, letting it out slowly.

"Thanks, Sam."

The tension in the air settled. Lee leaned back into the couch, crossing her legs and folding her arms.

"Have you thought about leaving, too?" she asked.

Sam bobbed his head, but didn't get more specific.

Lee scratched at her scalp through her beanie. "Family to go back to?"

His eyes widened. "Oh no. They're enormous. Three generations, uncles, aunts, cousins on the same block, parties all the time. I couldn't handle it. That's why I left." His voice cracked.

Lee tried not to feel jealous. Her own experience with a single, crackhead mother who had killed herself when Lee was twelve was much different. Foster care had been a blur of homes, none of them permanent, and Lee found her way onto the streets the year before she'd been infected with thaumaturgy.

She was alone.

A twig scratched the basement window outside. Lee

glanced up, seeing nothing but darkness beyond. Just that bush planted in front of the window. Its branches moved erratically. Had it been windy when she walked home? She couldn't remember. The bush stopped moving, and the washer buzzed. Lee jumped to her feet, fumbling with the sandwich plate in her lap before setting it down and crossing the room.

She opened the washer. A sleepy haze passed through her mind like a shadow. Something whispered.

"What was that, Sam?"

No response. She turned, wet clothes in hand, glancing over at him as she bent over and opened the dryer. He stared forward, back ramrod straight, mouth opening and closing soundlessly.

Lee straightened. "Sam?"

A bag jerked over Lee's head, and she screamed. Instinctively, she went Liminal. The burning itch spread across her body and then vanished. Soothed away by a suffocating blanket that coated her brain. She stayed tangible, paralyzed by the smothering influence. Mentally, she went belly-up despite the instincts that screamed she should run, despite everything that told her this was wrong.

An unintelligible whisper caressed the back of her neck, and footsteps came down the stairs to her left. A body moved behind her, but no one touched her.

Someone had set a trap, and she'd walked right into it.

CHAPTER 12

Lee's breath closed in around her, hot and frantic. The bag over her head tugged against her beanie, threatening to pull it off. Fingers played with Lee's hair against her back, and she shuddered. A long sniff came from behind. Creep. But as much as Lee wanted to squirm away, her limbs felt heavy, and a strange sedation lingered in her mind. She'd never encountered a mental ability like this.

A high-pitched male voice slid into her ears, saying, "As you can see, we are prepared for your particular antics. Leaving the realm is no longer an option." Then it dripped out again, leaving an oily sensation in her skull.

Lee wished she could shake her head, as if she could get rid of it. She'd only heard of people like him. They were called Mentalists.

"Who are you?" Lee asked. She tried to move, but her limbs wouldn't obey her. Where was Sam? Had they immobilized him too?

"What about this one?" a gruff voice spoke from across the room.

"Leave him," the man near Lee said. "We have what we came for." He slid his arm against Lee's side, locking arms with her.

Lee's mind moved like sludge, but she forced it to work. She couldn't go Liminal. What *could* she do? She'd removed her shoulder blade sheath while gathering her laundry. The only knife she still had was in the forearm wrap beneath her jacket. Her fingers twitched at her sides as she thought about it, and she breathed in, focusing on moving those fingers closer to the release catch that would put the handle in her hand.

The man looped his arm through Lee's elbow on the side where her knife was. She could still reach it and stab the man in the leg, possibly freeing herself if she could move fast enough, but even the tiny movement of curling her fingers towards the knife took immense effort.

A bellow erupted, and footsteps pounded across the floor. Several hundred pounds rammed into Lee and her captor. Lee smashed to the floor, and the suffocating mental blanket lifted. She flung the bag off her head, taking in a gasp of fresh air, and jumped to her feet. Reflexively, she drew her enchanted knife.

Only two strangers stood in the room. One was a man dressed in grey and black, with long, stringy hair and pale skin, his abnormally long fingers reaching for Sam's neck. Sam straddled him, his normally massive body bulked up beyond belief. Muscles on muscles. His clothes hung in tatters, except for a pair of biker shorts that strained at the maxed-out seams.

The second stranger was a nice piece of muscle with a shiny bald head, but he was no match for the hulking form Sam had taken. He aimed a gun at Sam's head.

Lee threw her knife at him without thinking. It struck the gun, knocking it off target as it went off. The bullet hit a pipe and ricocheted. Lee ducked, but the bullet didn't come her way. She shoved her leg into the bald man's shins, knocking him to the floor.

Sam throttled the dark-haired man, but he didn't struggle for air. Instead, he smiled with a mouth full of crooked, widely spaced teeth, and pulled an amulet out of his shirt. It glowed, coating his body in orange light, and then he vanished in a puff of orangish dust. Sam fell forward, grunting.

The bald man scrambled to his feet. Lee stood at the same time, whistling shrilly. The knife she'd thrown spiraled back into her hand. One of the best thefts Lee had ever made.

Sam stood, two feet taller than he'd ever stood before, head scraping the basement ceiling. Lee tried not to gawk.

She faced the bald man, panting. "Are you going to disappear in a cloud of dust too?"

The man growled and raised his gun again.

Sam opened his mouth and released a yell that made Lee slap her hands over her ears, and the bald man's cheeks rippled.

The bald man dropped the gun and fled back into the stairwell. Sam pursued, but his bulk got stuck in the doorframe. There was no way around him.

"Let me through, Sam!"

Sam grunted, turned, and nearly ran Lee over as he trundled away. Lee took the stairs two at a time, knife in one hand. No one else was around to intercept the man. If she could trap him, she could find out who sent him and that other creep.

The front door banged open as she crested the top step.

Chest burning, Lee ran harder, down the hall and across the doorway. She leapt the steps, glancing around.

A car drove past on the still suburban street. A dog barked in the distance, and wind rustled the trees, blowing a strand of hair into Lee's face. She dragged it away from her mouth, still brandishing her knife.

Drat. The bald man was nowhere in sight.

Metal clinked behind Lee and she crouched beside the pillar on the front porch, peering around it. Her heart pounded as she watched an older man and a tiny dog walk into view. Who walked their dog at this hour? It was nearly 2 a.m.

Lee stood, tucking the knife back up into her forearm sheath with a practiced move. The man nodded when he saw her, as if this was a normal neighborly encounter. Lee turned and entered the house, then shut and locked the door. She rested her back on it until her heart rate came down, and then she remembered Sam.

How had he changed forms like that? Better question, how had she not known he had more than one ability?

Lee walked down the stairs, then came around the corner and found Sam eyeing the couch.

"No, Sam, don't—"

Her warning came too late.

He sat, and the wooden couch frame crunched. Lee leaned against the doorframe, watching the muscled-out Sam adjust his seating, trying to get comfortable. He didn't seem to notice her, but she was glad for a moment to let her heart rate come down.

Who were those men and why had they wanted to capture her? The cloying suffocation of the Mentalist's influence lingered on her mind, and she shuddered at the memory of him touching her.

Footsteps on the stairs startled Lee, and she brought the knife out again. She slid around the wall into the laundry room and waited. Would the bald man be foolish enough to come back?

Risa walked into the point of Lee's blade, then backed up fast, holding up her hand.

"What just happened? We saw that man running, but he got away from us. Physically enhanced, for sure. It was like we were waking up from a trance."

"That was a Mentalist." Lee barely got the words out, her tongue feeling thick in her mouth like she had way too much to drink.

"A Mentalist? Why?"

Lee shook her head. A chanting started from the corner of the room. Her gaze landed back on Sam, whose mouth moved with the bass intonation. Make that double bass, or however one described a tone that was deeper than the human voice could make. His muscles started to deflate.

"Water. Food. Now." He reached out, making a grasping motion.

Lee darted forward, thrusting her half-eaten sandwich into his hand. He shoved it into his mouth like an eating contest contender and motioned for more. Risa and Lee both sprinted up the stairs, Lee grabbing water in two glasses from the faucet, Risa loading her arms with lunch meat, cheese, and bread. They ran back down the stairs and burst into the room.

Sam's eyes rolled to the back of his head, and he swayed. Lee shoved a glass against his lips, holding it so he could drink. His shirt soaked, she backed off so Risa could hand him meat and cheese slices in quick succession until he grabbed the entire loaf of bread and ripped into the bag.

Risa and Lee stepped back. Lee tried not to let her disgust

show on her face, but glancing at Risa, she saw her feelings mirrored. They both turned around, putting Sam's binge eating at their backs as they stared at the cement wall.

"Do we have any idea who those guys were?" Risa asked.

Lee shuffled her feet and swallowed. "I've never seen them before today. I don't know why they'd want me. They had no interest at all in Sam; they were after me."

"To hold you hostage, maybe?" Risa wondered.

"But we're a small-time crew! Why would they think we had the money to pay ransom?" Lee said. She bit her lip. It didn't make sense, unless they wanted a Liminal badly enough to kidnap one. But what would be the purpose of that? It unsettled her, the not-knowing.

Sam's chewing changed to swallowing as he chugged water. Lee closed her eyes against the sounds and tried to concentrate, to bring up the faces of the men who had attacked her, so that if she ever saw them again, she would be prepared.

"Are you all right?" Risa asked, lowering her voice. "They didn't hurt you?"

Lee shook her head, her throat tightening up.

"Thanks, guys," Sam said.

Lee turned around, relieved to find that Sam had finished. The remains of his desperate meal were scattered around the battered coffee table, bread crusts and crumbled bits of cheese. He'd eaten all but two slices of bread and half a package of the lunch meat.

"Want to tell us what that was?" Risa asked, folding her arms over the billowy, pirate-style shirt and corset she wore.

Sam swallowed, looking sheepish. "The real reason I can't go out in public."

"It's not anxiety caused by premonitions? Do you even get those, or is that made up?" Lee asked.

Sam waved his hand. "Oh no, I get those. But I have this...other ability, too."

"You turn into the Hulk."

"Sort of. It's not all Bruce Banner. I'm not a mindless killing machine, and I'm obviously not green. But...it's a bit like that. And it does happen when I'm agitated, but I can also do it intentionally. My premonition ability makes me anxious, which leads to me turning all bulky, and then I stop seeing the premonitions. So maybe it's a coping mechanism? Like I have to turn off my thinking brain and get into my animal brain, or something." He shrugged.

"That's actually pretty smart. A survival mechanism your body created so you don't go mad or combust. A balance." Risa bobbed her head.

"Yeah, I guess," Sam replied.

"Why not tell the crew, though?" Lee asked. She'd been in the crew longer than Sam, and she had never seen him do what he'd just done.

"Silas knew. He wanted me to keep it under wraps, avoid freaking anyone out." He glanced shyly at them, and Lee saw the fragile anxiety in his eyes and hunched posture.

"We're not freaked out. Are we, Risa?" Lee elbowed Risa, who shook her head dramatically.

"Not a bit. Although the eating is a tiny bit...freaky." Risa pinched her fingers together for emphasis. "It's gross to watch."

"Fair enough," Sam said.

Risa glanced between them. "I don't know how those men found us. They must have been watching this place for weeks.

Or maybe the Mentalist could sense something? We'll have to use the fallback. This place is compromised."

"How do we prevent them from finding me again?" Lee said quietly. First the Speller refused to give her directions, and then these men came out of nowhere trying to kidnap her. She did not need this kind of stress.

"I'll talk to Silas about increasing protections," Risa said. She headed for the stairs, her skirts swishing as she went.

Lee groaned. More protections meant more house arrest and less traveling between realms. How could she help the crew make a big enough score to pay the Speller if she was stuck inside?

"Thanks for not freaking out," Sam said quietly. He stared at his fingers in his lap.

Warm affection surged inside Lee. "Are you kidding? You saved me. Possibly my life. And you're still Sam. You'll always be Sam, whatever size you are."

Sam stared up at her, blinking back tears, and Lee squirmed. She wasn't good with the mushy stuff.

She slugged Sam on the shoulder. "Keep it together, big guy. You've got all that tech to pack."

Sam's eyes widened. "You're right! I've got to get up there." He stood, stumbling, and took off up the stairs, his steps thundering and sending tiny bits of debris showering down into the stairwell.

Lee wandered up to her room and stared blankly at the bed before blinking a few times and moving robotically to the dresser. She opened a drawer, grabbed a duffle bag from the closet, then started shoving clothes into it without worrying about wrinkles. There wasn't much to pack, and she stood there looking into the bag for a long moment before realizing that most of her clothes were still downstairs being washed and dried.

She sat on the bed.

She couldn't take the bed with her. Or the doorframe Shane used to lean against, grinning at her like a fool. Neither could she take the kitchen chairs he turned around and sat backwards in while they planned their heists, or the room they'd lain in together the first night they'd discovered that what they felt was more than either of them had planned.

Lee leaned back and put her palms over her eyes. She breathed deep, then sat up, swinging her duffle bag off the bed and racing out of the room with all of its memories.

Maybe this would be good for her. Maybe she could move past Shane.

Even as she thought that, she knew it was a lie. She would never forget. Leaving this house would just drive the memories deeper into her heart, where they would face her with every turn.

She started down the stairs and ran headlong into a muscled chest covered with a black t-shirt. Her gaze traveled up to meet a pair of sympathetic green eyes framed with curly hair. Finn.

He licked his lips. "I heard about what happened. Are you —are you all right?"

Lee nodded and gestured to herself. "As you can see."

Finn laughed breathlessly, then ran a hand through his hair. He glanced around. "We have to get you out of here."

"Yeah, that's what this is." She held up the duffle bag, then narrowed her eyes at him, remembering what Sam had said. He did seem disproportionally concerned with her well-being for hired muscle. Though if she died or disappeared, it was unlikely Silas would pay him.

Or maybe he was nervous because he was the mole who had told those other men about her. Sam had said that Finn's intentions were focused on Lee's Liminality. Maybe he was working with those men to some end, and now that the plan hadn't gone off like it was supposed to, he would try to find another way to make it work.

She stepped up closer, staring into his eyes as if some evidence he had betrayed her would appear like magic in his irises. After a moment, she backed down.

"Did I pass inspection?" Finn asked.

"Why are you here?" Lee blurted.

"Another day, another job. I told you, I'm a bit of a nomad." He shrugged, looking about as innocent as a kid who's hit a ball through a window.

"Everyone has a reason they're in this business. You're telling me you just like hitting people?"

He sighed. "For the last time, I'm not just a hitman. And since you keep insisting on prying into my personal life, I'm here because my...friend is sick."

He hesitated before friend, and he wouldn't meet her gaze. Not a friend, then. Family, probably. Someone he was protecting. The girl Sam had mentioned?

"Well, I hate to say it, but this crew hasn't had great luck lately. There's not much to go around. You'd be better off doing your nomad thing and finding a more lucrative job."

"I like what I see so far. I think I'll stick around. I like the sound of this museum heist." He jutted out his chin.

So much for scaring him into leaving. Lee gritted her teeth. "It's your friend's funeral." She ducked past him and rushed down the stairs, not wanting to engage with the infuriating conversation any longer.

"Hey, where's the fallback hideout?" Finn called after her.

Lee ignored him. If Silas hadn't informed the new guy, she wasn't about to.

They were out the door in fifteen minutes, the place stripped bare. Risa jogged in place as if preparing for a race, and her metal instruments clinked together on her belt.

Sam had an extra sack for food. He wore noise-cancelling headphones and dark sunglasses, which made him stand out in the dark hours of the morning, especially combined with his bulk and his brilliantly colored Hawaiian shirt.

"Split up, meet at the factory hideout by 0300. Finn, you're with Lee." Silas slid on a pair of shades and a ballcap, covering up his most recognizable cyborg features.

Lee spit to one side, then adjusted her beanie and tugged at her jacket.

Finn came to stand beside her. "You'd do better to take that off. It's like a beacon."

She resisted the urge to stick her tongue out at him and stubbornly left it on.

Scowling at Silas, she said, "Do you have to give me a babysitter?"

"You're safer if they don't find you alone."

"Alone I can skip across town in the blink of an eye," Lee argued.

Silas lowered his glasses, his cyborg eye shining at her. "I don't want you using your abilities until the job."

"But—"

He jabbed a finger in her face. "Don't forget, it's your fault we're in this mess. That Mentalist locked on your signature somehow. You're lucky I'm letting you stay with the crew. It's going to cost even more now to keep you protected." He raised his glasses and walked away.

Lee watched him leave, her heart sinking. With the mysterious men after her, this crew was her only lifeline. She could leave, but where would she go? No one would want a dying Liminal, and certainly not one that had a price on her head. She'd be picked up by those goonies within moments of being kicked out of the Gadai. Silas was right. Even if the way he said protection made Lee think of prison instead.

Finn clapped his hands together. "All right, which direction are we headed?"

"Through," Lee said. The tingling started in her fingertips. Screw Silas. If Finn was a traitor, she wasn't about to let him gift-wrap her for the Mentalist.

Finn raised his arm calmly and held it in an odd position, his fist rotating in the air.

The tingling stopped.

"What did you do?" Lee demanded. She could feel the Liminal realm, but she couldn't phase through.

"You're not going anywhere that way," Finn said. His grin looked twisted, and there was a gleam in his eye that Lee did not like.

A chill creeped up the back of Lee's neck. He could prevent her from going Liminal, and she had nowhere to run. If those men were working with Finn, now would be the time for them to strike.

Lee might have been cut off from the Liminal realm, but she wasn't helpless. She pulled her knife and lunged, putting the point right against Finn's neck.

CHAPTER 13

Lee snarled. She didn't have time to dance around or play guessing games.

"The men who attacked me—you're working with them. Who are they? What do they want with me?"

Finn stumbled back, but she grabbed his shirt, holding him tight. He threw up his hands, eyes wide. He didn't try to get away. Still playing the innocent.

"Woah, woah, woah. I'm not working for any other crew, and especially not those men," Finn insisted.

"You stopped me! Why would you do that except to make me an easy target?" Lee bristled. The blasted man was a Neutralizer.

"I neutralized your Liminality," Finn said calmly. "Why do you think Silas assigned me to you?"

Lee shoved Finn back, relieved she could still move. He wasn't the source of the paralysis she'd experienced when the Mentalist attacked. She had been all but paralyzed then.

"Why Silas thinks I need a nanny is beyond me. Someone has to scope out the museum. I'm the best option we have."

"Why not get permission then?" Finn cocked his eyebrow at her.

"You know Silas won't listen. He's being unreasonable."

"Maybe he's afraid to lose an asset." Finn rolled his shoulder as if growing tired, but he didn't open his fist or drop his arm.

That stung. Yeah, she'd known for a while that Silas didn't care about her beyond her ability to travel through space and time, but hearing someone else say it—a stranger, nonetheless—hurt.

"You don't think it's awfully suspicious that you arrived and within *days* someone is trying to capture me from the hideout? How else would they know where to find me?"

"Nothing I say will convince you to believe me. I'll just have to prove it," Finn said finally. He dropped his fist and shook out his arm.

Lee didn't feel any different, but she touched the Liminal realm ever so slightly, just to be certain she could.

Finn glanced at her, but didn't say anything, and he didn't try to block her again.

"I would be stupid to trust you," she said.

Finn inclined his head. "I agree. I hope I can earn it."

"Few have." Lee turned away from the earnestness in his gaze and walked away. She tugged her phone from her pocket. 2:34 a.m. She had time before Silas expected her at the factory hideout, and she had the cover of darkness on her side. Silas would be glad she had done it. They needed to know what they were up against, and the sooner she scouted, the sooner they could clean the place out.

Finn footsteps sounded from behind. Lee stiffened, but kept walking, tucking her knife back into its wrist sheath as she did.

"You're pretty handy with those knives."

Lee didn't say anything.

"Why not a gun?"

"Anyone can kill with a gun. Pretty much any fool that knows how to point and shoot. Easy to misfire and kill by accident, too. If someone picks up my knife, they're less likely to know how to use it against me." Lee eyed him, noticing the bulge on his side under his t-shirt. "You're a gun man."

"I am. It's reliable. And I can take someone out from a distance."

Lee threw her knife in a swift motion. It struck a tree about fifteen feet away. Adam whistled.

"Impressive." His gun clicked, the nose of the barrel pressed into Lee's side. "But now you don't have a weapon."

Lee whistled, and the knife in the tree glowed blue and spun back into her free hand.

Finn smiled. "All right, I approve." He removed his gun, holding up his hands in surrender. Lee waited until his gun was stowed away in its holster before putting away her knives.

I don't need your approval. Lee rolled her eyes. She took off at a rapid-walking pace again, jamming her hands into her pockets.

Finn kept up with her. "This job—what are we facing, exactly? What security measures do they have in place?"

"I don't think they know what they have in their vaults. I've only ever seen a few regular security guards."

Finn raised an eyebrow. "And that doesn't concern you? That there's a literal vault filled with valuable magic items and supposedly no one else knows about it and no one is guarding it?"

Lee shrugged. "There aren't many people with my ability to see magical items through walls. Who else would know it's there?"

Finn hesitated. "I can sense magical signatures."

"You can?" This guy was full of surprises. "That's why you can block me before most people would know I was going Liminal."

"I haven't tried much with objects. It's more helpful with people who are about to use thaumaturgy."

Lee whistled. "That's a big word for a thug like you."

Finn rolled his shoulders. "Hey, there's more than you think beneath the surface."

Lee's mind turned toward the City Museum. If the crew was going to be successful, she had to scope it out more thoroughly. Once she got to the new hideout, Silas would have her under lock and key. But if she could give Finn the slip, she could finish her recon and no one would be any wiser.

She pictured the City Museum. It was an easy place to shift in and out of at this time of night, due to the brightly glowing ley line that led in and out of it. Moving between realms would take no effort at all, and coming back would be a piece of cake.

Lee breathed through the tingling in her arms and legs, the painful pricking of invisible pins and needles as her hands turned red with the outline glow of the Liminal realm. The world slowed, and she sighed with relief.

Finn stepped toward her, moving slower than usual, but still moving. Lee's heart about leapt out of her chest at the sight, her mind flashing back to the FBI man who had defied the laws of Liminality and come at her despite the slowdown. As if he had joined her in the Liminal realm. She stared at Finn, who stared back.

His words came out in the slowest of drawls. "Whhh—"

Lee didn't wait to hear what he would say, but focused her attention on the nearest ley line and clung to it, ready to throw herself into the void.

She hit a wall and crashed back through the veil between realms, stabbing sensations scraping across her skin. She hissed with pain, stifling her own exclamation to avoid anyone overhearing.

"If you did that, I swear I'll kill you," she said through gritted teeth, grabbing the bed and hauling herself up.

"I have a—"

"Job. I know. Go pretend to do it. Or better yet, do me a favor and find a new crew to bother." She readied herself again, grimacing at the lingering pain in her bones. It faded, but slowly.

"Silas said no using your powers," Finn said. "You need to rest."

"I need to see what we're up against," Lee insisted. "We can't go into this blind."

"Then take me with you. I can't show up to the hideout without you—Silas will have my hide." He gave her a wide-eyed look of concern.

Lee growled. "I'm not dragging you with me again. It'll wear me out and increase my chance of glitching."

"Did it happen last time? When we went to the laundromat?"

"Well…no. But that was a fluke. I'm not risking it. You'll just have to tell Silas I'm doing this for the crew."

Finn crossed his arms. "You're not going anywhere without backup. The Mentalist and his thug could find you, and then where would you be?"

A cold chill rippled through Lee's body. If the Mentalist

could track her signature, then he'd wait until she was alone and attack. Finn was right, and judging by the smirk marring his handsome face, he knew it.

"Fine." Lee threw her arms up, pacing a few steps forward, then back. He could stop magical attacks. Maybe he could be useful. "Fine. You can come. Don't be a drag."

"Har har!" Finn stepped forward, putting a hand on her shoulder, then pulled it away and put it on her arm instead. "Is this okay?"

"I'd prefer it if you touched my butt," she snarked.

"Can I get that in writing so you don't hang me for sexual harassment later?" A cheeky grin popped onto his face.

Lee rolled her eyes—something she seemed to do a lot around this new guy—and focused. She could still feel the ley line, though it was buzzing strangely. Someone else could have just used it, which seemed unlikely since she wasn't aware of another Liminal in the city, or perhaps there was a magical influence nearby. A Speller?

Lee leaned through the veil, parting it with her hands and allowing Finn to be pulled along with her. Moving with his hand on her arm was shockingly effortless. There were no painful prickles, just the slightest tingle in her nose of all places. She latched onto the ley line and tugged, and was jerked off her feet and into full transport mode, flying over the blurred city streets on the red arc of the ley line.

They came down where the ley line met another, a bulbous crossing point called a node, and Lee changed directions, taking them on another ley line, stopping at nodes and shifting lines until they came to the City Museum.

The building stood as a dark monstrosity of weird angles and jutting constructions that seemed to follow no known architectural logic. The airplane stuck out over the side, a dark mass lit up from beneath with a glaring security light.

Lee moved towards the building, fully intending to enter, but Finn's arm across her chest stopped her. She pushed him away and crossed her arms over her breasts with an indignant huff.

"Out of line," she said.

"Sorry. I didn't want you to walk into that." Finn pointed.

Lee couldn't see anything. She phased quickly into the Liminal realm, and the glare struck her so hard she was momentarily blinded. A glowing, pulsing mass surrounded the entire building, like the blob from those old sci-fi horror movies.

Lee phased back into Earth's realm. "What is it?" she whispered.

Finn stared at the mass, running a hand through his hair. "I don't know. But it isn't happy, and it knows that we're here."

CHAPTER 14

Adam put his hands on Lee's arms as she leaned into him to get away from the blob. She was tangible again, having slipped back into Earth's realm. Security was what he was going for, but Lee startled and slid away from his touch, giving him a stink eye. Gave Finn the stink eye, anyway.

"Have you seen one of these before?" she asked, thankfully not getting after him about touching her.

"No." But he had, in a drawing by a Speller. Not at this building, however. Someone *really* didn't want anyone getting in there.

"Do you think we can touch it?" Lee moved forward, and Adam snagged her shoulder, yanking her backward. She glared at him.

"I don't think that's a good idea. Someone put that there to keep people out. It could... absorb you, or something." *Or incinerate you.*

Lee chewed her lower lip, scanning the outside of the building. "What if it's supposed to trap us instead? Making us easy pickings for whatever bumbling cop answered the security call?"

"That would suck. Any way to test that out?" Adam asked. He knew the question threw off her perception of him as the mindless muscle. But he was tired of dumbing himself down.

Lee tapped her chin. Adam watched her hand turn red, and the world around them dimmed, except for the glowing beast surrounding the museum.

"No!" he said, his voice sounding an octave lower, like he was inside a bubble.

Lee drew her hand back and the world returned to its usual pace and lighting, the mass invisible once more. She frowned. "I thought you said you didn't know this creature."

Adam swallowed. He jammed his hands in his pockets. "I said I had never seen one before. I—I've heard of them."

Lee narrowed her eyes. "How?"

"A Speller I knew once. His passion was animals affected by thaumaturgy. He studied them. He had something like this in a jar, said that it could grow exponentially. It feeds on thaumaturgy."

"It's alive?" Lee said.

"Near as he could tell. Said it might be a fungus? Or a parasite?" Adam couldn't stop the shudder that moved through his body.

"Does it have a weakness?"

"I'm sure it does. But if you have any sort of magical signature, forget getting near it. It'll eat you for breakfast. Quite literally." Adam pulled his phone out of his pocket and mimed scrolling through his contacts. He knew which one to select. It was right at the top.

Logan, his brother, was working on developing a college-level curriculum studying the flora and fauna affected by thaumaturgy. He would know if this thing had a weakness, but Adam wondered if he should give the crew this much help to break into a building like the museum and steal everything inside. Director Hatcher wanted the Liminal in custody, end of story. His supervisors were hounding his tail. But if Adam helped Lee pull off this job, she would trust him. He could possibly follow her straight to the Ceteri.

And the moment she found out he worked for the FBI, that trust would be screwed. He glanced her way and caught her tucking her hair back behind her ear and frowning, her lips pouting.

Lee snapped her fingers in front of Adam's face, and he blinked, realizing he'd been staring.

"Earth to Finn. What's with the phone?"

"That Speller, I've got his number." Adam gestured with the phone. "I don't have to tell him what I'm doing, just ask him about this blob. He'll know how to handle it."

Lee crossed her arms, but nodded, those fantastic lips pursing as she watched him back away down the sidewalk. She glanced left and right, then turned slightly to check behind. They certainly didn't want to draw any attention.

Adam selected the number and it dialed, ringing twice before a familiar voice popped up on the other end.

"Bro! It's been ages. What's up?"

"It's been literally two weeks." Adam rubbed his eyes and sighed. His youngest brother was a pain in the ass.

"Right, ages. What do you want with the genius in the fam?"

Adam gave a breathy laugh. "Well, I've got a job involving that blob thing. The one from the jar on your desk? Did you ever figure out what it was?"

"Living fungus. Acid burns prey and it sucks in their thaumaturgic ability before it evaporates. Which we've figured out it does. Must be some sort of liquid form in the human body."

"So it just makes someone not magic anymore? It's not deadly?"

"Well, not exactly." Logan sighed. "Let me see if I can dumb this down. It doesn't affect normal human beings, but those with thaumaturgy in their blood turn into vegetables after physical contact. You spot one on the job? Steer clear."

"I know that. How could someone get past it? More specifically, into a building that a giant mass of living fungus has...er...consumed?" Adam turned away from Lee's scathing gaze and stared down the dark street on the other side.

Logan snorted. "Get past it? Dude, you gotta kill it."

"What, like, bleach it or something? What kills magic fungus?" Adam asked.

"Fire. But not your average light-a-match type. You need an elemental, or a Purple Heart," Logan said, the familiar excitement leaching into his voice.

"I'd like the building to remain standing," Adam said dryly.

Logan clicked his tongue. "Well, dude, I'd like to help you, but..."

"It's like someone hired it to guard this building," Adam edged, trying to catch his brother's interest again.

"Woah. I knew they were trainable; I didn't know anyone had made a business of it." Logan's lying voice couldn't have been more obvious.

Adam rolled his eyes. "Yes, you did. You sold yours to the government for what, half a mil?"

He put a hand against his hip and glanced back at Lee,

who appeared to be stretching her neck by holding it to each side. She looked back at him and tapped her wrist impatiently.

Adam eyed the translucent, undulating shape with a slight glow. The ticking sensation of his magic detection beat a rapid staccato in his chest every time he looked at it.

"Money is relative, man. What I meant is, I didn't know civilians had a hold of it. In any case, you probably don't want to destroy someone else's property, knowing your level of morality."

Adam scratched the scruff on his chin. "That's ideal, yes."

"I got nothing for you, man." Logan sniffed in a way that told Adam he was hiding something. He just had to ask the right question and his brother wouldn't be able to resist spilling what he knew.

"How do they tempt it away from the site it's guarding every morning and guide it back?"

"Weeellll, I don't want the general public to get their hands on this knowledge, you realize. If people knew how to handle the living fungus, how to trap it, I'd get in big trouble with some big people."

"I'll guard the knowledge with my life," Adam said, his tone filled with mock seriousness.

"You'd better. Listen, it's pretty simple. The living fungus will be drawn to small spaces, but only those in specific shapes. You need a hollow prism." He coughed.

"And where do I get that? Any particular size?"

"You can make one. Just take a reflective polycarbonate plastic and...nevermind. Just... meet me at my workshop tomorrow. No questions asked. But I'd need to be compensated for supplies. The FBI can swing that, can't they?"

"Yes, fine," Adam hissed into the phone, glancing towards

Lee. How much could she hear? She was contemplating the City Museum again.

"Eight o'clock sharp. I'll have it ready."

"Thanks. You're helping me out of a really tight spot."

"Can I borrow your badge?" Logan's voice raised in pitch, sounding youthful and hopeful.

Adam laughed and shook his head. "No. Thanks again." He hung up before Logan could ask him for anything else and pocketed his phone. He rubbed his hands.

"Okay, we've got a way to get rid of it tomorrow night. I'm meeting with a contact in the morning."

"Just a contact, huh?" She slid her tongue across her teeth and raised her eyebrows.

Adam sucked air through his teeth at the teasing expression on her face. Damn, she was beautiful.

He forced himself to reply. "We've worked together before. I trust him."

"Well, I don't. You didn't tell him the details about our job, did you?"

Adam rolled his eyes. Did she think he was incompetent? "No. He told me how to deal with this thing. We can use enchanted fire or trap it in a special kind of prism."

Lee pursed her lips. "Trapping it in a prism sounds more manageable."

Adam nodded. "It means we won't be able to check for anything else tonight. There could be other magical security measures that we won't discover until the night of the heist."

"It's the best we can do, then. Better than nothing." She scrubbed at her eyes with the heels of her hands.

"Let's get you to the hideout."

Lee stepped forward and stumbled, swaying on her feet. "You're too nice," she muttered.

"Woah, you okay?" Adam grabbed Lee's arm a split second before she phased into the Liminal realm. Adam hardly noticed, except that the red outline appeared on her hands. She'd brought him with her.

"You're in no state to–"

"Hold on," Lee said with a grimace, and she reached out her hand, grasping at an invisible thing. As soon as she appeared to reach it, the world around them dissolved.

An ethereal wind blew him to bits, the universe screaming in his ears. He screwed his eyes shut until the air stopped moving.

They landed crammed between two piles of towering garbage in a cluttered basement. Lee squirmed to get past Adam, who caught sight of a teetering suitcase on a stack of junk behind her and slammed his hand into it, trapping Lee against his chest.

"Um, thank you," she said, her voice breathy and light. Her face was barely visible in the bit of streetlight that filtered in through the dirty, broken windows. She closed her eyes for a long second, then blinked furiously.

"How'd we end up here?"

"A secluded, cluttered space is easier than a crowded, clear space," Lee muttered. She put her hand on his bicep, then ducked under and headed for the more open pathway through the center of the room. She tilted her head left, then right, and leaned against another unsteady column of garbage.

"Come on," Adam said. He might be role-playing some sort of thug in this crew of thieves, but he couldn't watch her struggle without stepping in. She must be tired. He took her arm, ignoring her protests, and draped it over his shoulder, then wrapped his other arm around her back.

"I'll just guide you a bit," he urged. He heard her cuss and he laughed, then awkwardly side-stepped around the piles of junk until they reached the stairs where they could walk side-by-side.

When they hit the top step, Lee pulled away from Adam and wandered into the main room, yawning. Everyone rushed her.

"You can't do that!" Risa scolded. "We were worried sick. I thought Silas told you to rest."

"I'm resting," Lee said, stopping to yawn. "Just point me to a couch."

Risa sighed and steered her to the nearest chair, and Lee curled up in it like a puppy. Sam brought a pillow from one of the beds and offered it to her. Lee dragged it under her head, then opened her eyes sleepily.

"You let her go?" Risa demanded, getting in Adam's face. She smelled like pizza, and Adam side-stepped as politely as he could, making as if he meant to sit on the couch.

"I'm intrigued, as well."

Adam's heart jumped nearly to his throat at Silas's statement from the back of the room. Damn cyborg always had to make a dramatic entrance from the shadows. Did he just like the dark corners, like a cockroach biding its time until everyone was asleep to spread its filth? Every word he'd heard from the man was tainted with lies and self-service. It left a bad taste in Adam's mouth just thinking about it.

"Lee thought we'd missed something. She wanted back-up." He didn't want Lee in trouble with the crew. The better they thought of her, the better they would think of him.

"We went to the museum and found this fungus covering every entrance, exit, and surface of the building and its grounds. Like some sort of guard dog. Fortunately, I have a contact who was able to tell me how to get rid of it. A case shaped like a prism will encourage it to shrink and hide in the small space."

"Peculiar," Sam said, tapping his chin with a finger.

"How convenient that you would have such a knowledgeable contact." Silas's mechanical eye swirled in its socket and flashed red, then blue. He grinned. "Glad you're with us."

Adam acknowledged his words with a slight nod. "Me too. Though keeping up with her"—he jabbed a finger toward Lee—"is a full-time job."

Everyone chuckled. Lee stuck out her tongue at him.

"So, we obtain this prism somehow." Risa rotated her hands around each other in a 'continue' gesture. "And…"

"We don't know what other magical measures might be inside, not with that monstrosity blocking things out," Adam explained. "Could be anything."

"We've gone into jobs blind before. Be on your toes. And get some sleep." Silas slapped Sam's shoulder and made as if to leave.

Was Silas that confident in the crew's abilities? Or was he being reckless so they could make a big hit? It didn't fit with the rhetoric Silas had fed him before about protecting Lee at all costs.

"Aren't you concerned about the safety of this job?" Adam asked.

Silas stopped and turned around, his head cocked and his tongue held between his teeth. "Listen, maybe it worked differently in your other positions, but here we trust the crew boss. We're a well-oiled machine. Moving faster to get ahead of the pack is a smart move, wouldn't you agree?"

"Yes, but…"

"And I make the final call here." Silas didn't raise his voice, but the tone changed enough that the fine hairs on

Adam's arm rose. He stiffened, but held his fingers away from the gun at his side.

"Of course," Adam managed to get out. No one else said a word.

"I hope Lee is better by tomorrow. She seemed wiped out." Risa glanced at Lee, who quietly snored in the armchair with her arm beneath her head.

"She'd better be." Silas said loudly from across the room. He bent over an array of tools on the table in the kitchen area and selected a narrow wrench, sitting with it. He powered down his arm and set to work on it.

Sam and Risa shared a look, then glanced at Adam. They looked just as bewildered as he felt about their leader dismissing the most valuable, and fragile, member of the crew off-hand, despite all the outward efforts he made to "protect" her. A feeling crept into Adam's chest, one he had learned to never ignore; whatever happened tomorrow night, he needed to watch out for Lee. Someone had to.

CHAPTER 15

Lee stared into her coffee mug, mindlessly fingering the white ceramic showing through the chip in the navy-blue surface. The caffeine buzz still hadn't kicked in after her second cup. She'd slept crazy deep. Was it possible she'd been drugged? More likely she was just exhausted.

She drank deeply from the mug, and the warm liquid seeped into her bones, chasing away the chill of the unheated factory.

No one spoke. They sat in different corners of the room, sipping away at their mugs.

Silas looked as if he'd been up all night, but then again, the military must have trained him to stay awake for days at a time.

"I don't think we can get past it," Sam piped up from the table.

Lee unfolded her legs from underneath her, then crossed one over the other. She set her mug on the side table next to her. "You're talking about the blob?"

Risa chuckled. "Is that what we're calling it?"

A crash sounded downstairs, and the entire crew jumped, except Silas, who simply shifted the gears in his hand until they formed the pistol. He exchanged a glance with Lee, who was already on her feet and sneaking to the basement door. He followed her, then slid against the doorframe and gestured for her to open the door to the stairs. Lee flung the door wide and Silas jumped into the entrance, shooting twice into the darkness.

"Don't shoot!" Finn's voice echoed on the stairwell. He grunted and another crash sounded. Empty ground coffee containers rolled into view, and Finn staggered around them, rubbing his elbow. He had a large clear prism tucked underneath his arm.

"Clumsy bastard," Silas growled, disengaging his firearm and stalking away from the doorway.

Finn glanced back over his shoulder at whatever mess lay behind him, then started up the stairs. He at least had the sense to look sheepish.

Lee rolled her eyes. "Real graceful there. The prism okay?"

Finn reached the top of the stairs, and slid it out from under his arm, inspecting it. "Just fine."

"Good." Lee shoved off from the wall and walked back to her chair.

"I'm fine too, thanks for asking," Finn called after her.

Risa busted up laughing, and Sam joined her. Lee flopped into her chair and grabbed her mug, sipping at the now-cool liquid.

"That's how we're going to contain the blob?" Sam asked, gawking at the object in Finn's arms. "It's so small! How's it gonna fit?"

"Oh, it's going to fit," Finn assured him, showing the

piece off. He rapped on it. "Nice and sturdy. My guy assures me this is foolproof."

Risa scooted closer to Finn and peered into the container. "How does it work?"

Finn shifted uncomfortably. "Unfortunately, I'm not supposed to tell you. But it'll work."

Lee narrowed her eyes. There was something odd about the way Finn skirted around the details about this prism. Lee scanned his body, watching for tells. The man rubbed his neck, and the slightest sheen of sweat glistened on his forehead. He was hiding something. Question was, would it prevent Lee or the crew from getting what they wanted?

"This contact of yours. Who does he work for?" Lee asked, cutting off Risa's next question.

Finn's gaze locked on hers, his blue-grey irises fierce and guarded. "He's an independent contractor of sorts. Clients all over the world." His words flowed smoothly enough, and he seemed to calm down as he spoke.

"You're pretty resourceful for a common crew thug." Lee circled around Finn. "Screener or not, it's unusual that you would have 'contacts' with such specialized knowledge."

Finn licked his lips, shifting his stance. He laughed uneasily. "Come on, now. You don't suspect me now, just because I'm friends with a guy with a 3D printer?" He passed the prism into his other hand and looked toward the table where Silas sat. "I passed the test with your crew boss. Isn't that good enough for you?"

Lee leaned in. "No, it isn't." Her gaze never left his.

A chair scraped across the stone floor, the sound grating on Lee's ears, but she didn't turn to look until Silas said her name.

"Lee." Silas leaned on the back of the chair he'd been

sitting in, his cyborg eye spinning in its mechanical socket. "We don't need infighting right before a job. You can pick the man apart after we've got what's in those vaults, but for now, you're going to take a nap so you're fresh for tonight. And we —" He spun his hand in an utterly inhuman way, indicating the rest of the group. "—are going to prepare to face whatever is beyond that blob."

Lee broke her stare with Finn. Once she had enough money to pay off the Speller, she'd be gone, and it wouldn't matter if Finn betrayed the crew. She wouldn't be part of it anymore. But her instincts pestered her with questions about this stranger who cared too much about her, had knowledge-able contacts at his fingertips, and skipped from crew to crew like thieving was some sort of game. She wasn't anywhere near done scrutinizing him, but it would have to wait, for now.

"I'm not going to sleep while the rest of you plan," she said. She downed the dregs of her coffee, accidentally inhaling some of the cold, thick liquid. Trying to suppress the resulting cough made her eyes water.

Finn brushed his mouth with the side of his hand, as if hiding a smile.

"Something funny?" Lee asked.

"You're dead on your feet, Lee. Get some rest," Risa insisted.

"Why doesn't anyone else have to take a nap?"

Risa didn't say anything until they'd moved behind the partition that marked off the corner of the room that Lee shared with her. "No one else is a Liminal on the brink of Fading. Damnit, Lee, you've got to take better care of your-self." Risa swiped the empty coffee mug out of her hand. "This is your second cup today. Have you eaten anything?"

"Half a bagel," Lee said in mock triumph.

Risa glared, and her hands rested on her hips. "You're going to sleep for a few hours and then eat whatever I put in front of you, or you're not going on this heist; I don't care what Silas says."

Lee blinked, staring at Risa's retreating back as the older woman left the enclosed space. Since when had Risa taken it on herself to mother Lee?

CHAPTER 16

A cold presence touched Lee's face, stroking her brow, trailing down her neck toward her collarbone.

Lee's eyes flew open, and she bolted upright in a panic. The cold touch fled. The blacked-out windows told her nothing about the time of day. She fumbled for the phone she kept in her pocket. 8:39 p.m.

She cursed and jumped out of bed, hastily combing through her hair and shoving it beneath her orange beanie, then stumbling into the main room. A single lamp lit the table they used for meals, and a white piece of paper gleamed on the scratch brown surface next to a fanny pack.

Lee strapped on the pack, filled with a few essentials for the heist, including her earwire. She plugged that in, tapping it to be sure it was secure, then she turned to the note.

Eat first. If you don't, Harro will tell me.
- R

Assuming Harro was a ghost, Lee glanced around. She couldn't see any wisps that indicated a ghost was in the room. Sometimes they appeared in the Liminal realm, but she decided she didn't want to know what sort of being haunted her right then.

A packaged dinner sat on top of the microwave. Lee's stomach lurched and clenched in anticipation of the heist. The last thing she felt like doing was eating. She crumpled the note and tossed it, turning for the stairs. As she stepped, an unmistakable wave of cool air passed through her, and the lamp flickered.

Lee closed her eyes. "Harro?"

The light flickered twice.

Lee let out an exasperated sound, tossing up her hands. "Fine. I'll eat."

The microwave buttons beeped and the motor whirred as it spun the plastic dish around. Lee pulled it out the moment the timer went off and slid into a chair, facing the steaming, soggy chicken and limp vegetables with a bad taste in her mouth.

The cold presence pressed against her back.

"I'm not hungry, I swear." Lee shrugged against the presence, but it didn't budge. She sighed and cut into the chicken breast. As soon as it was cool enough, she shoveled it in. The persistent ghost took his job way too seriously, not letting up until she'd cleaned the tray. Lee rubbed the goosebumps on her arms as she left for the stairs, muttering under her breath about stubborn ghosts and trying to think of a way she could get back at Risa for this unnecessary display of maternal concern.

As much as she hated to admit it, the food had given her more strength. Once outside, she summoned her ability, fading into the Liminal realm. The red glow around her body was a strong, solid line, and she moved with confidence to the nearest node where two ley lines crossed. She stood outside the next warehouse over and watched as the red line arched before her, leading her to the next ley line on her way to the children's museum.

Her hands shook as she let go of her tie to the physical realm and leapt across the ley line, but she didn't let her fear of the Fade surface. Instead, she soared, invisible, through the night air. At one point, she caught sight of another ley line, blinking into existence as she landed at a ley point and prepared another line to jump, but it was gone in a flash. That made her pause. She'd never seen a ley line disappear before, and it unsettled her.

She had to jog to a cemetery nearby to find her next ley line.

The glowing mass covering the museum could be seen for miles in the Liminal realm. Its gelatinous mass waved tendrils of globby light in her direction as she arched toward the ground, following the path of the ley line.

Lee landed on the sidewalk beneath a gutted airplane that jutted out from the top of the museum, and the glow from the glob vanished as she phased into the Earth realm.

Finn turned around, grimacing when he saw her. Had he hoped she wouldn't show? She shoved past him to face Silas.

Silas spun a dial on the firearm that replaced his cyborg hand. "Sleeping Beauty awakened after all. Thought we'd have to manage without you."

Lee ignored his statement and nodded toward the building. "I see our blob friend is present. Seems active."

"I'll take care of that," Finn said, hefting a huge clear prism. In his other hand he carried a pair of steel forceps.

"Get on with it. We don't have all night," Silas growled. He turned to Risa. "You have the backpack?"

"Ready, boss," Risa replied, snapping her gum and showing off the large black backpack she carried. She nodded to Lee. "Did Harro give you a hard time?"

Lee crossed her arms. "I don't need a babysitter. Phantom or otherwise."

Risa winked. "But it got you to eat, didn't it?"

Lee pressed down the urge to give into Risa's goading and watched Finn place the prism on the sidewalk. She bounced lightly off her heels. She couldn't see what was happening with the blob. Was it reacting to the container at all?

She phased into the Liminal realm. Finn glanced over his shoulder, glaring at the place she'd been standing. He'd felt her use her Liminal ability, and he didn't like it. What was his problem tonight? Lee stuck her tongue out at him, knowing he couldn't see it.

Finn turned back to the container and unhinged the lid, then used the forceps to slide it closer to the blob, which Lee could see now, glowing fluorescent green. Light rippled through it, and it started moving.

Lee gasped. The prism was about the size of a microwave, but there was no way the blob would be able to fit inside. Not when it could cover the entire children's museum. Would the blob compress itself?

Voices outside her Liminal bubble made Lee phase back into reality. She couldn't properly hear what they were saying when she stood outside of time.

"—doing?" Silas finished asking as she emerged.

"Well, I assume it's going into the prism. My b—" Finn paused. "Sorry. My buddy said wait ten minutes and it should be safe to close the lid. If we leave any part of it outside of the container, that part can let off a warning signal that's detectable for miles. And it can still suck the thaumaturgy from us."

"Ten minutes? That's absurd. Lee," Silas barked and made Lee jump and tear her eyes away from the blob. She clasped her hands, then unclasped them, feeling stupid.

Silas's cyborg eye honed in on her. "You can see it. Report."

"Er, just a sec." She popped into the Liminal realm, then blipped back out again. Her hands stung, the pins and needles feeling lingering. Lee rubbed them.

"It's moving in pretty rapidly. I'd say only a few more minutes. Ten is generous."

"Good. Time to scatter. Turn on your earpieces and meet at the vaults." Silas pressed a button inside his ear and reverted his hand back to its humanoid form, sticking both hands in his pocket as he strolled away from the group gathered at the entrance to the museum. Risa took off in the opposite direction.

Lee fumbled with her earpiece, having left it in her pocket. She stuck it in her ear and static crackled as the device activated.

"Lee online," Sam's voice crackled through the tiny speaker. "Hey, Lee."

"How are you doing, Sam?" Lee asked.

"Fine," he said. Lee suspected his brief answer hid more than he let on, but she let it be. A heist wasn't a time to get emotional.

She blinked in and out of the Liminal realm to glance at the blob again. Nearly there. Damn, her hands stung. It was stronger than usual tonight. She needed to be more sparing with her ability.

Finn looked at her and raised his eyebrows. Right. She needed to get moving. She adjusted her beanie and walked the same direction Silas had gone—around the block to the side of the museum, where a giant slide stood sentinel behind the tall iron fence.

"The fungus is contained. Proceed to the meetup point," Sam's hushed voice came over the line.

Lee couldn't resist checking. She blinked into the Liminal realm, wincing at the stinging in her hands, just long enough to confirm that the glow of the fungus was gone. She looked both ways down the empty sidewalk, noting a car turning at the corner. She waited until it passed, pretending to pick something off the ground as it went by, then rubbed her hands together and jumped, gripping the top of the fence and pulling herself up.

Lee landed on her feet on the other side and took off running. There was an entrance through a silo-like building attached to the museum. Lee entered, her pounding footsteps echoing on the cement floor. She stopped, breathing hard, and glanced around for any lights or other signs that a human security guard might be nearby. The air in the silo was still and musty-smelling. Lee sniffed and edged her way to the ladder that reached to a walkway at the top of the metal tower.

She scaled it swiftly and walked along the bridge to a tunnel constructed of rebar. It stretched over the ground below. In the dark, Lee fumbled her grip, and fingers slipped on the bars. It slowed her down more than she'd like. If she went Liminal, she could see better, but she didn't want to wear herself out. Besides, the intense tingling she felt tonight could make scaling the bars more difficult. She moved quickly and carefully, placing each hand and foot with intention.

"Something's up in the museum," Sam's voice startled Lee, and she froze mid-movement, inhaling deeply through her nose.

"Want to get more specific there, Sam?"

Static crackled, but no sound came through. Lee took a moment to catch her breath as she climbed out of the tunnel, but her internal alarm went off as soon as she stopped. She stood in the midst of the mezzanine, a spacious ocean-themed event room with columns that gleamed with silver streaks and mosaic mermaid. The problem was, the mezzanine was on the first floor.

She had entered on the third.

Lee pulled a flashlight out of the pack at her waist and shone it around until she found the entryway to the next room. She crossed the room swiftly, her shoes squeaking on the tile flooring. Before she reached the doorway, she heard a low grinding sound and her body swayed with unexpected motion.

The entire room rotated as the floor sank, taking Lee with it.

CHAPTER 17

Lee went Liminal. She gritted her teeth through the burning that spread like fire up her arms and to her throat, chest, torso. The room's shifting slowed to a crawl, and Lee had a moment to breathe, to get her bearings.

The room was moving. The museum often changed various features of its attractions, but certain things had always stayed the same—including the walls and floors. Apparently, things were different at night. How could she find the vault room if nothing was where it was supposed to be? She had to rely on Sam. He'd be in contact with the others, who could share their locations and that way they would meet up.

Lee gripped her flashlight in her gloved hand and breathed out, phasing back into the Earth realm. The grating of the building's shifting made her screw her eyes shut and grimace. It was louder than she would have thought possible. She waited for the room to come to a complete standstill. If her guess was correct, the mezzanine was now in its proper place on the first floor. Had the entire building reverted to the original floor plan?

Lee took off at a sprint, dashing through the hall and into

the familiar caves. She was used to playful, multi-colored lights turning these tunnels into a funhouse. The erratic bouncing of her flashlight beam made it a much spookier experience, and she found her breath coming in gasps, panic rising.

She pressed the receiver on her earpiece. "Guide me, Sam. I'm running blind. In the cave tunnels on the first floor."

"If you can get to the vault room before the building shifts again, you'll be golden. I'm not sure how often it moves, so just keep going."

"Is everyone else all right?"

"Risa got stuck outside, but she's found a way back in. Don't worry about the rest; they'll meet you at the vaults if they're able."

And if they're not? Lee shivered and took a sharp left, then a right, and ended in a narrow hall outside of the caves. At the end was a ladder going straight up.

She put the flashlight in her back pocket with the beam facing out and started to climb, the light bobbing into the void above her. Every creak and bang made her startle, thinking the building was about to shift out from beneath her feet. She sped up, jumping out onto the second floor.

Something barreled into her from the side. Lee gasped as she hit the ground, her elbow scraping the mosaic tiles that decorated this part of the building. She lashed out with her feet and connected with a solid object that wheezed at the force of her kick.

"Damnit, Lee!" said a male voice tight with pain.

"Finn?" Lee pulled one of her knives out, just in case, and scrambled to her feet, backing away.

He rolled over, making pained noises that Lee had only heard a man make when he'd been kicked between the legs.

"You really nailed me," he finally gasped out.

"Had to make sure you never have kids," Lee said, putting her knife away at last.

Finn snorted, then straightened up, grunting. Lee shone her flashlight on him, catching his eyes. He threw up his hands.

"Watch it!"

"Sorry. Had to be sure." Lee angled the flashlight down and glanced around. "No one else with you?"

"Unfortunately. Which way again to the vaults?" Finn asked, hands on his hips.

Lee walked past him in answer, headed towards the vaults.

A jolt beneath Lee's feet knocked her off balance, and she toppled back into Finn, who grabbed her around her waist. The floor split off in four directions, the piece they stood on together rising into the air. Lee shrieked and ducked, expecting to hit the ceiling, but it, too, had moved, and as they sailed to the top of the museum, she pressed her face into Finn's shirt. The roof opened and the bit of floor they balanced on halted once it got there.

They were at one peak of the building, at the top of a climbing structure that had a ladder going down one side of the platform and an extremely long slide going down the other.

"Do you think it's sentient?" Finn asked. He still had one arm wrapped tightly around Lee, the other reached out to the rim of the slide, stabilizing them.

"What? The building?"

"Yeah. The building. Seems odd that the patch of floor that we were standing on was the one to zip up here. Where does this lead?" He craned his head to look inside the white slide.

Lee licked her lips, her hair whipping into her face and sticking to her skin, which prickled with sweat. "I-I think it comes out on the second floor."

"Excellent. Ready?"

No. She wasn't. But she wasn't about to tell him that. She nodded.

Finn looked at Lee's hands, which still clutched his shirt in a death grip.

"Ah." She released him and stepped onto the platform for the slide, then dropped into the enclosed tunnel of the slide and grabbed the metal bar above her head, suspending herself at the top of the slide. She stared into the darkness, a terrifying thought paralyzing her. What if the building shifted while she was in the slide? Would it spit her out two stories up with nothing to catch her fall? Would it crush her somehow if something sliced through the slide, or if a wall made the slide into a devastating dead-end? She licked her lips and adjusted her hands on the metal bar.

"Uh, Lee? Any time now." Finn said. That blasted tone of concern was so obvious in his voice again. If he was faking, he was damn good.

Lee breathed in through her nostrils and let go. Air rushed past her, and a thrill rose inside of her, making it hard not to scream with excitement. The slide was dark until she rounded a bend and a spot of light flashed into view. It grew steadily brighter and rounder until she came out onto the landing area with a thud. She grinned, allowing herself a moment to enjoy the ride she'd gotten, and then she stood and rapped the outside of the slide.

"It's safe," she called. Then she stepped out of the path of the slide's opening.

Finn was down in a moment, a juvenile grin on his face,

curly hair tousled from the ride.

He beamed at Lee. "Remind you of being a kid a bit, doesn't it?"

"No," Lee said flatly. She didn't have time for this nonsense. The building could shift again any second. She turned away from him and walked swiftly, not waiting to see if he would follow.

In the hall of mirrors, reflective even in the dark museum, glints of light streamed in from streetlights and the moon outside, catching the mirrors at odd angles. Lee's face flashed in one as she passed, skin pale, expression intensely focused. She jogged the last few steps until she saw the large faux vault door that stood next to the rows and rows of small bank boxes, each one holding within it a treasure waiting to be found.

A figure stood at the other end of the wall of vaults, peering around the opposite corner. A dark ponytail swished as the figure jerked her head at the sound of Lee's hurried footsteps.

"Lee!" Risa exclaimed." Thank the Reaper. I thought you'd gotten lost or…"

Or worse. The walls could have smashed her, trapped her somewhere. But she made it through just fine, and judging by the mouth-breathing behind her, Finn had too.

"Let's do this."

"I had my ghosts check the vaults. I marked some interesting ones with chalk." Risa pointed out the white X marks at the bottom right corner of several vault doors.

Lee rubbed her hands together. "All right. Where's Silas?"

Risa licked her lips. "He left to investigate a sound earlier. I couldn't hear it, but then my hearing isn't digitally enhanced."

"I'll take this side, if you've got that one," Finn said, jutting his thumb back toward the hall of mirrors he had come through with Lee.

Lee nodded, sucked in a deep breath, and watched the red glow flow over her fingertips. The red line wavered, flickering like a strobe light, then held. Lee let her breath out, shaking off the pinpricks that traveled along her arms and legs in waves. The world muffled around her, and time held its breath.

The vaults lit up like Christmas lights on the wall in front of her, and fortunately she could still make out the white X's marking the ones she should start on first. By shifting, she could see that three of Risa's ghost-marked boxes were duds. The items inside barely glowed, which was a good indication that they weren't powerful. She skipped over those, finding one that pulsed with blinding white light. She shifted back into the Earth realm, letting her hands go tangible.

The museum was silent, except for the scratching and clicking of her pick in the lock and the occasional shuffle from Finn or Risa. The museum creaked, and Lee froze, bracing herself on the wall. As if that would save her if the floor suddenly dropped out from beneath her.

Nothing happened. Her breathing slowed, her heart rate still pounding. The lock finally released beneath the tip of her pick, and the vault door opened. A ruby the size of her fist gleamed darkly at her. Lee reached in and grabbed it, staring down with a smile widening on her face.

She didn't know what the gem did, or what power it held, but she knew it would fetch a pretty penny at the black market in Kaloyadu. After this, she could pay triple what that blasted Speller had originally offered, and he would show her the Ceteri. How could he refuse a king's ransom?

Fabric slid across the floor, thumping against Lee's sneakered foot. A backpack. Risa had slid it to her. Lee placed the ruby inside and went back to the wall. Phasing into the Liminal realm wasn't entirely necessary, but it helped her move faster, eliminating boxes that held nothing or items that didn't seem to have much power.

She unlocked a second box in record time, pulling out a hammer. Not the type found in anyone's garage, but an ancient one formed of pure iron, with a block-like head and strange rune-like symbols that glowed with a subtle purple sheen. Lee shuddered as she picked it up, power coursing through her uninvited.

Whispers started in her mind. Lee hesitated, then rummaged in the backpack until she grabbed hold of a sack at the bottom. They'd brought a few bags to separate items of potentially greater value. This hammer seemed like it shouldn't come in contact with too many other powerful items.

She stuffed it in an outer pocket of the bag for good measure, then went Liminal for the third time. Given her trouble with phasing earlier that night, she was surprised she was doing so well. A particularly bright light gleamed in the upper left vault, but Lee couldn't reach it on her own.

"Finn," she hissed, coming out of her phasing, and he turned Finn's toward her. "I need a boost."

He walked over and knelt without speaking, his pine-fresh scent washing over Lee as he bent down, offering his back for her to stand on. Lee stepped up, finding balance on her worn sneakers, fully aware that it was a human back that she stood on. She didn't want to be up there any longer than necessary. Her gloved fingers fumbled at the lock and she dropped a pick.

"Damn," Lee muttered.

Risa was there in an instant, quiet as the ghosts she talked with. She handed the slim metal piece back to Lee.

"Go easy, now," Silas's voice rumbled behind her, nearly sending Lee off balance. "Rushing leads to mistakes."

She wobbled, adjusting her position on Finn's back. The man beneath her moved slightly and exhaled.

Lee breathed in. She worked two picks in the lock until the tumblers fell into place. The lock clicked, but the vault door didn't swing open like the others had.

Lee frowned. She touched the edge of the little metal door, intending to pry it open. Perhaps it was stuck, wedged by time and age. The moment her fingers made contact with the unlocked door, Lee was thrust backward by a silent, explosive force. The raised numbers on the surface of the vault burned orange and red in her vision as her head cracked back against the cement flooring—vault number 104.

Lee blacked out, then woke a moment later, vision tunneling in and out, her hearing sharper and louder than normal. Why were they yelling? Sam's voice crackled in her ear, but she couldn't make out the words.

She spotted her pick case lying a few feet away and reached for it, when a booted foot came down on her hand. Lee followed the black heeled boot up the shapely leg inside it, past a curvaceous waist to a familiar and bewildering face.

"Risa?" she asked.

The black-haired woman tossed her curled tresses and laughed, glancing at someone behind Lee. "She thinks I'm you. Though I'm the better dressed one, I do think. Only one of us got our mother's fashion sense."

Lee squinted. The woman looked like Risa, but she wore too

much makeup. She had a mole on her left cheek, and her hair was a waterfall of lovely curls. Risa never did her hair outside of a sharp bun, and she had a mole on her neck, not her face.

Lee tugged her hand out from under the woman's boot and slowly got to her feet. She glanced behind, confirming that Risa was, in fact, standing there next to Finn. The darkness in the vault made it difficult to discern faces, but the people standing next to the woman who looked like Risa had flashlights pointed at the ground. Lee could make out five of them total. The two men looked exactly alike, and two of the women had identical faces but had dyed their hair opposite colors. Which left the tall, porcelain-faced woman who could have been a mirror image of Risa.

"Meet my twin," Risa said grimly. "Rosaura."

Lee glanced between the two. Risa had never mentioned a sibling, much less a twin.

"Don't say it like that. Like we're strangers. Rosa and Risa. We were once quite close. Closer than most, as we shared a womb, sister." Rosaura tilted her head, smiling.

"Who are your friends?" Risa asked, gesturing at the four others that stood beside Rosaura.

Rosaura swept her hand out, gesturing to two males. They raised their flashlights, finally illuminating their identical faces. "Kellan and Sawyer; Isis and Sage." Rosaura indicated two women with similar features on her other side, one with black hair, the other with blonde.

"And your friends, Risa?"

"You know Silas. Then there's Sam, Lee, Finn," Risa said shortly.

"No twins? So drab, Risa. You never should have left."

"I left because you're a psychotic bitch," Risa snapped.

Rosaura leveled her gun casually at Risa. She let the hammer click. Locked and loaded.

Risa raised her hand. "One wrong move and my denizens of the otherworld will rip your throat out."

Rosaura laughed and tossed back her hair. "Oh, baby sister, you forget I know what you can do. Intimidation won't work on me. Especially a bald-faced lie like that. They can't do more than spook me, and I assure you, I can't be spooked the way I was when we were kids."

"We haven't spoken in two years. You think things haven't changed since then?" The air around Risa crackled with a light-sucking energy streaked with crooked purple veins.

Lee took advantage of Rosa's distraction and snatched the pick off the ground. She lunged for the vaults, hoping her crew would get the hint. They hadn't emptied nearly enough vaults.

"Don't move, Liminal," Rosaura shouted. "Unless you like the feeling of lead in your spine."

Lee froze, panting, hands splayed out across the vaults.

"This is our job, Rosa." Silas's voice carried from the stairs. His robotic arm held the form of a plasma cannon, the center glowing with an icy blue light that slowly changed to a rich orange as it heated. Lee glanced at his leg and noticed it was smoking. That couldn't be good. He must have dragged the malfunctioning leg up the entire staircase.

"What, we play finders keepers now? Since when?" Rosaura barked a laugh. "I say we split it. There's enough loot in those vaults for both our crews to walk away rich."

It didn't seem like an unreasonable offer, but Lee saw the hardening of Silas's eyes before he spoke.

"I won't be the sucker who gives his loot over to the likes

of you," he growled.

Lee opened her mouth to argue with him, then shut it.

Rosaura's eyes gleamed gold.

"Drop dead," Risa snarled.

Rosaura shrugged. "Very well."

A cool wind played with the fine hairs at the back of Lee's neck, trailing along so much like a finger that Lee swatted at it without thinking. The air trapped her hand and wrapped itself around her neck, choking her.

Silently, Lee fell to her knees. No one of her crew noticed, until a smirk twitched on one of the other female twin's faces, betraying the attack. The females, at least, were elementals.

Risa glanced around at her companions and screamed in rage when her gaze landed on Lee. Her hand flung up into the air and a string of Latin words erupted from her mouth. Lee couldn't see the ghosts Risa called, but through the spots forming in her vision she saw Rosaura shriek and duck. She swatted at them from a crouch, then aimed her gun at Risa and shot twice, but Risa dove to the side.

Every attempt Lee made to gasp was met with another layer of wind consuming the breathable air before it reached her. She slumped to the floor, lockpicks rolling out of her hands and clattering against the floor.

Silas barreled past Rosaura, headed for someone behind Lee that she couldn't see. One of the female twins was a wind elemental, and the other…

Electricity crackled and Silas bellowed, his large body crumpling. The smell of singed human hair wafted through the air.

Then a different sound. An exasperated scream, and the air around Lee's throat drifted away. She rubbed it, gasping as her vision returned. She pivoted from her seated position on the floor and saw Finn, a fist raised and turned in a specific way. The female twins faced him, guns ready and murder in their eyes. Finn had thwarted them with his ability to block magic.

Silas lay unconscious on the floor ten feet from Lee.

Lee's knuckles scraped against the floor as she gathered her picks.

Risa was locked in a fight with Rosaura and the male twins, who seemed to have enhanced physical abilities, one with super speed, the other super strength. If only Sam were there, he could have beaten the punks, no problem. The usual low hiss of static in her earpiece was gone. Possibly the lightning strike had taken out their communication with Sam.

Lee hoped Finn could handle the elemental twins on his own. This was her last chance to grab something of value from the vaults.

Her fingers trembled as she pried a vault door open. A single gaudy clip-on earring sparkled in the depths of the vault. Lee grabbed it and shoved it in the fanny pack belted to her side. She left the door swinging and moved on, selecting another glowing vault at random and picking the lock.

A pair of glasses. A pen. A golden paperweight. A torn piece of paper.

All of it went into the fanny pack, and when it was full, she snagged the backpack she'd dropped earlier and unzipped it, ignoring the chaos around her. The sights and sounds dimmed each time she entered the Liminal realm to remind herself which vaults still contained items.

Her Sight from the Liminal realm slipped as she looked for her eleventh item. She put a hand to her head, body swaying. Someone slammed into her and she crashed face-first into the vault boxes, grunting with the force.

"Sorry!" Finn shouted, thrusting off of her as he pushed back against the dark-haired elemental woman. Her eyes sparked, and Finn yelped. His forehead beaded with sweat. He couldn't keep holding them off.

"I've got enough. Let's go!" Lee said. She thrust her pick set into the backpack and threw it on, releasing a knife from her wrist sheath as she went. Picking her target was harder when Finn kept changing directions and getting in the way.

"Risa!" she hollered.

The woman didn't respond. Only the whites of her eyes showed. Her head tipped back and wind streamed through her hair, but everything around her remained unaffected.

The light outside increased. It couldn't be daylight already.

But it wasn't the sun, and it came from the same staircase Silas had come up. A roar shook the floor beneath Lee's feet.

Everyone paused their fighting, like a spell had been laid over them. The light from the stairs flared in the mirrors' reflections again, the red-orange of flames. A shadow stretched on the wall, a twisted image of a beast that Lee had hoped was nothing more than myth.

"The chimera!" Risa shrieked, irises returning to her eyes.

"Sure, little sister. You would believe in that..." Rosa's insult trailed off as a giant maned face emerged at the end of the hall of mirrors. The beast roared, a bleating and a hiss escaping from the additional heads on either side.

Rosa's eyes bulged. "Muvengi, out!" she barked, diving across the slick floor to a hole in the wall that led to one of the dozens of slides in the museum.

Lee bolted to Silas's side, grunting as she rolled the massive man onto his back. She slapped his face and shook his shoulders. He woke with a gasp, eyes bloodshot and murderous. She clenched as the mechanical arm gripped her throat in reflex.

"Silas!" Finn shouted.

Silas jerked and released her, recognition flooding back into his eyes, the mechanical one spinning wildly in its socket. He took in the situation, then looked back to Lee.

"Which way?"

She nodded the way the Muvengi had gone. "That slide is the fastest way out. The other way leads to the roof."

"No telling if they're waiting for us at the bottom. We go up." Silas grunted and pushed himself to sitting, but his mechanical leg slid out from under him.

A blast of fire came from the hall of mirrors. Lee looked at Finn, who grabbed Silas's arm and threw it over his shoulder amid the crew leader's protests. Risa took his other side, being taller and stronger than Lee.

"We won't make it like this. We have to chance the stairs," Lee said.

"Or you transport us out of here," Silas growled.

"Silas, I can't move this many people. I've never…"

"Try!" he bellowed.

Lee swallowed. Her hands shook as Finn and Risa's arms landed on her shoulders. She'd never attempted this many people, and she already felt shaky from so many transitions to look in the vaults. But behind her, a fiery beast of legend with three heads was squeezing itself down the hall.

All it took was one glance at the mad goat head with its rolling eyes bleating in terror while the lion head roared and the serpent head wound around the other two hissing and spitting for Lee to squeeze her eyes shut and fade into the Liminal realm, consequences be damned.

CHAPTER 18

The ley line faltered beneath Lee. Sometimes ley lines moved, but Lee knew this time it was her. She felt the weight of the three passengers with her, and she didn't have the strength to compensate for their souls added to hers traveling through space and time.

A hand squeezed her shoulder, and strength surged through her, bridging her across to the landing point at the other side. They'd only jumped one, but it would have to be enough.

The crew landed in a heap on the pavement beside a dumpster, terrifying several alley cats rummaging through the garbage. They scattered, yowling and hissing. Lee heaved herself out of the pile of bodies, scooting backward as fast as she could, trying to still the trembling muscles in her jaw.

Finn and Risa sat up first. Finn rubbed his head, while Risa muttered something about her elbow, but she rotated her arm just fine and stood up.

Silas lay prone on the pavement.

"He's unconscious." Risa prodded the man's neck gently

and grimaced. "It's hard to tell with all the wiring in there, but I think something short circuited. Has he ever done that before?"

"Not with me." Lee swallowed. If she'd killed him...if she was responsible for another death of a member of their crew...

Finn crawled over and put a hand on her knee. Lee stared at it.

"Hey, look, it's not your fault. You can't control what happens to people you bring over. If you hadn't gotten us out of there, we'd be chimera toast."

"He's breathing," Risa announced.

Lee covered her quivering lip by wiping her hand across it. She nodded, but she knew inside that she was a curse to everyone around her. Sure, her abilities came with advantages. But eventually they would cripple her, and with other crews trying to kidnap her, it was only a matter of time before her crew would pay the price and wind up dead.

"How far are we from the factory hideout?" Risa asked, glancing around. Lee didn't recognize this part of the city. It was easier to travel to places she'd been to before, but in the height of emotion she could end up anywhere with a strong enough signature.

"I think we're close to the Energia District, but I'm not sure which side." She stood, brushing off her hands, and slipped out of the alley onto the street. It was dim, littered with broken and burnt-out street lights.

Well-to-do people didn't live here among garbage-packed streets filled with grime. A few stragglers loitered on the side-walks, even after 3 a.m. Druggies and magic users looking for hits to hide their troubles.

"It's getting Silas out of here I'm worried about. People will think we killed him."

"What if we call Sam? He could bring a car around," Finn suggested.

"Let's do that." Lee took her phone from her pocket and dialed Sam's latest number. He answered on the third ring.

"I lost communication with you guys! What's wrong with Silas?"

Lee didn't think her concern was strong enough for him to read it so clearly through the line. She swallowed. "He's unconscious. We're not sure what's wrong, but he's breathing. We need you to pick us up."

Finn walked swiftly away, getting closer to the graffitied street sign. With the shadows and the dark paint, it was nearly impossible to read, but he jogged back soon after.

He rattled off the street name to Lee, glancing to the side at a woman across the street. She had frizzy, curled hair and wore an oversized jacket. When she saw Finn staring, she shrugged off the wall she leaned against and put her cigarette out, then entered a door to the left.

"He'd better hurry," Finn added. "That woman is a Xurga."

Lee's mouth went dry. She gave Sam the street name, then hung up, shifting the backpack strap that dug into her shoulder.

Xurgas worked in packs, poaching on the magic abilities of others. They could project the abilities onto regular humans and sell them a taste of what it was like to have magic. A one-off spurt of watered-down magic that was dangerous in the hands of those who didn't know how to use it. Each member of the Xurga pack took a share, leaving the thaumaturgic user an empty husk, if they didn't just kill them to cover up the crime.

Lee wiped the base of her neck and her hand came away damp and cool with sweat. She turned back to Risa. "We've got to carry him somewhere safer if we don't want Xurga company in five minutes or less."

"You can't take us out of here like you did before?"

Lee shuddered. "No. Not all of you."

"Just Silas, then," Finn said. "Risa and I can hold our own."

"But Sam is headed here. What will he do if he doesn't find us?"

"Call him with your new location. Take him somewhere safe." Risa started to lift him.

"Wait!" Lee cried. She licked her lips and backed up a step. "Look, I want to, but I...I can't. I can't risk it." She darted a glance at Finn, then down at her dirty sneakers. Shame tinged the fear in her chest. She was too afraid of the Fade to save the life of a crew member. Did that make her a coward?

Finn's eyes hardened. He stalked over to Silas's prone body, dragged the unconscious man's arm over his shoulder, and hefted him over his shoulder. He grunted, and his knees nearly buckled, but he held steady. Lee's eyes widened until she thought they might pop out of her head. She'd never seen anyone lift a man as big as Silas. With all of his metal attachments, the man had to weigh well over two hundred pounds, and Finn wasn't anywhere near that muscular.

"Come on," Finn gasped. "You can cover my back."

"Not so fast, there, mister." The frizzy-haired woman was back. Her voice was unexpectedly smooth, a rich alto that didn't match her frazzled appearance.

Knives in both hands, Lee faced the Xurga. Seven of them. Seven was a huge group. How did they all get fed? *That's why they're set up so close to the Energia District,* Lee realized. Here, they could find enough unfortunate, drugged up magic-users to satisfy their urges. She tightened the backpack straps so it didn't move around so much.

"Stop there. You don't want to mess with us. You'll find easier prey somewhere else," Lee warned.

"Tainted," The woman with the frizzy hair hissed, flicking her tongue in the air, as if tasting it. Her eyes flashed gold. "We need...more." She lunged.

Lee lashed out with the knives and made contact. The Xurga yelped and retreated, gesturing to her pack. The six others closed in around Lee and her crew. A brave one darted in under the knives and tackled Lee to the ground, knocking the wind and one of her knives from her grasp. Lee plunged the other one into the broad back and the Xurga howled, thrashing off her and arching its back on the ground.

Lee left it there, scrambling to her feet and retrieving both her knives. Risa had some kind of spectre helping her ward off two Xurga, the invisible blows and the chill in the air clues to Lee, who couldn't see the otherworldly spirit.

Two other Xurga had Silas's legs in their grips, and Finn was barely hanging on as a third Xurga crept up behind him and caught him in a chokehold.

Lee grimaced and ran forward, swiping with her blade and catching the stomach of one of the Xurga holding Silas. It gurgled as it fell, and Lee yanked her blade back, trying not to think about the body on the ground, its blood spilling out.

She'd killed a person. Magic sucker or not, it had been a person once. She wiped her mouth with the back of her hand

and breathed in, the stink of the alley strong enough to distract her mind from the horrific reality at her feet.

The Xurga choking Finn hissed at her, then bit down on his shoulder hard.

"No!" Lee shouted. She wanted to throw her knife, but she was too afraid that she'd hit Finn. The Xurga blinked with confusion. It bit Finn again, who yelled and lashed about, bashing his head into the Xurga's face. Its yelp of pain startled Lee into action, and she brandished her knife.

"Want to end up like your buddy there?" She nodded towards the body, holding her gaze carefully away to avoid sickening herself again.

The Xurga released Finn, spitting. "Broken," it said. It turned on Lee.

A strong arm lashed around Lee's shoulders from behind. She kicked and screamed, but the Xurga that had abandoned Finn rushed forward and knocked the knives from her hands, then held her legs. Hot breath crossed her cheeks, smelling of fast food. Two other Xurga approached, practically salivating as they each took an arm.

Risa shouted, her words garbled at first, then clear. "Shift, Lee! Go Liminal!"

Lee yanked at her limbs. She tried to slip into the Liminal realm, but she couldn't concentrate. Four sets of teeth descended.

A thousand crackling sparks burst between Lee's skin and the Xurga's teeth. They dropped her, smoke rising from their faces as they clawed at their skin. They gathered and retreated with a chorus of screeches, taking off down the pavement with loping gaits.

Lee blinked, dazed, and glanced over at Finn and Risa.

"Did...er, one of you do that?"

Risa shook her head slowly. "It wasn't something you did?"

"No way." Lee stood, brushing off her pants. She found her knives on the ground and sheathed them, then scanned the buildings around them. A few faces flashed away from the glass in various sections, but she suspected they weren't anything other than curious onlookers. Or maybe one of them was something more.

"Holy hell," Finn said. He met Lee's gaze. "I've never seen anything like it."

"Well, I'm glad they were on our side. Whoever it was." Lee scanned Risa, checking that she was all right. Risa gave her a nod, hands on her hips as she caught her breath. Lee looked back at Finn.

"You all right?" she asked.

He hoisted Silas up again, doing his best to see the wound on his shoulder. "It's bleeding. Xurga aren't venomous, right?"

"What did it mean when it said you were broken?" Lee asked.

Finn grunted, adjusting his grip on the unconscious cyborg. "I couldn't keep it from biting me. That's a physical action. But they can't suck my ability away."

"Fortunate, that." Risa bent down and picked up a piece of paper.

Lee opened her mouth to ask why Risa was so interested in trash, but closed it again when she saw the scripted writing scrawled on the paper in brilliant blue ink.

"Leanna. Isn't that your full name?" Risa asked, handing the note towards Lee.

Lee stared mutely at the note. No one used her full name. Risa gestured again and Lee took the paper. The rest of the note wasn't in English, or any other language she recognized, but touching the paper made her fingertips tingle, and then the edge of the paper outlined itself in red, and Lee knew what she needed to do. She took a deep breath and stepped into the Liminal realm, watching as the words rearranged until she understood.

You will be retrieved tomorrow.

There was no signature, and no indication otherwise whom the note could be from. Lee crumpled the paper and shoved it into her pocket, phasing back into the regular timestream.

"It's just some gibberish. Lots of people named Leanna."

"Weird coincidence." Risa eyed her, rightfully not trusting Lee's words at face value.

Finn cleared his throat. "Uh, ladies? Car's here."

The darkened window rolled down, and Sam leaned out, waving. As Lee slid into the front passenger seat, she dug her fingers into her pocket and pulled out the note again, then stared at the foreign words. They didn't look like any language she'd ever seen before, at least not any Earth language. The way the letters formed, they looked suspiciously like the few writings that had been found from the Ceteri.

She'd been trying to contact them for years; she just hadn't anticipated that they would reach her first.

CHAPTER 19

The backpack of items buzzed against Lee's back as she emerged from the top of the staircase at the hideout. She felt haggard. Coffee would help. She dropped the backpack off on the kitchen table and headed for the coffee pot.

"I lost the connection after I heard the roar. Visuals went out before that. What happened?" Sam said, walking up to the table and eyeing the backpack.

"There was a chimera," Risa said in a sing-song voice, exiting the stairway behind him.

"Woah, no way. What was it like?" Sam's eyes got wide as saucers, and despite her exhaustion, Lee had to smile at his awe.

Risa launched into a detailed description, and Lee frowned at the residue in the bottom of the clear coffee pot. She turned on the hot water and scrubbed it out, then set to prepping it for coffee. She shook the coffee can. A few grains rattled in the bottom. She set it down.

"Who didn't buy more coffee?"

Sam waved at her sheepishly. "I finished it off just now. Sorry."

Lee straightened her beanie. "Well, I need some."

Risa and Sam stared at her.

"It's 1 a.m., darling. I'm sure someone can go for coffee later. Try eating something." Risa tucked a loose strand of hand behind her ear.

Lee crossed her arms. She *needed* coffee. She wasn't about to let everyone look over the items she'd snagged without her.

"Unless all of you want to wait until morning to take a look at these things, I suggest someone makes a coffee run. I'm happy to. Snap of my fingers and I'll be at Beans and Things." Lee raised her fingers and snapped, fully intending to go Liminal and watch the slow-motion shock on all of their faces as she shifted realms and disappeared. Dang, she was feeling catty.

Her fingers clicked together with an audible snap and everyone stood blinking at her. The lighting didn't dim, and Lee's skin didn't glow with the red outline of Liminal travel.

Sam fidgeted, glancing down and giving himself away as a guilty party who could possibly explain why her powers didn't work.

"Sam, what do you know about this? Why can't I go Liminal?" Lee stuck her tongue against the inside of her cheek, crossing her arms.

Sam shuffled, his bulky form twisting nervously from side to side. He steepled his fingers and put them against his mouth, looking at Lee with his big brown eyes.

"So, while you were away, Silas left me with specific instructions for safeguarding this place. He wanted it locked down so the signatures of the magical items you were bringing back wouldn't be able to escape and inform others of our location, both rival crews and law enforcement. He wanted to protect *all* of the crew's assets." He paused for emphasis, keeping his eyes on Lee.

Understanding struck her like lightning. She threw her hands into the air and placed them on her hips. "He considers me an asset."

"Exactly," Sam said with an exhale.

Risa sat in a kitchen chair and loosened the laces on her boots. "You've gotten us out of some pretty tight places in the past. Take tonight, for instance."

A grunt sounded from the bottom of the stairs, and Lee remembered Finn and Silas.

Sam went to go help, and a moment later the two men emerged with Silas between them. They walked him over to the couch, making sure he was settled before they rejoined the conversation.

"I'm hardly able to do that anymore. I almost dropped you guys back there. If I hadn't gotten that weird shot of strength in the middle, I would have." Lee tried not to look at Finn. She didn't want to think about how every time her power was clear and strong lately, like it had been when she'd first manifested her powers, Finn was nearby. That damned Speller couldn't be right about soul mates and their insipid bonds acting as protection from the Fade. And Finn couldn't be her Anchor.

"That doesn't change the fact that you're valuable to us. To the crew. We want to help you find a cure," Sam urged. "Part of that is making sure you don't burn yourself out first."

"Is that what Silas told you?" Lee snapped. Tears pricked in her eyes. She tried to tell herself it was fatigue or a post-heist adrenaline crash, not the surge of warmth in her heart at the earnestness in Sam's voice and body language that he wanted to help her find a way to stop the Liminality from claiming her, body, mind, and soul.

The large, open room fell silent, except for Risa's boots hitting the floor. No one spoke, and no one looked at Lee.

"Am I the only one who can't leave?" Lee asked, all the anger gone out from her words. Damn, she was tired. She didn't want to be standing anymore.

"Until Silas wakes up and gives permission, no one comes or goes," Sam explained.

Lee snorted. Typical Silas to give a broad order like that and expect it to be followed even while he was unconscious. To be fair, though, no one had expected that to happen. If nothing else, Silas had a plan for everything.

"At least we have something to occupy the time until he wakes up." Lee started for the table, but Risa held up a hand.

"Hold on. We need to wait for Silas before looking at these items."

"What, worried I'm going to pocket one in plain sight? I just want to look," Lee said, frustration leaching into her voice, making sound like a whine. She couldn't stand the pitying expressions on everyone's faces. "Oh come on, don't tell me you all agree with her! Sam? Finn?" She glared at them both.

Finn's expression was so gentle it frightened her. "Get some sleep, Lee."

Lee stalked over to an armchair and curled up tightly in the seat, resting her elbow on the arm of the chair and putting her chin into the palm of her hand.

She jerked herself out of a heavy, thoughtless stupor when a hand tapped her shoulder. She could have sworn she hadn't slept, but the trail of drool on her cheek suggested otherwise.

Lee looked into Risa's eyes.

The woman held up a tea bag between her index and forefinger. "It's just green tea, but it'll give you a buzz if you still want it."

Lee snatched for it, but Risa held it out of reach, the dim lamp light glinting off her goggles. "Promise me you'll eat."

"I don't feel like having a meal." Lee's stomach flip-flopped at the thought.

"I'll make toast. And the tea. You just sit here. You did a lot tonight."

Lee felt guilty as Risa walked away. Lee had acted like a brat over not getting coffee, but Risa's own twin sister had attacked her, and no one was helping her process that.

Lee wiggled further under the blanket that covered her lower half, barely registering that she hadn't put it on. She would ask Risa about it when the moment was right, try to get the woman to talk about it. Prove that she wasn't just a selfish coffee monster...

Lee yawned and shook her head. The toaster popped, and a knife scraped the crisp bread. An obnoxious beep indicated the water for her tea was hot. She opened her eyes as wide as they would go. She would stay awake. She wouldn't drift off...

A tugging sensation in her navel woke her up. She was floating on a boat in the ocean. No, that wasn't right. She was spinning through a galaxy on a rotating rocket shaped like half a dozen ragged armchairs. Damn this dream was trippy.

Not a dream.

Lee clutched for the arms of the chair, but they weren't there. A red line extended before her, arching to a distant point she couldn't discern. She hurtled through the air along it, her entire body pulsing with red light. She was in the Liminal realm and traveling, only she hadn't activated the ley line, and she had no idea where she was headed.

The ley line was longer than any she'd travelled before. Time stretched and blurred. Panic gave way to trepidation first, and then boredom. She couldn't *see* anything. Before, she'd been dreaming. Much more interesting than the nothingness she saw now. It was a black void, only disrupted by the occasional red shine of the activated ley line she traveled.

A flash of gold blinded her vision after the extended intensity of the utter blackness. She blinked rapidly, shrinking the spots filling her gaze.

The ley line ended, dropping her onto a cool floor. She rolled onto her back, staring up at a glistening black ceiling. Polished, curved walls gleamed black. The floor shone so smooth that Lee's reflection looked back at her. The surface felt like glass.

Lee stood. Her exhaustion was gone for now, chased away by the pounding of her heart in her chest, blood and adrenaline pumping through her veins. Where was she? And who had brought her here?

"Hello?" Lee's voice echoed in the space. She couldn't identify a light source in the glossy black room. It was like being in a hall of mirrors. She remembered the wavy glass, filled with bubbles and other imperfections, twisting her body out of shape. She took a step now and her reflection bounced from a hundred surfaces, scattered the visions of herself. Lee instinctively reached for a knife from her thigh sheath.

The familiar weight of the weapon gave Lee confidence. She stood still, staring into her own warped reflections on the walls of the room.

"Who are you?" Lee asked, hoping to address whoever had brought her to this place. Her voice sounded flat, like the room was on the smaller side. The mirrors could make it look much larger than it was. Lee sniffed, drawing in a cloyingly sweet scent, like sticky melted popsicle juice on a sidewalk in July.

A chittering sound from behind made Lee's hair raise on end. She whirled, but saw nothing move.

Lee slid her feet along the floor, hoping to catch a trap before she triggered it, if any existed in this strange place. The chittering sounded again, this time from her left. Lee whirled, blade-first, nearly tripping herself. Chest heaving, hair over one side of her face, she peered at the reflective blackness.

"Hello?" Her voice echoed out, a lonely sound. She licked her dry lips and crept forward again.

A warm, fast-moving mass hovered behind Lee for an instant, freezing her mid-step. Rapid, insect-like clicking vibrated in her eardrum.

The mass did not move after the chittering stopped. Lee slowly rotated her body, stepping back a single step to view the impossibly tall figure standing over her. Its grey face was long and pointed at the chin and ears, thinner than humanly possible. Its almond-shaped eyes had irises that glowed turquoise with slits like cat-eyes with golden centers instead of black. Thick, clumping locks of wrapped silvery hair moved stiffly with every turn of the creature's head, and its sweeping, tattered robes flowed down its arms and to the ground like gathered smoke.

Lee's heartbeat stopped for three long counts. Her eyes locked in the creature's gaze as it smiled to reveal jagged teeth.

"Welcome, Leanna," it said, with a voice like the voice of hundreds speaking at once.

Lee couldn't speak. Her mouth was glued shut, her arms

and legs locked, every fiber of her being screaming to run in the presence of this predator. The being opened its arms and others melted through the obsidian walls, surrounding her in a sea of glittering eyes and clicking tongues.

"Who are you?" Lee choked out.

A hundred voices spoke in unison. "We are the Ceteri."

CHAPTER 20

Shit. Adam ran his hand through his hair as he looked around the cluttered basement of the hideout. He knew Lee was gone, but he put on the pretense of checking every corner with Silas's mechanical eye blazing at him.

"She isn't here, sir," Adam said at last. His shoulder twinged as he swung around to face Silas. Damn that Xurga.

"I'm aware she isn't here. The question is, how did she get past you?"

Adam had felt the faintest of clicks in his chest, now that he thought about it. But he'd ignored it because he'd seen her falling asleep in the armchair in the middle of the room and there was no way she could make it through the magical barriers Silas had set up. Then she had vanished, leaving the blanket and a slight depression in the floral fabric of the chair.

"Never mind. If I'm going to find her, you need to let me out of here." Adam swallowed, hoping the eagerness didn't show on his face. He hadn't reported in more than 24 hours. Hatcher would send agents in after him if he didn't check in soon. Not to mention Millie…

He broke out in a cold sweat as the cyborg's blue eye swept over him. Silas lifted a lit cigar to his lips. "Go do your job."

"Yes, sir." Adam withheld a sigh of relief and headed for the back entrance, weaving between towering stacks.

"Finn."

He froze mid-stride.

"Don't come back until you find her," Silas warned.

Adam swallowed and went to the door. A moment later, he felt a tingling as one of the spells lifted, and another, and then the lock on the door clicked and it swung open.

He checked his messages as he walked briskly down the sidewalk. His car was parked three blocks away. Plenty of time to listen to the six missed voicemails and make a few calls. He pushed play on the first one.

"... I hope you're coming home soon."

Adam glanced around at the empty street, passing beneath a street light as it flickered on. It was late. She was probably asleep. He punched the dial button anyway and listened to the rings. No answer. He left a brief message, promising to call in the morning.

Next, Hatcher. He didn't bother with the voice mails, but dialed the number with a dry throat. Adam had been gone for days and had nothing to show for it, except he had helped rob a building, defacing public property in the process, and potentially gained the trust of a Liminal. That last one would hopefully be enough to get Hatcher to shut up and listen for thirty seconds and not retract his support of Adam's pet project.

"Finley. About time. Where are you?"

"The East Side. Don't worry about me. I got tied up in the case."

"Hope that's not literal," Hatcher grumbled. "I got

Kimball from the council breathing down my neck. What've you got for me?"

"I've gained the target's trust. Listen, we need to talk in person about this." Adam's gaze darted across the street to where his car stood parked on a dark, out-of-the-way street. No one else was visible, but that fact made him more nervous. He hesitated on the corner, jingling his keys in his pocket. A drop of rain struck his arm.

"You aren't kidding. Meet me at Mal's in twenty minutes." Hatcher hung up the phone without waiting for a response.

The feeling of being watched followed Adam to a bar near the center of town. The rain picked up in earnest. It dotted his windshield too slowly to need the wipers, but enough to make the lights in front of him divide into a hundred shining dots.

Adam pulled up to Mal's. It was the Goldilocks of bars; not too busy, not too dirty, and people mostly came to nurse drinks after the workday or do business. He joined Hatcher at a table against the front wall, near a window.

"I ordered your usual."

"Thanks." Adam shook his arms a bit before sitting down. When the drinks arrived, he couldn't help but think of the unique mixture he'd tried in the supernatural bar with Lee. This beer wouldn't hit the spot in quite the same way.

He sipped the drink. It tasted flat.

"Something wrong with your beer?" Hatcher swigged his jack and coke, smacking his lips.

"Nah. Just thinking."

"What went down last night, exactly?" Hatcher tapped the table for emphasis, raising his eyebrows.

"A rival crew and a chimera blew up the original plan. But

the Liminal got away with a number of valuable magic items."

"And how close are you to bringing this girl in?"

"We could swarm the place and try to nab her, but you know how unlikely that is with her abilities. We'll either need to wait until she's vulnerable or until she trusts me. And..." Adam trailed off. He shook his head and took another drink. This was his job on the line. He had to think about his future, his and Millie's.

"The lab is ready for her. They're eager to get started."

"Do they have a plan to contain her?" Adam suppressed a shudder. The 'lab' wasn't a place he would want to end up. But the knowledge gained by the researchers and technicians there had become invaluable in the fight against thaumaturgic crime.

Hatcher nodded. "The material is insanely expensive, but they've formulated a compound to put into building materials that creates a room that cannot be used to travel realms. They have given us the use of a single such room where this Liminal will live under observation."

"You know, we could try asking her to help us. She's human after all."

Hatcher's eyes flashed. "Human? There's hardly anything human left in her cells by now. The magic has consumed it. That's what this magic does. You want us to ask her to donate her body to science while she's still alive? Not likely. But a criminal might do it in exchange for a reduced sentence." Hatcher turned his glass, staring at Adam.

"The most she'd get is a few years. She's a petty thief. She's never killed anyone." *Until the Xurga.* Adam shuddered. If his ability didn't involve blocking magical attacks, he'd have been drained. And Lee hadn't wanted to kill it. It had been a desperate act of self-defense.

"And how are we to know she won't be at it again once she's out? She can do a lot of damage as a Liminal. Imagine what someone with her powers could do in politics."

"So you're saying she'll be threatened." Adam swirled his drink and sipped the beer again.

"The judge will be easily persuaded into making her time at the lab required 'community service', if you will." Hatcher raised his eyebrows and smiled. "We have something to persuade everyone."

"But for life? That seems excessive." Adam shifted, scooting back and sitting up in his chair.

"How long do you expect her to live, Agent? From your reports, this one could pop off any time."

"She's stronger than I imagined. I've traveled with her."

Hatcher's eyes narrowed. "Just remember your goal, here. We need a live subject. We've studied corpses enough. We need to find out why these people are dying and how thaumaturgy is passed on."

"Why are Liminals the key, though? You could learn that from any other magic user."

Hatcher hesitated, and then leaned in over the table, gesturing for Adam to do the same. "With a live Liminal, we could get to the Ceteri, negotiate for the removal of thaumaturgy from humankind, and find out why they cursed us in the first place."

"That's why?" Adam laughed. "Lee would do it in a heartbeat! She's trying to get enough money to get directions to the Ceteri's realm so they'll remove the Liminal ability from her body. If the government could pay her way, I imagine she'd cooperate."

Hatcher sat back. "You don't say? Well, this girl certainly has high ambitions. Petition the Ceteri herself! But how do we set it up so you don't blow your cover if it goes wrong?"

"I could maneuver her into a position to be approached. And stay nearby to keep her from entering the Liminal Realm." Excitement built in Adam. Lee could have what she wanted, paid for by the government, and Hatcher and his supervisors would have what they wanted, access to the Ceteri.

A phone rang. Both Hatcher and Adam went to their devices, but it was Hatcher's that had lit up. He stood, finishing his drink in a gulp. "I'll have to take this. We'll talk soon, Finley."

"Yes sir," Adam replied out of habit. He watched in confusion as Hatcher tossed a bill on the table and left, not answering the phone until he'd cleared the bar doors.

Adam stewed in the weird feeling that hung around after Hatcher had gone. The director seemed flighty lately, and though Adam knew the man had a lot going on, the pieces weren't quite fitting together.

A woman left the bar, digging in her purse. She wasn't looking where she was going, and a moment later she tripped, landing in Adam's lap and spilling the rest of his beer.

"Oh, I'm so sorry! Terribly sorry." He got caught in her intense green-eyed stare as she pushed herself upright. She crammed something in his pants pocket, and Adam sputtered.

"Excuse me?"

The woman flashed him a smile and ran out the door, remarkably fast for someone wearing heels.

"Here." A barkeeper came over with a towel. He glanced at the door, shaking his head and pursing his lips. "I'll be unlikely to let her in here again."

Adam sponged at the beer on his shirt. "It's not that big of a deal." He glanced down and noticed a crumpled paper sticking out of his pocket. He frowned, taking it out and smoothing the wrinkles. It contained a scrawled address and two double-underlined words that made him abruptly stand from his chair.

Breeding Liminals.

He ran out the front door of Mal's bar, looking both ways down and across the street for the brunette woman, but she was gone, blended into the crowd or vanished entirely. Both were valid possibilities. He ran a hand through his hair. Did he have time to pursue this lead? Or would he risk Silas's suspicion if he didn't bring Lee back soon enough?

Silas be damned, Adam had to do this. If someone was breeding Liminals…what would it all be for? Liminals might have a powerful ability to move through time and space, but children born with this ability were condemned to shorter lifespans. What would be the advantage? Get to the Ceteri?

Adam made it to the address in less than ten minutes. He parked across the street from the tall, tan office complex. A single light was on, shining from a basement floor from a narrow slit of a window.

He couldn't tell anything from the building's surface. It looked like any other building on the street. He took his gun off the passenger seat and strapped it on, then locked the doors and crossed the street at a leisurely pace that belied the pounding in his heart. He jammed his hands into his jeans pockets, and closed one fist around the paper.

Please be wrong.

He walked down the alley between the buildings and stopped just before the lit window, trying to see inside. A row of cots lined up against the wall he could see, about a half-dozen of them. Each one contained a female, ranging in ages from teen to middle-aged.

Adam lay on the ground to get a fuller view, army-crawling to stay out of the direct line of sight from the window, trying to see if anyone else was in the room.

The light inside the room flicked off, plunging his view into darkness. Adam rubbed a hand down his face. He'd have to come back during the day, tell Hatcher and get a team on this.

On second thought, he didn't need to involve anyone in this. There was nothing here to observe. There was no crime in a few women sharing a room.

A soothing blanket coated Adam's mind. His pulse lowered to a resting rate, and then continued to drop until he found himself nodding off on the pavement. He really ought to get home, get some shut-eye…

Adam's military training kicked into high alert, and his thaumaturgic ability flared. His senses flooded back, adrenaline spiking so high his heart felt like it might explode. He leapt to his feet and pulled his gun. He turned and faced a lone man.

The man smiled and brushed a lock of greasy black hair behind his ear. He stroked a medallion on his chest.

"You're stronger than I expected." The man's voice oozed calm and complacency. Adam could barely hold onto his own mind with the block he'd thrown up.

"Who are you?"

"I'm glad you asked. I'm the Mentalist."

"You're coming with me," Adam huffed out. With one hand on his gun and one hand holding the sign he made to hold the thaumaturgic block, he couldn't pull out his badge.

"So much authority in that voice. What gives you such confidence that you can demand I come with you?"

"FBI." Sweat dripped from Adam's brow. The man he faced seemed perfectly unfazed by the gun, and he showed no outward evidence that he was increasing his mind attack, but Adam could feel it pressing into his mind, trying to smother his consciousness.

"Well then, it's a good thing I'm not alone."

"Wha—" Adam heard the footsteps shuffle behind him a second too late. He swung around to meet the person and felt the burning blow delivered to his head.

Agent Adam Finley crumpled to the ground, his gun skittering toward the Mentalist. Blinding pain incapacitated him, and he rolled on the ground moaning, then his training kicked in and he fell silent, pretending to be unconscious so the men would let their guard down. He cracked his eyes ever-so-slightly. At the very least, if he could stay awake he might discover the location of their operations.

The Mentalist bent down and picked up Adam's gun, handing it to his bald associate.

"Shouldn't have come alone, little agent. Bring him," the Mentalist barked at the muscled man beside him. "The boss will be quite interested in this one."

CHAPTER 21

Everything Lee had hoped, searched, and stolen for stood in front of her, and all she could do was stand frozen, blinking and staring. How had she gotten here? Were the Ceteri so powerful they had broken through Silas's shields?

A wave of anxious-sounding chittering erupted among the Ceteri, and their golden eyes winked and glittered, reflecting in the obsidian walls.

"Perhaps we made a mistake bringing it here," one Ceteri said. Gender was irrelevant. Every single one of the thin-faced beings looked just as terrifyingly beautiful as the last, and there were no obvious indications of male and female.

"It seems broken. Can it speak?" another said.

The Ceteri that had appeared first leaned in toward Lee, who couldn't help but lean away from the nine-foot being as it drew closer. Lee gripped the edge of her beanie on her head for comfort, breathing in a strange cinnamon and burnt-rubber scent that came from the Ceteri's mouth as it spoke.

"We intimidate you? Speak, small one. We have brought you here of our own accord and will not deliver any harm."

A Ceteri behind the first chittered and clicked, ending with a slight popping sound.

"That is a good point," the first said in response. "Perhaps my name will bring it comfort." Its eyes scanned Lee's. It put a hand on its chest, impossibly long fingers stretching across its robes. Six fingers. It had six. Lee's gaze fixed on the fingers, then drifted back to the golden eyes.

A string of insect-like chirps and rhythms came from the Ceteri's lips, then it paused, cocking its head. "In your language, you would call me Xochitl."

"Xochitl?" Lee repeated, finally finding her voice. "How do you know my name?"

"You are the one called Leanna. We have been watching you ever since the power chose you to be a messenger." Xochitl straightened back up, joining his fellow Ceteri. At least, Lee felt as if it were a he. Just an impression.

"Yeah, about that. No one wants your powers," Lee said boldly. "If you could take them back, that'd be great."

The Ceteri withdrew from her as a group, hissing and baring mouths filled with teeth like broken glass.

"The human eschews our gift!" a tall Ceteri in the back shrieked. Angry clicking filled the obsidian chamber.

"Ingratitude," another said. "We should have—"

Xochitl let out a keening whistle-like sound, silencing his fellows. "What is the meaning of this offense, human girl?"

Lee crossed her arms. "I don't mean any offense, certainly, but your so-called gift is killing people back on Earth. Our bodies weren't made to hold this power."

Xochitl nodded, as if he understood. "You humans are so fragile. It is part of the reason we chose your world for our gift. The magic makes you stronger."

"It seems that way at first," Lee said. "But more of us are

dying of thaumaturgical illness than ever before. I promised myself I would find a way to your world and do whatever it took to convince you to remove the magic. If not from all of Earth, then from me."

Lee spread her arms. She swallowed past the dryness in her throat. "Give it to someone else, someone who would be grateful."

A Ceteri pushed past Xochitl, muttering or chittering, Lee couldn't tell. She tried not to wince as it leaned in and passed its hands over her arms, legs, back, and then clamped onto her head.

"Xever, unhand the human girl," Xochitl demanded.

The Ceteri, Xever, held onto Lee a moment longer, then stepped back and addressed Xochitl, popping and occasionally grunting, even whistling. Lee watched with interest, unable to identify any patterns to the language, and nothing was revealed in Xever's flat expression.

"What's he saying?" Lee demanded, watching the two Ceteri exchange sounds.

Xochitl looked at Lee. "He says your essence has holes. And the power we gifted humankind appears to be the cause. We could not have anticipated the speed with which the power has affected your frail body. There are others of your species that are stronger, correct?"

All of the green and gold eyes bore down on Lee.

"Well, yes, I guess so. But strength, size, gender, none of it seems to matter. The magic disables us, makes us ill. Some are killed, consumed by this so-called gift." Lee swallowed as the discontented chittering started up again. Would the Ceteri attack her? She didn't truly have anything to lose. The thought emboldened her.

"And how do you know they wouldn't have died or been

disabled anyway?" Xochitl asked.

"Our doctors don't know anything that can stop the disease caused by your magic. The more I use it, the more it consumes me. And I've known people who have been crippled, and those who have disappeared. You can't tell me it's in my head." Lee stepped forward, hand clenched into a fist.

Xochitl waved a hand. A hum thrummed through the cavern, and an opalescent light rippled across the dark glossy walls, liquifying them, turning them into a gleaming crystal. Quick as a flash, the wave of rainbow translucence vanished, and the cavern seemed darker than ever. Lee blinked the spots out of her vision, but she couldn't get rid of it fully.

"Do you know why the Ceteri blessed humankind with power?" Xochitl asked.

Lee bit back a smart alec remark. She tapped her foot and bit the inside of her cheek, then shook her head. She didn't subscribe to any of the dozens of theories. She wanted to hear it directly from the source.

"The light you saw is a miniscule taste of what our realm used to be. But it is dying, and as it dies, beauty and light and power leech from our atmosphere. Our light has nearly gone out, and we need your planet in order to survive."

Lee gritted her teeth. *Hear him out*, she reminded herself. She wouldn't get anywhere with unnecessary anger.

"We planted four...seeds...on your planet." Xochitl hesitated, then gestured to his right. "Your planet was perfect. Close to a living, burning star, but not too close. With water and beings with intelligence. That intelligence is found in one out of ten galaxies. There are billions, but not within reach of our capabilities to travel, which dwindled to a near devastating point. Making it to Earth took all the concentrated power we could muster."

"You didn't come to invade?" Lee shot out, unable to resist. "Everyone assumed that when aliens landed, they would want to take over Earth. Some bull about humans wasting it."

Xochitl's expression changed, drooping a bit. "We cannot live on your planet. It took much out of us to exist there for the brief time we did. Once the atmosphere filled with our power, the seeds we planted could grow and take root and develop into the items that would save our planet."

"Wait, seeds?" Lee asked. She shivered, but the temperature of the room was neither hot nor cold, which in itself felt unnerving.

"We planted what our planet needed to be restored to its former function and glory," the Ceteri's voice dropped almost to a whisper. "The fruits have reached maturity. They must be returned to our realm."

A dramatic pause filled the room. Lee glanced around at the Ceteri, who all stared at her. "So, why do you need me again?"

Their chittering sounded like laughter. Xochitl spoke over the noise. "Because we have lost the ability to travel."

"But you're the ones who brought me here."

"Relying on the power that has taken root in your body, not the power within our bodies. It took much less to track you and bring you here than to go and fight against the unwelcome atmosphere of your planet. We need you to find the items we seek and bring them back to us."

Lee tapped her foot, crossing her arms as she considered the impossibly tall beings standing before her. "I'll do it," she said at last. An audible sense of relief broke across the group of Ceteri.

"If," Lee raised a finger. "If after I bring you the items you request, you remove my Liminal ability and restore my body to its full function. And also, you have to provide a life of luxury for myself and my crew."

Xochitl tilted its head sideways. "Your crew?"

"Yeah, my crew. They're, uh, a group of humans that can help me be more successful getting the items."

"They must not know of the nature of the items. Humans are selfish. They will try to sell them, to undermine you, to take it for themselves." A third Ceteri stepped forward. Lee did not know this one's name, but her voice sounded more feminine.

"Xuxa," Xochitl barked.

The Ceteri stood her ground, staring at Lee, who locked her eyes on the strange golden glimmer within the Ceteri's irises.

A sweat broke out on Lee's brow. Did she trust the Ceteri? Not entirely. Their story of a dying realm sounded legitimate, but she was still confused about how a race of powerful beings such as these could have killed their planet. This was her best chance at returning to normalcy, and at very least she could give her crew the reward of a lifetime for helping her.

Finally, Lee nodded. "I'll keep the items' true nature a secret." She turned her gaze to Xochitl. "Are you going to tell me anything more about them? Do you know where they are hidden?"

"We can find them the same as we found you, using their magical signature. The first is near you, in a glass palace in your human city."

Lee searched her mental map of St. Louis for a building that matched Xochitl's description. A palace? Made of glass? Her brain sparked.

"The Jewel Box?" she asked.

Xochitl nodded solemnly. "Indeed. The item is called the Barat. It is a foot-tall statue made of lapis lazuli and gold, and it is valuable far beyond what can be seen or utilized by humans."

"Are you going to give me a description or...?" Lee gestured with her hands, rolling them over each other.

Xochitl blinked. "It is a statue of particular value—"

"I got that," Lee interrupted. "But what does it *look* like?"

"It will be obvious. Can you not sense magical items and their energetic signatures? It is one of the abilities you were gifted." Xochitl emphasized the last word, and Lee stopped herself from rolling her eyes.

"What will I see with my eyes? A physical description will make it easier," she insisted.

"Our eyes do not see the way yours do. Any description I could give would be useless to you," Xochitl explained. Around them, the cave trembled. Lee's arms flew out to steady herself, but the Ceteri barely moved. A few chittered urgently.

"Our time with you grows short, and we cannot remain here for much longer. The walls and ground will shift, and you will be lost. You must leave," Xochitl said.

"You can send me back." Lee said, adjusting her beanie and then sticking a thumb in her jean pocket.

Xochitl shook his head. "Getting back is up to you. I can give you a direction to set your ley line and a push to get you started. If your powers fail mid-flight, you will be lost."

"You brought me here without a guaranteed way back to my planet?" Lee said, her voice rising. "You do know that if I fail, you won't get the items to save your planet."

"You assume you are the only one we have contacted this way. There are others we've given the same information to.

And if all fail, we will reserve our magic and contact others, even if it takes a thousand of your years," Xochitl explained, his voice so calm and monotone Lee could hardly believe what he was saying.

"So, you don't care if I fail. You don't care that your magic has already fragmented my soul into a hundred million pieces, that I made this jump once but it's unlikely I can make it again without your aid. You are sending me to my death," Lee said, gritting her teeth.

"Your death, or your ultimate restoration and success," Xochitl said with infuriating calm.

Lee ground her teeth. Fear hardened in her chest, restricting her from taking full breaths. She narrowed her eyes at the Ceteri, wondering if this was somehow a trap, but she wasn't important enough to them to deserve this level of manipulation to achieve her death. She was just a pawn to them, a being they bestowed their power on as a gift—a gift that would eventually kill her if she didn't do what they asked of her.

Shane would want her to do it. He would tell her this was her chance.

Lee squared her shoulders and faced the Ceteri straight-on.

"Show me the ley line I should take." She didn't have a choice. Either make the jump, or be crushed in this obsidian cavern far from her own realm.

CHAPTER 22

Lee fought to hold onto the ley line that grew dimmer with each passing moment. She'd never had a ley line disappear while she rode it before. Would she be flung into the nothingness and lost forever?

The line vibrated through her body, threatening to rip her to shreds. She burned. Every part of her burned as she fought to hold on, fought to keep the fading red line in her sight.

A brilliant flash of red light consumed her vision, and a scream ripped from her throat. Her hands broke from the line, and she was thrust through a wall of crimson pain.

Cold, damp air struck her face as she gasped for air, hands scrabbling against the pavement. Pavement. Ground. Earth. Lee blinked her eyes open, staring at the bits of gravel and broken glass beneath her hands. She closed them again, panting through the bright pain shooting through her spine. Her face, hands, and knees all burned with scrapes from her landing, but she had made it.

After a long moment, when her breath stopped shuddering

through her lungs and her body didn't tremble, Lee tried to sit up.

She couldn't move her legs.

Scrapes burned on her knees and shins, so she wasn't truly paralyzed, but the muscles refused to obey. She grunted and heaved herself up on her arms, willing her legs to bend beneath her. Pain shocked through her spine and she cried out, collapsing to the ground and panting. She turned her head side to side, getting her bearings.

From her position lying flat on the ground, she could see fluorescent lighting in the distance, but around her it was dark. A few run-down buildings, an auto-parts store. Where was she? She hadn't paid much attention to where the ley line was leading her. Was she even in St. Louis anymore? Missouri? The U.S.? The auto shop sign was in English, at least. That ruled out countries where they wouldn't speak her language.

Pain blazed through her spine as she laid her head back down. She was injured, somehow, but she couldn't be sure it was her back or the effects of the Fade. If she could reach her phone, which was trapped beneath her body in her jacket pocket, and if it still worked after being taken out of Earth's realm and the hard landing, she could call someone. Shane. No, Shane was dead.

Wincing as she moved, Lee slid her hand against the rough ground and pushed it beneath her abdomen. She felt the outline of the phone in her pocket, but it took several minutes of grunting and rocking side to side before she maneuvered it out. The cracked screen stared ominously back at her. She rested her head on the ground so she could see the screen and pressed the side button to turn the screen on.

It flickered to life, and Lee sighed with relief, navigating through the lock screen and clicking the first name on her contacts list.

Finn. He would have to do.

Footsteps. Lee bit her lip, hitting the dial button. She didn't have the energy to roll over and see who approached, but it turned out she didn't need to. A familiar, false soothing sensation passed through her mind, coating her thoughts and making them sluggish. The Mentalist.

A black boot came down on the phone in her hand. Lee registered the pressure of her hand being crushed, but the pain was muted under the Mentalist's influence. With him there, she wouldn't be able to go Liminal. Not that she could anyway in her condition.

Lee rolled so her face angled up. "How'd you find me?"

Her voice croaked like she'd come down with something. She coughed past the dryness in her throat. Unless the Mentalist could teleport somehow, his presence meant that Lee was still in St. Louis, which gave her a small measure of relief.

"I told you, we've been watching you. All of your movements are known to us." He moved his foot and reached down, grabbing the phone out of her hand. Lee glimpsed the screen. The call had dropped.

"How?"

The Mentalist smirked. "Our secret, I'm afraid." He dropped the phone on the ground and ground his boot heel into it, shattering the screen beyond repair and grinding until the back popped off and he could smash the computing bits inside.

"Ed will carry you if you're unable to walk."

Lee grunted and tried again to push herself up. Her legs tingled now, which she took as a good sign, but it wasn't enough to get away, or even take herself wherever they were headed with dignity. She had no choice but to allow herself to be lifted and carted away like a corpse.

The bald man who had attempted to kidnap her before approached from behind the Mentalist, his bald head gleaming in the far-off street lights. He bent and hefted her with ease. Obviously enhanced. Just the way his muscles didn't even strain. Lee whimpered.

"You're injured?" The Mentalist surveyed her. "You've taxed your body, possibly beyond repair. You should take better care of yourself."

Lee didn't bother responding. Take better care of herself only to die young in a few months or years? After the stunt she'd just pulled, she probably cut years off her life expectancy. Why did the Mentalist care?

He didn't speak again. Lee forced herself to stay awake and observe her surroundings. They walked across the street to a silver car. Ed placed her in the back seat with surprising gentleness, and as he did, she thought she heard the Mentalist mutter, "Carefully."

Despite her best intentions, Lee passed out on the drive. It couldn't have been long, but it felt like an eternity later when she woke to Ed moving her again. The Mentalist's influence kept the pain thankfully dull, but she could still feel it beneath the blanket of mind control he held over her.

They entered an office building, and Ed carried her down two flights of stairs. A door opened, and a smiling woman in a white coat greeted her. Her hair curled softly around her shoulders. Her hands felt cold when they touched Lee.

"This one is in bad shape," the woman said. "Where did you find her?"

"Exactly where we were informed. She made a realm jump."

The woman paled. "In her condition it should have been impossible."

She ushered them into the office and smoothed the crinkling paper on the bed. Like a doctor's office.

"She's stronger than she looks. Be sure to remove her knives first." The Mentalist's expression became grim.

Lee smiled. He remembered that much, at least. Her arms hung heavy at her sides, drenched in the soporific effects of the Mentalist's control. She couldn't reach her knives; she couldn't do anything but wait until she regained the use of her limbs. How would she retrieve that item for the Ceteri now?

The female doctor bowed. "I'll take good care of her. Thank you."

The Mentalist and Ed left the room.

The doctor smiled at Lee, who watched her with wary eyes. "I'm Doctor Janet Ozawa. I'm going to clean you up and give you a look over to make sure you're not injured. Is it your spine giving you trouble?"

Lee hesitated, then nodded. The Mentalist's touch didn't fade, and she wondered how big the range of his abilities was. Could he control her across the building? Across the city? How many people could he influence at once?

The doctor patted her down, removing knives where she found them on Lee's back, wrists, and in her boot. While she was busy looking for weapons, Lee slipped the Way Mary from her pocket to her wrist. It might come in handy, and she'd rather risk the doctor noticing it versus losing it if they took her clothes. The doctor gently took Lee's jacket off one sleeve at a time, pausing at the Way Mary on her left wrist.

"That's a beautiful bracelet."

"Thank you." She barely glanced at it. The faster they moved on, the less likely Doctor Ozawa would be to suspect it was more than just a trinket. "I like your earrings," Lee returned lamely.

Doctor Ozawa laughed and touched her earring. "Thank you! My husband gave them to me."

The doctor pulled up Lee's shirt and rolled her onto her side. She prodded at Lee's mid-back. "How does that feel?"

Lee shrugged. It was hard to tell with the Mentalist clouding the pain.

"There's deep bruising. You may have damaged some nerves, to say nothing of what that Liminal jump did to you. What were you thinking, trying to go so far?"

Did the doctor know where Lee had been? Lee clamped her jaw shut. She wouldn't say anything more than she had to until she knew who these people were, and why they wanted her alive badly enough to kidnap her and give her medical care.

The doctor tugged down Lee's shirt and squeezed each leg, bending them. The tingling in each worsened, but Lee couldn't move them herself.

"The bruising. Will that…will my legs move again? On their own?" Lee could hardly organize her thoughts and make the words come out coherently. She needed sleep, but she'd be damned before she slept in this place without some answers.

Dr. Ozawa smiled. "Yes, the feeling and movement will return. It shouldn't take long. Meanwhile, I'll help you change. You'll be more comfortable in softer clothes." The woman produced a gown from a drawer, powder blue and styled like a hospital gown, but without as much gaping in the back. A nightgown?

"No, thanks."

"It's not optional." Dr. Ozawa's sweet voice clipped at the end, and her eyes widened as if in warning. She came towards Lee with the gown, setting it on the table nearby. "Would you like to remove your clothing with my help? Or I can do it."

"Over my dead body," Lee hissed, crossing her arms.

"Oh, we'd much rather not." The doctor reached for a syringe sitting on the table just out of Lee's sight. She held it up. "You can comply, or we can make you comply."

The syringe moved closer. Lee knocked it from the woman's hand and sat up in spite of a lightning shock of pain.

She grabbed Dr. Ozawa around her neck. "Let me go, or I swear I'll kill you."

"You can't walk," Dr. Ozawa choked through Lee's death grip. Her fingernails scratched against Lee's skin.

The exam room door opened, and the Mentalist strode in. "Enough."

Lee's muscles melted inside her body as relaxation flooded her system. Her pulse slowed until she struggled to breathe, and her eyelids flickered. Her body was shutting down. Her arms slid away from Dr. Ozawa's neck, and Lee fell limply to the table, unable to even manage a proper glare at the Mentalist.

"I'll stay for the remainder of this appointment," he said.

"You'll do no such thing." Dr. Ozawa straightened her coat and replaced the gloves on her hands, then retrieved a glass bottle from the counter near a small sink and filled a new syringe.

"Why waste supplies when you have my abilities?"

"Because keeping this tight a hold on one girl will limit your ability to control the others," the doctor snapped. She plunged the needle into Lee's arm.

"You underestimate me," the Mentalist growled.

"I'm not risking my job—or my life—on your metaphysical abilities. I trust medicine. It works every time."

The volume of their arguing voices faded in Lee's consciousness as she drifted into blackness.

Coming out of it felt like wading through mud. Lee dragged her mind into the light, literal light streaming into her eyes as she cracked them open. She blinked a few times, then looked around. She lay on a cot in a beige-colored room with a blanket laid over her body. An IV fed into one arm, bandaged heavily to discourage any prodding. Her other arm was chained to the bed. How medieval.

Lee reached for the Liminal Realm, but felt a dampening numbness. No spark. No curtain through space and time. Nothing.

"Haven't seen one they had to tranq in a while," the voice spoke up from the bed next to her. Lee hadn't realized until that moment that she wasn't alone in the room.

The woman looked to be about late-thirties. Her honey-blonde hair was curled and she wore makeup, of all things, and read some frilly magazine showcasing a perfectly manicured garden on the cover.

Lee propped herself up on her elbows. "Who are you? And what is this place?"

The woman put down the magazine. "I'm Helen. They don't have a name for where we're being kept, and I wouldn't know the location, but we're part of project 276041."

"There she goes again," A lower female voice spoke from across the room. Lee glanced around. Eight beds, seven of which had an occupant, if she included her own. Some girls seemed to be asleep, despite the lamps still on throughout the room.

"Someone should tell her before they take her back for the first time," Helen replied. "I've been here the longest, so I take that charge on myself. And they've never said we can't inform newcomers."

"It won't do her any good." The strange female voice belonged to a woman about Lee's age, with dark, stringy hair that she wrapped around her finger and watched as it unraveled, never looking at Lee or Helen. "They do what they want with us."

"What do they want with us, exactly?" Lee asked. She pressed her hands into the cot and slid her bottom backwards slowly and steadily, adjusting the pillow behind her so she could sit up. No one moved to help her, and fortunately, she didn't feel any pain. The IV must have been set up with a painkiller, in addition to the Mentalist's touch stifling her senses.

Helen sighed, her eyes and tone changing to one of compassion. "They require your ability to bear children. Which involves some...unpleasant processes."

"It's not rape, if that's what you're thinking. God, Helen, you don't need to milk the drama. Look how pale she is." The dark-haired girl snorted and dropped the strand of hair she'd been wrapping.

Lee touched her face. A breeding ring. But if they didn't require these women to have sex with selected men, how did they...

"Very well, Aster. Insemination. There, happy?" Helen looked displeased at her delivery being interrupted.

Lee blinked rapidly, glancing among the beds. Aster, in

particular, had a rather round stomach. And at least two of the others were obviously pregnant.

"I'm still confused. Do we have something in common? Why get Liminals pregnant?" Lee asked, furrowing her brow. The Mentalist had clearly staked her out, not picked her as a random victim for his scheme. So why her? Lee's heart rate picked up, the monitor tracking it and showing it for the whole room to see.

"You're a Liminal, right?" Helen asked.

Lee nodded.

"They are working on modifying our DNA, to alter the effects of thaumaturgy and prevent it from eating at our cells. The babies that are born are supposedly going to live longer, and with fewer negative impacts." Helen brushed through her hair with her fingers.

"They're studying us? Have any of you had a baby?"

"I have," Helen said quietly. "They took her away, but not before I saw she was a girl."

"Aster is due any day now," another girl said, sitting up over her own obvious belly. "I'm not for a few months. It's not so bad. They feed you well and the doctors look after you. And after you've given them a few babies, they promise to let you go if you promise not to talk about it to anyone."

They. Lee knew about "they". "They" rarely let anyone go. Because anyone could talk. She swallowed, her mouth filled with cotton and a slight sour taste. All the girls in the room—six, besides herself—were sitting up and staring at her.

Not at her. Someone behind her.

"We strive to be transparent here, Lee. No one is a prisoner." A deep and rich male voice said.

Lee froze, unable to even turn her head. She didn't know

the voice, but it made her body's alarm system go off. Adrenaline rushed her system, the alarms on her monitor beeping incessantly.

She forced her head to turn, to meet the ice-blue eyes of the man in the doorway. He wore a lab coat and an expensive-looking suit but no tie. His black hair spiked up from his head, held by a stiff gel.

He smiled at her. Or rather, smirked, because despite the genuine expression, Lee sensed an undercurrent of ulterior motives from this man. He was a con-artist. Used to getting what he wanted.

And Lee had a bad feeling that what he wanted was her.

CHAPTER 23

The man held out his hand. "Doctor Bruce Tanaka."

Lee glared at the offered hand until Bruce withdrew it.

"Liminality is the least understood of all thaumaturgic abilities, and the number of people suffering from it is increasing." Bruce crossed his arms behind his back. "This project aims to change that. We need to know if the Liminal ability is passed on through genes, from parent to child, or if it's caught, like a disease. If we can isolate the cause, we can eliminate the suffering of thousands, if not tens of thousands, of people."

"Why not find volunteers instead of kidnapping women, then?" Lee shot back. "If the authorities find out what you're doing, you'll go to jail."

"I think we have that in common, Miss Lee." Bruce raised his eyebrows.

Was that how he was getting away with it? All of these women had records or something he could blackmail them over? Lee folded her arms over her chest.

"Are you the creep impregnating all of them?" She didn't

include herself in their number, not yet. And she wouldn't, if she could just think of a way out.

"You assume I'm not Liminal. You also assume I'm a donor. It reduces variables to have Liminal donors, and while I am Liminal, it's unethical for me to be a donor. Call it a conflict of interest." His tongue rested on his teeth, and he gave Lee a smug expression that did nothing to dissuade Lee's belief that this man didn't do things ethically. The only question she had now was how many of these babies were his?

Her hands shook with rage. She closed them around the blanket in her lap, gripping it instead of reaching for the man's neck. The Way Mary bracelet gleamed, catching her eye. Of course. Once activated, the beads would collect luck.

Slowly, she moved her finger towards the jade-colored beads, feeling along until she found one with a symbol etched into it. She rubbed the symbol with her pointer finger until it heated up. A slight purple glow accompanied the bead's activation, and she hurriedly covered it with her finger, obscuring it from Bruce's view.

"I hope you'll see our true purpose is noble," Bruce said. "And while you're in our care, you will not be expected to shift through realms, or worry about anything. Every need will be taken care of. You couldn't ask for more luxury."

"It's not luxury if I'm in chains." Lee moved her arm, making the chain attaching her to the bed clink.

He opened his mouth to respond, but the door opened, interrupting him. He clasped his hands and rubbed them together.

"Ah, Dr. Ozawa! Just who I wanted to see." He put his arm around the woman's shoulders. Dr. Ozawa looked as if she'd eaten something sour, but she pasted a smile on her face.

"Bruce, it's good to see you." Dr. Ozawa took a breath and stepped out of Bruce's reach, focusing her attention on Lee. "How is our newest patient?"

"Fiery. I like her," Bruce said, winking at Lee.

Lee looked away, swallowing the sound of disgust that had risen in her throat.

"Lee, how's your pain level?"

Lee didn't answer. She owed these people nothing. Did the doctor have a phone? She could use it to call for help.

All of the doctor's pockets seemed flat and empty, except for one with a single pen sticking out. Bruce, on the other hand...Lee's gaze lingered on his right pants pocket, where a rectangular shape showed through. If she could get him closer...

Bruce saw her staring and smiled in a predatory way. "Maybe we should skip the procedures and do this in a more traditional style, doctor."

"I should think not!" Dr. Ozawa straightened and put a hand on her hip, facing Bruce. "I'll not have that sort of insinuation from you, especially in front of the ladies. We are a respectable operation, I'll remind you."

Bruce narrowed his eyebrows together. "Of course. Forgive me, I shouldn't have spoken out that way." His eyes still sparkled with mischief, and he crossed the room to Lee's bedside next to the doctor, putting his hand on Lee's shoulder.

Dr. Ozawa made a protesting sound.

"I'm impressed with our latest candidate. She'll make an excellent carrier," Bruce said seriously. His pocket was within reach, now. Lee eyed it, her fingers twitching. She looked across the room and caught the redhead's gaze. The girl seemed to understand Lee's intention, and she immediately doubled over, crying out in pain.

The doctor rushed to the girl's side. "Lily, Lily, tell me what you're feeling."

"It hurts!" Lily moaned. "I think it's the baby!"

Bruce's hand slid away, and so did Lee's. She quickly slipped the phone beneath her pillow.

As quick as she'd started, the girl, Lily, stopped her caterwauling and straightened. She panted, making it believable, but looked at Lee, her mouth twitching up at the corner, before turning to the doctor.

"That was so strange, the pain is gone now," Lily said.

"Are you sure? We'll have the ultrasound brought in. We should monitor...you'll let me know if it comes again? It's too early for you to go into labor now."

Lee felt bad for the doctor. She seemed like a good person. She cared. Even if the cause she supported was madness.

"How soon can we get this one through the procedure?" Bruce asked, gesturing at Lee.

Dr. Ozawa glanced over at him, blinking in surprise. "Well, we wouldn't recommend that until we've had her for at least a full cycle. We need to know more about her, about her body and how it will tolerate pregnancy."

Bruce's hand curled into a fist. "Where is she in her cycle?"

"We've had her for less than 24 hours, but the ferning results show that she's in or near the follicular phase."

"Then it's the perfect time."

"But sir—"

"Who signs your paycheck? Oh, yes. Me. Dr. Ozawa, I'll make this as clear as I can. If I hear you've hesitated and missed this window, I will personally deliver your notice to the board. These girls are getting harder to find and take valuable resources to bring here and care for. If the last one hadn't turned out to be a dud..." He shook his head. "Never mind. Just...do what I've asked." He straightened his suit and stalked out of the room without another glance at any of them.

Dr. Ozawa turned to Lee. "I'm sorry. I'd prefer for more time to allow your back to heal. This isn't how it's usually done, but my hands are tied." She tsked and shook her head. "I'll return for you in an hour."

The stolen phone seemed to burn a hole through Lee's pillow against her back. She looked at the other girls, most of whom avoided her gaze. Would any of them tell if she brought out the phone to make a call? It was too risky. She'd try a text message once they fell asleep. Lily eyed her, though, and Lee knew she would have to collaborate if she didn't want the girl to turn on her.

"You've all been through this?" Lee asked casually, as if making small talk.

A few nodded.

Lee took a breath. "What happened to the last girl?"

"She was infertile. She underwent nine months of the treatment and never got pregnant. They said she was a liability and let her go home," Lily explained.

Aster snorted and shook her head. She laid down and pulled the covers up to her shoulders. "Wake me when they bring the meal cart around."

"You're all Liminals?" Lee hadn't met many others like herself. "Why haven't you tried to escape?"

"Look," Aster sat up. "I don't know your story, and I don't want to. Most of us don't have families, and those that do are given money to send home. We might have been brought here under duress, but once they explained it all, none of us refused. It's better than the life we would have had."

"What would happen if you had refused?" Lee looked

from woman to woman, trying to meet their eyes. Aster and Lily both held her gaze. "Are you prisoners or not?"

Aster's lips pursed, and she faced away from Lee.

"Don't mind her. Hormones, you know." Helen laughed and patted her own curved stomach, then went back to her magazine.

Lee stared at the woman. She'd been forcibly impregnated, chained to her bed, given a choice between death and bearing children for a billionaire scientist with grand delusions, and she sat complacently reading a magazine.

"Don't fight them." Helen didn't look at Lee, gazing at her magazine like it contained the most precious information in the universe. "They'll just knock you out again."

Like hell. Lee would fight. She lay down on her pillow and slid her hand underneath to touch the phone she'd swiped off Bruce. The stuck-up scientist wouldn't know what had hit him when her crew ripped through here, and Lee knew if she called them, they would come.

CHAPTER 24

Adam took a hard blow to his jaw, his head snapping back with the force of it. He spit blood onto the floor, tongue roaming his mouth to feel the teeth in that side. They seemed to be holding. He lifted his head, glaring at the bald man.

"What did you all want Lee for?"

The muscle rifled through a box of clanking metal items, taking out a set of brass knuckles and trying them out in his hand. "I don't care what they do with the girls, so long as I get paid. This room is my office. Nice, eh?"

Adam gave it a cursory glance. Floor to ceiling concrete, a set of metal shelves filled with odds and ends, no doubt devoted to torture. A box of papers. A bare bulb hovered above his head, trembling occasionally.

"You get a lot of…clients?"

"In my industry, there's never a shortage of fools sticking their nose where it doesn't belong." He put the brass knuckles back and drew out another pair, the metal shiny and black, with ridges on the knuckles.

"Is this because I meddled, or do you just enjoy pounding people?"

"Both. And the feds killed my cousin." The man slapped his fist into his palm, an ugly sound that made Adam flinch, despite his attempts to stay stoic. The man laughed.

"Mafia, then. Ex mafia?"

"Don't have to be mafia to be loyal to family. You feds don't know anything about that."

"Don't we?" Adam muttered, staring at a dark spot on the concrete floor, trying not to think of Millie. If he did, he wouldn't make it out of there. And dammit, he wanted to make it out. It had been foolish to come without backup, but he couldn't let that mistake end him.

Adam's mind spun into action. He had to get out of here, get past the ringing in his head and come up with a plan.

"Now, enough talking." The bald man flexed his fingers, adjusting his grip on the band of metal around his hand. He grinned at Adam, who twisted his hands in his bonds one more. The ropes held firm, contorted in such a way that even his extensive training didn't give him a way out.

He'd have to resort to alternative means, a desperate measure that he'd sworn he wouldn't take unless his life was in danger, and in this case, it was.

Adam Finley wasn't only a neutralizer of thaumaturgic ability. He was an enhancer.

As the bald man swung his fist, Adam thrust his arm up to perform a block, but at the same time activated the fire in his belly that burned the power hot and fast through his body, enhancing the block and bringing it into the physical realm. A boom shuddered through the room, and a force field threw the bald man across the room.

Adam picked up the chair he was tied to, adrenaline

holding him up. He inched toward the table, glancing at the bald man, who groaned on the floor a few feet away. The box held a dozen different brass knuckles, but nothing sharp enough to cut him loose. He hobbled to the metal shelf. A drawer full of sharp, dental-like tools sat on the second shelf, just within reach. He maneuvered around the chair and grabbed one of the sharp implements, sawing awkwardly against his back. He nicked himself once, twice, and then a piece of rope fell free.

The bald man bellowed, looking from the blood on his hand, which had come from his head, to Adam, who stood chair and rope free with nothing but a short scalpel to defend against the heavy, muscled man.

Adam licked his lips and gestured. "You know you want me."

The muscle obliged, charging full power aimed at Adam.

It couldn't be that easy. Adam side-stepped, and the man barreled past, caught in his own momentum. Adam bolted for the door, knowing that if he stayed to finish this fight, he wouldn't turn up winner. Already his stomach grew cold and heavy, as if a rock sat at the bottom. The coldness would travel through his body, through his limbs, and put him into a virtual coma. He had minutes to spare.

The heavy metal door flung open. Adam pushed it, but he didn't feel it as the tips of his fingers turned numb. He gripped the scalpel, his only weapon.

Get out, get out, get out, he chanted mentally and slammed the door shut behind him. No lock on the outside.

Run. He bolted down a hall. He hadn't been conscious when they brought him in, so this was a blind guess. His lungs heaved.

The first corridor had one door at the end, no exit sign. He spun the other direction. The metal door opened and the red-faced, berserk bald man tumbled out.

Adam leaned into his sprint and turned down another hall. Doors lined the walls. The one at the end was lit with the familiar green light. *Through there.* He yanked the door open and ran into a fully lit room filled with beds and screaming pregnant women in nightgowns. He blinked.

Last moment he remembered the raging madman in the hall behind him and turned the lock on the handle of the door. It clicked into place. The bald man bellowed outside, and Adam waved cheerily through the security window slit.

"I'm not here to hurt you," he shouted to the cacophony in the room. He held his hands up, dropping the scalpel. A few of the women had burst into tears. The rest stopped their screaming and stared at him.

"Who are you?" demanded a middle-aged woman from the far side of the room, fists on hips, belly protruding with undeniable pregnancy beneath the blue nightgown she wore.

This time he did get out his badge. "FBI. I was scouting the place and got captured. Can you show me the way out?"

"There isn't any way through here," a red-head piped up. She pointed at the exit sign over a door next to her bed. "It's been cemented."

"How do I get out of here, then?"

"Through the medical offices." A dark-haired woman rolled out of her bed, her purposeful stride more of a waddle with the advancement of her pregnancy. "They're through here. Locked, but you just need the code." Her swollen finger poked six numbers on the keypad next to the door and it clicked, unlocking.

The rattling of the door Adam had come through stopped. The bald man was no doubt on his way to intercept him.

"You'll go right," the dark-haired woman said.

"Thank you, very much. I'll return with help."

"Don't bother. We're not prisoners." The older woman waved her hand.

Adam stared, dumbfounded. He wanted to stay and reassure them, to get more information about their situation, but he couldn't afford getting beaten to a pulp. A full-scale argument broke out as Adam opened the door.

The red-head scowled at the other woman. "Speak for yourself. If you can find a way to get us out, my name is Lily Abbott, and you'll find me filed under missing persons. If they move us, I'll try to leave a sign. There was another girl, too. They took her back for the procedure."

Adam spun on his heel and took the dark-haired woman by her shoulders. "What procedure?" A panic he had never felt before surged through his chest.

Lily's eyes widened. "Y-yeah. The—it's—she's being inseminated."

The words hardly processed in his mind. He just knew they weren't good. "Where?"

"End of the hall."

The coldness made his right leg drag, starting in the hip and working its way down. His left arm dangled uselessly, and his lungs felt smaller than usual. He couldn't draw a full breath. The bald man would have no such limitations, and Adam had a new mission: he couldn't leave if Lee was in the building.

At the end of the long corridor, another exit sign gleamed with tiny arrows pointing to the left. Adam half-dragged himself down the hall, pulling his bum leg as fast as it would allow. He glanced through the window slits in the doors, but most of them were dark.

In the last pitch-dark room, however, a man stood alone and stared through a wide window pane. Adam froze. He turned the door handle slowly, so it wouldn't click. The hinges stayed silent as he slipped into the room.

His heart pounded. He took slow, deliberate breaths, reminding himself that he could still breathe, no matter how far the coldness creeped up his chest.

The man made no indication that he knew Adam was there. Adam followed his gaze through the window.

A single female doctor prepped at a small cart next to the table. The patient seemed drugged as her head lolled to one side to look at the doctor. Her eyes fixed on the area where the window was.

Beside her, a woman with indigo streaks in her hair lay on a steel exam table, wearing a hospital gown, her legs in stirrups.

Lee.

A strangled sound escaped Adam's throat. His legs gave out at the same moment, and he collapsed into a nearby chair. The man turned around, his shadowed expression showing mild surprise.

"Well, hello. I didn't realize I had company." He came closer and frowned at Adam's appearance. "What position do you hold here?"

"F... B... I..." His badge was still clasped in his hand from showing the women. He flexed every muscle he could and managed to flop it onto his lap, showing the man.

"Ah. My men must have apprehended you. But you escaped? Well done. I suppose you're wondering what all this is for?" He gestured to the window, where the doctor picked up a metal contraption.

"Why haven't you apprehended me?" the man asked.

"Can't... move." His lungs had constricted to a point Adam couldn't hardly speak. He felt breathless and faint. He couldn't pass out, not yet. Lee needed him to get her out.

"That's all well and good, then. I'll call my men to collect you." The man reached into his suit coat, then checked another pocket. He chuckled. "I suppose I left my phone somewhere. Never mind. Once the procedure is finished, I'll call for someone. I do like to watch."

He turned back toward the window. Adam couldn't seem to tear his eyes away, nor could he close them. The air around him swirled in an unusually cold way, like fingers brushing across his skin. He shivered. The air around him distorted. Was this the Mentalist's doing?

"They're all mine, you know. The babies," the man said.

"Why?" Adam croaked.

"Discovery, of course. For the good of mankind. And my name will be known across the world when I create a line of medications that neutralizes the Liminal Fade." The man was insane. His eyes gleamed as he watched the doctor take a strange syringe with tubing on the end of the table. "There they are. Precious."

Absolutely off the wall. Adam rarely wanted to hurt someone the way he wanted to hurt this man. He could imagine wrapping his fingers around the man's throat, snuffing out the madness in him. But he was helpless, the effects of his thaumaturgic enhancement costing him the movement that would save Lee from being impregnated against her will and get them both out of this madhouse.

A light flickered in the procedure room. The doctor glanced up. A crunching sound made the doctor startle, and she dropped the syringe.

"No!" The man stood. "She knows how critical this is. The fool woman, I'll—"

He didn't get to finish his sentence. A door in the procedure room burst open and a hulking man charged through, bellowing at the cowering doctor. The slight woman knelt on the floor, begging noiselessly. The mirror kept out everything but the loudest sounds.

The man slammed the window with his fist, and then he froze. Adam felt a click in his chest. Someone was about to use thaumaturgy, and he didn't have the energy to stop them. The man's outline turned red, and just like when Lee went Liminal, he faded from view.

CHAPTER 25

Sam bellowed, and Lee's heart lurched. Her crew had come
for her. The phone was still hidden beneath her pillow, the
incriminating text sent into the void moments before Dr.
Ozawa had returned. And then the Mentalist had practically
knocked Lee out, keeping her sedated mentally. She couldn't
have struggled if she'd wanted to.

"Hold on, this won't be pleasant." With a metallic click,
Risa released the speculum, and Lee could finally relax.
Except for her legs trembling in the stirrups. Risa gripped one
and lifted it, slowly bringing it down to the cold surface of the
metal table, and then did the same to the other.

Lee held back a whimper at the pain in her back, but Risa
was right there next to her head, cradling her.

"Are you all right? Did they hurt you? That woman
didn't… She didn't do what I think she was trying to do, did
she?"

Lee shook her head, trying to clear the mental fog. She
didn't think so, but it was hard to be sure. The Mentalist
wasn't letting her go. He seemed distracted, and his influence

had lessened, but her memory of the past twenty minutes was hazy at best. The last thing she remembered clearly was Sam's roar as he broke down the door.

Lee's teeth chattered from the adrenaline and the chilled air that permeated her flimsy gown. She gripped Risa's arm and sat up, staring at the doctor on the floor.

"I'm sorry. I'm sorry. Don't hurt me," Doctor Ozawa whimpered at Sam, who loomed over her with his bulk.

"She's all right, Sam. I'm all right."

He grunted and nodded, but kept his bulk. Right. They still had to break out of here.

Risa helped her down from the bed. Lee stepped gingerly, afraid to put pressure on her back. She gasped and would have crumpled if not for Risa's support.

"You *are* hurt!"

"It's a bruise," Lee said, waving her hand. "I'll be fine to leave in a moment."

"No, you won't," a smooth male voice spoke, and everyone turned to look. Bruce stood behind Sam, adjusting his cufflinks and grinning madly. "I've worked too hard to have this effort thrown away now. Do you know how rare our kind are? How hard I searched for you and those like you?" He laughed, high-pitched and on edge.

Sam raised a fist and swung faster than most men could react. Bruce's body outline in red, and Lee's stomach jerked as he left Earth's realm. Sam spun, nearly falling to the ground, and Bruce appeared behind him.

"Try all you like, monster, you won't strike me. And I'll be taking Lee with me." He disappeared again.

Lee shouted a warning, flailing her arms, and Bruce appeared at her side, pushing Risa off of her and gripping her around the waist. They blinked out of existence.

And the Mentalist's influence vanished. Here, he didn't exist. Here, he had no power. Here, Lee was her own. She twisted in Bruce's grip, then stopped and she smiled. He smiled back. He was insane if he thought her smile genuine.

"There, now, isn't that..."

Lee decked him, using the base of her palm to jam his nose into his skull as hard and fast as she could, and in the second he let go to grasp his precious face, she jerked away and fell.

Her body wouldn't walk the way it was supposed to. Pain flared in her back. Even as she fell, she reached for Earth's realm. It was close, so close, and a red line arched before her. She grabbed for it, pulling, and suddenly she could move enough to get back.

She landed back among her friends. "Hurry," she panted. "He'll be coming."

The Mentalist's influence descended like a smothering blanket. Lee felt it close around her mind and though she struggled, he was stronger in this. Risa screamed, and Lee's consciousness flickered.

"Let me see her," Finn's voice came through the air.

"What do you think you're doing? Let go of her."

Her body jostled. She wanted to cry out, to tell them to be careful, but the pain was dull beneath the Mentalist's control. A small benefit to becoming someone's mind puppet.

The red light flared again, arching from Lee's chest into the chest of the person holding her.

"Hang in there, Lee. We're getting you out of here. Can you go Liminal?"

Her lips moved. Did sound come out? She couldn't be sure.

"Okay, don't worry. No worries. We've got this." Finn's

voice came through muffled, but it soothed the panic that raced in her mind beneath the Mentalist's influence.

"Mentalist," she burst out, using all of her strength to get the word past the power coating her mind.

Finn froze. "I don't know if I can...never mind. You're right. Sam, take her," he barked.

Sam didn't hesitate. Despite his bulked-up size, he handled Lee as if she were a priceless artifact. With eyes half-closed, Lee watched as Finn moved his arm in a specific, practiced motion.

The sky broke clear in her head. She gasped as if coming up from underwater. Over Sam's muscled arm, she saw a familiar bald head gleaming, and another man beside him, blood streaming from his nose. Bruce.

"Go, go, go!" she yelled.

Finn held his fist up and ran beside Sam and Risa. There was a hole in the wall where the exit was supposed to be. Lee regretted that she couldn't bring more of the girls with her.

"Lily!" She flailed. Sam shook his head, avoiding her arms.

Risa grabbed her arms. "You better calm down, chicka, or I'm knocking you out."

Lee gasped for air. Coming out from under the Mentalist's influence made every thought and feeling broadcast in her brain like it was on a loudspeaker.

"Lily was the red-headed one?" Finn asked.

"Yes. The others might not care, but she does. She doesn't deserve this life."

Finn ran his free hand through his hair. The other still held in the position that kept the Mentalist blocked. "None of them do. You're sure they won't come?"

"I don't think so."

"We have to get you to safety." Sam's deep bass rumbled through her body like thunder. It vibrated her spine, making it ache.

"I can go through the Liminal realm if Finn comes with me."

The others glanced at each other with shocked expressions.

Lee rolled her eyes. "He can keep the Mentalist off my back. Without his blocking ability, I can't go Liminal."

"We aren't a rescue team, we're a thieving crew. We leave together," Risa said firmly.

Lee looked at Finn. She saw in his eyes the same thing she felt: they couldn't leave Lily, or any of the other girls, not if they wanted to leave.

Lee reached out her hand, and Finn took it. She looked at Risa. "Meet you back at the factory."

The pins and needles felt like daggers across her skin, through her muscles and bones. She pushed forward and that red light flared again, easing her into the Liminal realm as smooth as can be. The stabbing sensation vanished. Finn pulled her out of Sam's arms and into his own, smiling at her.

"Think they'll forgive you?" he asked.

"Eventually. If they're smart, they won't follow us. Do you think you can get back to their room?" *Without attracting Bruce?* she added mentally.

Finn nodded. He strode forward, moving more easily through the Liminal realm than he had before. It was this strange connection between them. If Lee looked out of the edge of her vision, she could see the line gleaming, almost like a ley line. At that moment she didn't care why it worked, just that it did.

"I don't feel the Mentalist's influence here, but as soon

as we leave the Liminal realm, I'll need you to block it again so we can get back." Lee fidgeted her fingers in her lap.

"Do you think you can take more than one person over? What if they all want to come?"

"Then we go a few at a time. Somehow, I think it's different with you. Are you sure you're only a Screener?" She grinned.

Finn's expression darkened slightly, but he didn't answer for a long moment.

"And if that guy shows up? He's like you, isn't he?"

Nice. He'd ignored her question. Which made Lee think despite her joking intention, she'd struck a chord. There was more to this guy than it seemed. Did Silas know?

Where was Silas?

Through the hallway, dimmed through the filter of the Liminal realm. They stood before the locked door to the women's room. Lee took a deep breath, then nodded to Finn and phased back through the veil between realms, back to Earth, back to real time. Finn set her down and held up his arm in the blocking position. So far, so good.

"You'll have to go in. I'm not crawling," Lee said.

"They aren't going to listen to me."

"I'll wave from the door. Just hold it open."

Finn knocked on the door. The lock clicked and the door opened, revealing a stern-faced Helen, her coiffed hair falling in scattered strands around her face. She looked stressed. And unsurprised to see them.

"Hello, Helen," Lee said from the floor, waving.

"We don't want whatever you're selling." She started to shut the door.

"Wait," Lee called. The door remained open, thanks to

Finn's foot at the bottom. "Some of the girls don't want to stay here. Will you let us talk to them?"

"It's only Lily. Everyone else has chosen to accept their place, and I won't have you distressing them."

"We'll speak to Lily, then. Thanks." Finn smiled. Lee hadn't known he could look so charming, even with his disheveled hair and rumpled, bloodied clothes. He had a fat lip, too, and a black eye forming. What had he gone through to get to her?

Helen disappeared. A freckled face appeared in the cracks, tear-streaked and red-eyed.

"They don't like that I want to leave. They say it's stealing if I do."

"Stealing?" Finn echoed.

"The baby," Lee said after a sudden realization struck. "They're claiming it's Bruce's property."

Lily sniffed and nodded. She glanced over her shoulder. "I don't know if I should...if the police come after me..."

"We'll vouch for you," Finn said, at the same time as Lee spoke, "We're used to it."

She glanced up at Finn, then back to Lily. "Look, we've got your back, okay? We'll take you wherever you want to go, keep you hidden if you want, for a while. Until you have the baby. Or get you a doctor. You can take on another name."

The door widened. Lily slipped through, took one last look at the other women all gathered around the same few beds, some glaring, some looking longing.

Despite what Helen said, Lee couldn't leave them that way. "The invitation is for all of you. Any other takers?"

Shoulders twitched. Heads bowed. No one spoke.

"We have to go," Finn said.

Lee nodded. "Okay, let's do this."

Finn bent down to Lee, Lily stepping shyly out of the way. Lily's eyes widened as she got closer to Finn.

"The fog—it's gone."

"I would...hope so." Finn grunted with effort, holding his arm up in the block position. "Ready?" He looked at Lee.

"Lily, Finn is going to keep the Mentalist off us. Can you go Liminal?"

"I...I don't know. Last time it...didn't go well. That was a year ago." Her face paled beneath her freckles.

"You can do this. It's in your cells." Lee held Lily's gaze.

The woman placed a hand on her swollen belly. Her bottom lip trembled.

Lee's heart fell. She wasn't going to do it. She was going to go back into that room and...Lily's outline turned red. Lee grinned and slapped her hand over Finn's wrist, bringing him into the Liminal realm with her. He picked her up.

Lily was there, beaming. "Everything feels fine! My baby is still moving."

"Let's not push our luck," Finn said.

"What luck?" Bruce strode around the corner, waltzing through the Liminal realm like he owned it. He examined his nails. "You're taking far more than you have any right to."

"Like hell," Lee spat. Finn's arms tightened around her. If he dropped her, he'd be thrust out of the Liminal realm and the side effects could be severe. But if Bruce attacked...

Lee moved her arm and the bracelet slid down it. *Luck.* She had activated it only a few hours ago. Would it have gathered enough from Dr. Ozawa to get them out of there?

"*Ungai.*" Lee muttered the word under breath, and one of the jade beads burst into powder and fell to the ground. She held her breath.

Nothing happened.

"Hand over the girls and you can go," Bruce told Finn.

"Let them both go. I'll come back," Lily cried.

"No!" Finn and Lee shouted.

It wasn't enough. It hadn't charged enough luck. A triumphant expression spread across Bruce's face. He motioned toward Lily, who glanced sadly at Lee.

"Thanks for coming back for me." As soon as she entered Bruce's reach, he grabbed her and pulled her close, laughing. She squirmed, but he held her tighter until she shrieked.

"Your turn." He gestured to Finn.

"Whatever you say," Finn said, voice measured, face impassive.

"What?" Lee shrieked. She wanted to kick and flail to make him drop her, but the residual pain in her back was strong enough that she just bit her lip and searched Finn's face for any indication that he had a plan. He didn't look back at her. He walked towards Bruce's eagerly waiting arms like a programmed robot, and Lee was helpless to stop him.

CHAPTER 26

Finn had to be faking...didn't he? Lee didn't know if she should slap him or go along with it, but she wasn't about to let him deliver her to Bruce the creep, either. She tensed as they approached Bruce, making eye contact with Lily.

She felt for a ley line in her mind. Not too far away, but in an obscure place, a place Bruce wouldn't think to follow.

She nodded to Lily.

"Wait!" Lily cried, reaching a hand out as if to stop them. Her hand landed on Lee's arm and the brief confusion from her exclamation was just enough time. Lee blinked, and the world flew out from underneath the three of them.

They soared along the ley line, Lily's abilities boosting Lee's. They landed, rolling in the dirt at the foot of a giant stone statue of an angel wrapped in unmoving cloth.

Finn coughed, coming to his hands and feet, looking up with dirt falling from his face. "A graveyard, Lee?"

She lay unmoving, focusing on the act of breathing. They'd made it. As far as she knew, ley lines held no signature to follow, no magical footprints to track. She could have gone in half a dozen directions at least, but she wouldn't put it past him to try each one. She rolled onto her side, gasping. Lily and Finn both looked at her with concern. She put a scowl on her face.

"What were you trying to do back there?" Lee snapped.

Finn blinked. "What are you talking about? You read my mind perfectly, Lee. You did exactly what I knew you would do."

"And if I hadn't gotten it? If Bruce had grabbed me from you and taken me and Lily somewhere and you had no clue where to find us?" Her chest heaved as she pushed up on her hands. Her heart pounded far too fast. She scooted backward, moving through the deep bone-throbbing ache in her lower back to lean against a tree trunk.

Above, the leaves swayed and the golden afternoon light gleamed as it came through. A graveyard was always Liminal, Lee had learned. Even during the day, it exuded a quiet reverence, like this part of the world held its breath while the rest went on.

Bruce. She had to remember Bruce was after them, that he could appear and tear this peace apart at any moment. But even with Finn and his strange ability to make Liminal travel easier for her, she didn't have another ley line jump in her. Finn looked haggard as well, and he kept rubbing his jaw, where a large purple mark had formed.

Lee opened her mouth to suggest a plan, but Finn beat her to it.

"Lily, could you get Lee to a certain location if I give you instructions? I know you probably can't carry me, but I figure with Lee being Liminal too, maybe you can help each other? I'll grab the next transit and make the necessary connections."

Lily rubbed her belly. Her eyebrows creased. "I think so.

But it might be better if we all took the bus. Lee doesn't look good."

Lee sat numbly as they talked. Her thoughts kept slipping out of her head. What if this bruise in her back was actually a deeper, much worse injury? What if she would never walk without pain again? She leaned her head back, vaguely aware of Lily and Finn carrying on the conversation around her.

When Finn jostled her shoulder next, Lee woke with a start. She'd fallen asleep against the tree, maybe only for a moment, maybe for minutes.

"We have to get out of here!"

"We know. Bruce. But you're not fit to go Liminal. And I don't know if we can pass without suspicion on a city bus," Finn said. He kept his voice careful, like he was afraid to wake a sleeping tiger.

"Are you kidding? Have you ever ridden a city bus? They get all sorts."

"But in your state, if I carry you on, they're going to think I'm abusing you. The cops might be called." He swallowed visibly. He didn't want that to happen. Which was possibly sweet...or self-serving. Either way, Lee didn't like him babying her.

"Lily can take me. I'll tell her where to go," Lee insisted.

But Lily shook her head.

Finn glanced at her, then back at Lee. "She's not comfortable going Liminal right now. She said her intuition says she should limit that kind of travel while pregnant."

Lily gave Finn a grateful smile that bordered on adoring. Lee rolled her eyes. She hoped this wasn't going to become a thing. If it did, she might gag. Had the others felt that way when she and Shane became a couple?

Lee shook her head to clear the memories. First things first. They had to get out of the graveyard before the manic psycho found them.

"Just tell them I'm crippled and hate my wheelchair. Tell them someone stole my wheelchair. That'll get 'em."

"You're downright wicked." Finn grinned.

"It's my job to be a good liar," Lee pointed out. "Now pick me up."

"And you're bossy when you're injured," Finn joked.

"Hey, you signed up to take care of me."

"To follow you. There's a difference."

Their banter made Lee smile, and she hooked her arm around his neck as he slid his hands beneath her upper back and knees and hoisted her up.

"You make that look easy," Lily commented.

"I could say the same about you," Finn said, jutting his chin towards her stomach. "How is the baby?"

"Active. Where are we headed?" Lily asked.

"We can't tell you," Lee interrupted Finn, who looked about to say something.

Lily's face creased. "But a few moments ago you were fine telling me, if I traveled Liminally with you."

"I would have told you which ley lines to take, not the exact location." Lee was exhausted. She wanted to hold herself up as much as possible, but it was too hard. She drooped in Finn's arms, resting her head against his shoulder for just a moment.

. . .

She woke up ten stops later, where they had to make a connection. She didn't even remember getting on the bus. But at least they were nearly home. She lifted her head and yawned, embarrassed by the obvious spot of her saliva on Finn's shoulder. He pretended not to notice, glancing down and smiling briefly before looking back at the buildings passing out the bus window. Lily dozed in the seat across from them, both hands demurely cupped around the curve of her belly.

"Sleep well?" Finn murmured.

"Shut up." Lee lifted her head and glanced around. "How close?"

"Next stop."

The bus was quiet, except for a group of teenagers chattering in the back, wires dangling from their ears as they traded headphones to listen to the latest hits. What would life be like as a normal teenager? Appearances weren't everything, and since thaumaturgy often struck around puberty, some of them might have powers. One could never tell for certain from the appearance of a person.

Finn stood before the bus stopped, and Lily followed suit, swaying as the vehicle stopped, hissing. The folded doors opened.

Finn carried Lee off the bus. She felt more refreshed after the nap, but the clinging helplessness she felt was unpleasant, to say the least. If it weren't for the Liminal ability she had, she wouldn't be in this position.

Down two blocks, left and right, until they reached the warehouse with its filthy windows barely lit from inside. Finn took the lower door and gave the special knock. There was no answer.

He looked at Lee, eyebrows furrowed in concern. "Uh, do you guys have a key?"

Lee kept her voice hushed. "Silas keeps it. He's always the first one here. He says if he's not here to open the door, consider it compromised."

"Might take him a minute to manage those stairs with his leg."

"What's wrong with his leg?" Lee asked.

"He was still assembling it when we left. He might have reattached it by now, who knows." Finn shrugged. He was obviously straining, holding her as long as he had.

Lee squirmed. "Put me down."

"Can you stand?" Finn asked.

"No," Lee admitted.

Finn shook his head, trying to hide a smile. His eyes crinkled up in the corners, giving him away. "Then no. It's really dirty here."

Lee snorted but didn't argue. A long moment passed, with Finn adjusting his grip twice and shifting stances. He knocked again, louder.

The door swung wide. Silas swayed in the entryway, eyes bloodshot, one leg missing from the thigh down, pant leg dangling. Finn nodded to him, then to Lily behind him. She waved.

"We had to do a bit of a rescue. Did Risa and Sam make it?"

"In," Silas grunted. He waved them into the building with the screwdriver he held in his hand.

Lee expected him to throw a fit about Lily, but if his temper was flaring, he was saving the reaction for a bigger audience. She held her breath as Finn edged past Silas, but still caught a whiff of the sour scent of the drink he'd been consuming copiously.

"Put 'er down. What is she, a princess?" Silas snapped, hopping ahead of the small group.

"Can't, sir. She's injured," Finn explained.

Silas's eyes looked like they would pop out of his head. He raised the screwdriver and stumbled towards Finn.

"You had one job," Silas said, spittle flying from his mouth.

Lee hadn't seen him like this since Shane's death. He'd been cool and hard and reasonable. This man before her was the opposite of all those things, shirt beer-stained and untucked, some of his mechanical parts missing. Had he worried that much about her?

"I'm okay, Silas. I'm just bruised," Lee said. The man would hurt himself if he carried on that way.

"Bruised enough she can't walk," Finn insisted.

Silas turned without another word and jumped up the steps two at a time. Lee had to admire the man's insane physical strength.

Lily's quiet voice came from behind. "He seems angry."

Lee had forgotten she was there. "He is. You'll want to avoid him. We can set up a cot for you, or you can use mine. Get some rest before you confront him," Lee said, thinking out loud.

Lily crossed her arms over her chest. "I'm stronger than you think. Being pregnant doesn't change that."

Lee had forgotten. Prim as she seemed, Lily was Liminal too. Who knew what people had used her for in the past? Aside from her current state, which was too horrific to think about.

She trembled involuntarily at the memory of what had almost happened. What she hoped had not happened. Had Finn seen? Had any of the crew arrived in time to see if Dr. Ozawa had succeeded with the insemination? Lee's entire body tensed, and Finn glanced at her, but he didn't say anything.

She didn't want to ask. She didn't want to know. But she would find out soon enough if the crackpot scientist had succeeded in impregnating her.

CHAPTER 27

"What sort of shit have you gotten us into this time, Lee?"

Lee tucked her arm under the blankets, hiding her wrist and the Way Mary that was now missing a bead. She watched Silas twisting the screwdriver in his hand, as if he imagined boring it into something. Probably someone's skull. Probably hers.

Finn stepped up. "Let her rest. She's been through an ordeal." He was sweet to defend her, but it wouldn't earn him any points with Silas.

"And the rest of us haven't?" Silas snapped. He jabbed the screwdriver into the chair seat and it went straight through with the power behind his mechanical arm. "Are we a charity now, taking in homeless pregnant women?"

Lily sucked in her breath beside Lee and cradled her stomach, bowing her head to avoid the fiery beam that swept over them from Silas's cyborg eye. Lee met his gaze, stomach pinching with fear, but she held steady all the same, cocking her chin up in defiance.

"This 'shit' wasn't my fault. Unless you count being

Liminal a fault, in which case I'll have to own that." Lee knew it was true. The Ceteri wouldn't have taken her to their world if she wasn't Liminal, and she wouldn't have been captured by Bruce. Everyone wanted access to her ability. She doubted any of them would choose it for themselves.

Silas glanced at the chair he punctured with the screwdriver, then chose a chair beside it and sat down. He rubbed his hand down his face and sighed, waving in Lee's direction.

"Tell us, then," Silas said. "Where've you been?"

Where to start? Should she tell them about the Ceteri? Lee's lips twisted as she thought.

"And don't leave anything out," Silas snarled. He wrenched the screwdriver from the seat and dropped it on the table.

Lee watched it rolling and swallowed. She didn't want to attempt the Jewel Box by herself. She could if she had to, but the Jewel Box was a mystery. The building had a tragic past, and there were many rumors about what was inside.

If she was going to have help, she needed to trust her crew enough to tell them about the Ceteri.

She rubbed her fingers together. "That note Risa found on the street after the museum heist was from the Ceteri."

A collective gasp went up among the crew. Even Lily seemed shocked. Had she never met them? Lee supposed most people never had. Occasionally, you'd get some nut on the news going on about it, but given the descriptions she'd heard of those encounters, they were pulling everyone's legs. The Ceteri were nothing like she expected.

As she told them what the Ceteri had said, Lee watched their faces for their reactions. Sam alternated between awe and terror. Risa looked impressed. Lily gaped. Finn...she moved on from him quickly, his piercing green eyes filled with questions she couldn't answer. Silas, predictably, held a practiced impassive stare as he listened.

"I didn't think I would make it back, but I found the ley line for Earth's realm and clung to it all the way here. That's when I hurt my back. My landing wasn't so graceful." It ached now, in fact. Lee tried to adjust herself and let out a grunt of pain.

Finn leapt up and gripped underneath her arms, lifting her slightly. Risa stepped in and adjusted the pillow at Lee's back, eyeing Finn.

"Thank you," Lee muttered.

"Is that it?" Silas demanded.

"That's not where I found her," Finn said before Lee could get it out. "The Mentalist grabbed her while she was vulnerable. I followed them to an old office building. They were operating a breeding program in the basement."

"Breeding program?" Risa asked, twisting her face in disgust. "Breeding what?"

"Not what. Who. They wanted Liminals. Had about ten, including Lee and Lily." Finn sat back down, this time behind Lee. She wished she could see his face.

His hand landed on her shoulder. "Do you want to tell this part?"

Lee made a face. "Not really, but I don't think you know all the details. The man's name is Bruce, and he's another Liminal. And a freaking mad scientist. He's been using his wealth to gather women with the Liminal ability and have them inseminated. I suspect at least some of them with his own sperm. He claims to be studying the genetics of thaumaturgic abilities, specifically Liminality. Apparently, scientists don't know if Liminality is contagious or not, as the numbers seem to be increasing. I don't think Bruce is working for himself, though. Someone bigger wants him to do this."

She shocked herself with the last words that fell out of her mouth, but as she said them she realized it was true. Bruce was a brilliant madman, but he was getting something else out of this, and someone was using him.

"Did they do this to you?" Silas asked, chin resting in his hand with one finger resting on his cheek. "This insemination?"

Lee sputtered. What could she say?

Finn came to her rescue. "I made it to an observation room, outside of where the procedure was to take place. Fortunately, Sam arrived and disrupted the process. The doctor dropped the syringe."

"Are you certain?" Silas's eye flashed blue and aimed straight at Finn.

Lee's pulse throbbed in her neck. Could it be true? Had Finn seen what had happened? Why hadn't he been the one to rush in and stop them, then?

"Yes." His voice held no room for doubt, and Lee felt the wound-up place inside of her relax. She couldn't be pregnant. If Finn could be trusted.

Beside Lee, Lily swayed. "I need to lay down," she muttered.

Risa led her to the beds in the closed off corner of the wide room, then returned.

Silas slapped the table. "That's it. Lee, you're out."

"What?" Her focus whipped back to Silas as he stood. Risa and Sam both started protesting, their words garbling together.

"She is a danger, a liability. Wherever we go from here, we go without her and her infernal ability. She's gotten herself wrapped up in some interdimensional conquest, and like as not this man Bruce works for the government. The risks are outrageous." His furious gaze swept over them, cowing them all into silent submission.

Risa glanced at Lee, then straightened on the couch where she sat. "Lee has been with us long enough. I think we owe her some loyalty."

Silas stalked back towards the group, fists flexing. "Enough loyalty to get us all killed? To have government hitmen taking us out every few days or weeks when they find our new hideouts? That Mentalist can recognize Lee's mental signature and track her down any time he wants. We can't protect her from that."

"I can make it worth it," Lee shouted above the protesting that arose.

Everyone fell silent.

Lee adjusted her beanie, grateful Sam had retrieved it for her. "The Ceteri told me to name my price. I mentioned my crew would be helping, and they offered to set us up. For life."

She made eye contact with each of them, letting it sink in. Everyone except Finn, who her eyes couldn't reach. He didn't make a sound behind her. Would it mean anything to him? Would he stay with the crew, despite the dangers?

"It won't be without risks, but it's the score of a lifetime. Risa, Sam, you could be done with this gig. Finished with the rat race. Silas…" What did the man want? She'd never bothered to ask, and he'd never offered to tell. "It's a lot of money, no matter how you slice it. Maybe you were never in it for the money, but you could take your share and start a new crew with an unending amount of capital. Just imagine it."

"And what do you get?" Silas jutted his chin towards her.

"Just doing it from the goodness of your heart? You become one of them? Take over the human race? What?"

Lee clenched her fists at the ugliness in his tone.

"You'll be healed," Risa offered, the realization lighting up her face. "No more fragmenting. No fear of a slow death."

"No more Liminal ability," Finn said from behind.

Lee nodded. She hadn't wanted to tell them, didn't want them to know how much she hated the magic that made up the fiber of her cells, but there it was, hanging out for the world to see. She didn't want to be Liminal anymore.

"And why would the Ceteri offer such a priceless gift? Healing from the malady they themselves inflicted? You're not thinking this through. They want our souls, Lee. They don't want to throw money at us," Silas said bitterly.

"Their world is dying," Lee blurted. "They are trying to save it. They need some items to do that, items that were... birthed, essentially, when thaumaturgy was combined with Earth's atmosphere and rained down on everything here. We just have to find the items. It's exactly what we've been doing, just on a bigger scale."

"How many of those items are here, in St. Louis? Do we have to leave the state? The country? Who is going to pay for that?" Silas swung his arms wildly. He was still frustrated, but Lee had his attention now.

"The first item we need is here. After that, maybe I can convince them to give us a partial payment, an advance, to find the others." She stopped, sucking in air. She felt like she couldn't draw in enough oxygen.

Silas raised the eyebrow over his human eye. "I'm listening."

"The Jewel Box." Lee let it out in a rush, barely containing her excitement. "I've always felt this insane energy coming from there, you know? And how often have I mentioned that we should scope it out, do a run on the place and clean it out?"

Silence followed her words, except for the quiet shuffling of feet. No one would look directly at her.

"What's wrong?" she asked.

Sam rubbed the back of his neck. "No one knows much about the Jewel Box. I mean, it's a wedding venue now, but it's hiding a lot of secrets. No thief who has gone in has returned. Just gone, without a whisper of a hint of what happened. I think you're in over your head, and you'll take the crew down with you."

"Risa?" Lee craned her neck to look at the woman, who was cleaning her goggles with her shirt. She breathed on one, circling her shirt across the lens again.

"You have a tendency to jump into things without looking first," Risa said at last. "A job like this requires months of recon. We have no idea what we're up against. It's not fair for you to ask us to risk ourselves that way."

Finn remained silent, and Lee didn't dare ask him directly. He'd only been part of the crew for a few weeks. And even if he agreed to help her, which she doubted he would, she still didn't trust him fully.

"None of you?" Lee shook her head in amazement. "A score this big requires risk. We won't get anywhere without taking some chances. Danger is part of this job, and you're saying no to an opportunity that could retire you from the profession. Don't you want that? No more grind, no more jobs, no more hiding?"

"You sound insane," Silas said. "The Fade must be getting to you. Making you desperate. You'd do well to forget about this whole business with the Ceteri. Probably a delusion anyway."

Lee balled her hands into fists. She wished she could stand and get up in Silas's face, to stare him down properly in her full strength. She glared at him from the couch.

"That's not fair. Just because my body is failing doesn't mean my mind is. I saw them. The Ceteri. They spoke to me. Their world is fragmented and dying. They need help."

Silas's arm swept through the air. "If they're powerful enough to send you to their realm, why don't they come here and get the items themselves? You know what I think? I think this is a cry for help. You're upset that I've asked you to stay put for once in your damned life, for the safety of the crew, and you'll look for any excuse to make yourself indispensable."

Silas paused, then shook his metallic finger. "Well, I won't have it. We're not doing this supposed job for the Ceteri, and as soon as you can walk properly, you're out on your own. Then you can storm the Jewel Box or go live with the Ceteri, whatever you damn well please."

Chest heaving, Silas stared at each of them, his gaze landing on Lee one last time before he stalked from the room, slamming the door at the top of the stairs as he went.

No one spoke to Lee. Gradually, each of them returned to their chores. Sam stirred ramen in a bowl and put it in the microwave. Risa continued cleaning her gear. Finn followed Silas out.

Lee spun in her own thoughts. She knew the crew would take some convincing, but she thought the reward offered by the Ceteri would be enticing enough to persuade them. Apparently, none of them trusted her enough to give her the benefit of the doubt. They thought her mind was addled, and they weren't willing to risk it all like she was. Could she blame them? After she'd gone after the Way Mary on her own, they must consider her selfish. And then she had the gall to get kidnapped.

She wiped furiously at her eyes and sniffed. Concern furrowed Risa's brow, but Lee stared straight ahead and breathed deep to calm herself. She wouldn't cry. Not in front of them.

Her breath shook, then levelled out until she could pretend nothing was wrong. She fidgeted with the bracelet on her wrist, and as she twisted and rolled the round jade beads between her fingers, an idea dawned on her.

She had done the Cupples' mansion by herself. Even without Risa, Lee could have handled it alone. Possibly better than with Risa being a literal drag. The ghost hadn't meant them any harm, and Lee could have popped in, grabbed the bracelet, and popped out again before the security personnel and that FBI agent arrived.

Lee's fists clenched the blanket over her legs. If the crew wouldn't help her, she'd do it herself.

CHAPTER 28

Lee could be a model patient, but it nearly killed her to do it for an entire day with the weight of her mission bearing down on her.

Risa waited on Lee hand and foot, feeding her and reminding her to take her medication. Lee rejoiced internally when she took the trip to the bathroom by herself with only minimal pain. She was drugged, and she took a nap afterward, but it convinced her that Doctor Ozawa's assessment was accurate: her back was only bruised. In a day or two, she would be well on the mend.

But she didn't have time to wait for one hundred percent healing. Another Liminal might already be on the trail of the Barat, scoping out the Jewel Box, or worse, moving to steal it tonight. Lee's whole body itched to get off the sagging couch and find the item that would lead to her freedom.

If she traveled using ley lines, she could get pretty far without walking. And she could move through the Liminal realm, taking time to rest as needed. With a stronger drug, she'd be better able to move.

Risa started turning off the lights in the main room. "Do you need anything?" she asked.

"Water, please," Lee said. Her throat blocked up, and she almost chickened out and didn't say anything, but then she blurted, "And do you have anything stronger than Tylenol? My back is killing me. I don't think I can sleep."

Risa hesitated. Lee saw the debate on her face. She considered Lee, who tried to look pained without overdoing it. The truth was, she only felt a slight ache in her back when lying down. As soon as she stood up, that's when the real pain started.

"I know it hurts, but you might not want what I have. It isn't technically...legal," Risa admitted.

Lee cocked an eyebrow. "I'm a thief, same as you."

"I've never even seen you drink, Lee. I didn't take you for the type who would want street drugs."

"Same." Lee stared at her, unblinking. Whatever Risa had, if it helped Lee get to the Jewel Box, then she didn't care where it had come from.

Risa dug around in her pocket and took out a tiny baggie with a single blue pill in it, then eyed Lee. "What's your weight?"

"Wet or dry?" Lee joked. When was the last time she'd stepped on a scale? Oh yeah. Doctor Ozawa's office.

Risa rolled her eyes.

"Sorry. It's 132."

"Skinny miss," Risa muttered, snapping the pill in two with her teeth, and then breaking the half into a quarter. She offered the quarter of a pill to Lee.

"Should I ask what that is?" Lee asked.

"Only if you're allergic to anything. Otherwise, it's probably better if you don't know."

Lee took the pill, turning it in front of her face. "It's a painkiller, right? I won't start hallucinating?" That wouldn't help her cause at all.

Risa laughed. "Nah. It's just enough to give you a buzz. Some people feel sick or drowsy. And after it wears off, the pain catches up to you. Speaking of, you should probably eat something with that." Risa stepped into the kitchen area and rummaged around, bringing back a granola bar and a glass of water.

"Thank you," Lee replied. She took the glass of water first and used it to gulp down the tiny portion of the pill. Next, at Risa's insistence, she chewed the granola bar.

"Don't drive," Risa joked.

Lee smiled weakly, pulling the covers up to her chin. A shiver went through her. Having never taken any strong medicine before, she wasn't sure what it would do to her. Hopefully, it would take away the pain and enable her to move, albeit slowly. She didn't have to be fast, just first. And if anyone else was already at the Jewel Box, she could always catch a ley line home.

Lee lay awake, listening to Risa talk to Finn. Apparently, he'd decided to stay the night. To keep an eye on Lee? She'd have to wait until he and Risa both fell asleep. All the lights went out, and the painted windows of the run-down factory made the interior nearly pitch black. Lee waited. She was glad she'd taken so many naps. She barely felt tired now, and the pill she'd taken was starting to take effect.

Buzzing was normal, right? She felt keyed up, like she'd had an IV of espresso. Her hands quivered. Lee grinned to herself, holding her hands in front of her face. Now for the real test. She sat up slowly.

No pain.

She twisted at her waist.

No pain.

She braced her arms against the couch and stood in one swift motion, almost throwing herself off balance with her momentum.

She felt no pain from the bruising in her back, just a lingering stiffness. Whatever Risa had given her, it was a freaking miracle drug. Lee walked toward the bathroom, the final part of her cover. If anyone heard her get up, they'd assume she was going to the bathroom. Walking slower than she needed to help her keep up the appearance of having a sore back. She opened the door, then shut it without going inside.

Lee reached for the Liminal realm, hardly daring to breathe as her arms took on a red glow and the world around her brightened slightly, giving her better night vision. She turned back around and walked toward the basement.

A ley line went out of the factory at the farthest corner, tucked in an alcove blocked by junk. Her emergency exit. She hoped it would get her around the magical "protections" Silas had supposedly set up. After all, the Ceteri had gotten around them. Maybe this ley line was the way they'd accessed her.

The ley line glimmered red, arching out of the factory. Lee stepped onto the starburst of red light on the floor, the node, and she was sucked into the air, caught in the jump. The world blurred, and a slight stirring of air passed over her face. She landed under a streetlight across the city and chose the center of three lines that passed through that particular node. She jumped again.

Only two more jumps to the Jewel Box. She'd never traveled into the building before, not knowing where the ley line would put her. But she had nothing to lose, now. The crew didn't want to help her, and if she didn't get the Barat before another Liminal, she would lose her chance to be healed and Liminality would eventually claim her life.

Lee breathed in, then out, and stepped onto the final node, feeling the familiar magic hook into her navel and vibrate through her body. She thrilled in it, not even feeling the pins and needles she typically felt while in the Liminal realm. She'd have to ask Risa the name of this stuff. If the Ceteri didn't follow through, or if she failed to get the item, maybe she could last longer using these pills. She wouldn't be in pain, at least, and her mind was clearer than ever.

Lee passed through the top of the Jewel Box roof, following the glowing red ley line into the building's basement. She landed in a crouch, silent, barely breathing, and peered into the pitch dark, still wrapped in the relative safety of the Liminal realm.

Her eyes adjusted. No sounds reached her hearing, not even muffled ones. Lee pushed through the veil between realms and became tangible again. Her senses regained full clarity, which was currently an off-putting silence.

Lee crept to the wall, putting her hand on it and walking until she reached a corner. She turned. She should have brought a flashlight. How was she going to find the Barat? Just sense it out, like the Ceteri assumed she could? Did she dare turn on a light?

A sudden sound stopped Lee in her tracks. A distant bleating, like a farm animal. It came from behind her. Lee retraced her steps, pausing occasionally to listen for the sound again.

It repeated. Her mind raced faster than it should have been able to. A possible side effect of Risa's pill? Lee didn't know. But she knew that there shouldn't be any animals down here, and if there were, she probably didn't want to meet them, but curiosity drove her forward until she saw, dimly lit by a silver nightlight-type device low on the wall, a cage. In the cage a white goat with frightened eyes.

It bleated when it saw Lee, and she stumbled back. Why was a goat in the basement of the Jewel Box? The goat bleated again, and somewhere in the distance, Lee heard a distinct, canine-like howl. Her blood froze, and the trembling in her hands started again. Sweat beaded on her brow. The howl sounded again, closer this time.

Whatever it was, Lee was standing between it and its midnight snack.

CHAPTER 29

Risa had looked at Adam like he had two heads when he asked if there was a bed available. He never slept at the hideout—he'd made it clear that he preferred his own sleeping quarters, but after Lee's kidnapping, he wanted to stay close and keep an eye on things.

Risa dragged a blanket and pillow out of the mess in the basement and had Adam carry a cot up the stairs. The main floor had office walls set up in the back, partitioned into rooms.

"Sam, can Finn crash here?" Risa asked, standing at the edge of the room lit with a purple blacklight. Posters glowed on the flimsy portable walls.

Sam looked up, moving his headphones. "Sorry?"

"Can I sleep here?" Adam asked.

Sam's eyes grew wide, and then his smile broadened. "Sure, man! Come right in. Let me just move this." He jumped off the bed and moved a pile of laundry to the other corner so there was space for the cot across from him. "You get kicked out of your other place, or what?"

Adam forced a smile. "Nothing like that. Just...needed a change of pace."

"He's worried about Lee," Risa said. She examined a bit of her hair.

Adam stared at her. "This is not about Lee."

"It is. Don't pretend. I see the way you look at her, and I'll have you know that if you hurt her, you'll be haunted for the rest of your life." Risa jabbed a finger at him and stalked away.

Adam looked away, shaking his head, and caught Sam's stare.

"She's serious. I'd listen to her," Sam said.

"Thanks for the advice." Adam wrestled the cot open, his injured shoulder complaining at the effort, and tossed the pillow and blanket down. He tried to get comfortable laying down, but between his sore shoulder and the beating he'd taken to his face, everything felt bruised and any pressure was miserable.

Adam stared at the light filling the room. "Do you leave the—"

"Light on? Yeah. It's a special lamp that helps my nerves and everything. But I can turn it off for one night..." Sam trailed off, his voice getting squeaky at the end.

"No, don't worry about it. I could sleep anywhere." It was just one night. Adam could put up with anything for one night, as long as Lee stayed safe.

He rolled over, facing the wall, and wondered if he should check on Lee one last time, but then he heard Risa talking to her. That was good enough. He could get up later to see if she was still there.

Adam set a mental intention to wake up in two hours and

drifted off to the sound of Sam humming some sort of show tune.

His eyes opened. It hadn't been two hours yet. Somehow he knew that, despite not having a clock. The purple light glowed from the opposite side of the cubicle-like room, and Sam snored softly on his bed.

Quietly, Adam rolled off the cot and soft-stepped across the floor. The old factory was pitch dark. He could barely make out the outline of various pieces of furniture, and the green numbers on the microwave.

He padded to the couch and peered cautiously over the edge. He didn't want to startle Lee if she was awake; he just needed to make sure she was still...

Damn.

The covers lay strewn on the bed, her pillow still holding the form of her head. He touched the pillow's surface. Still warm.

He heard the bathroom door close, and his breathing slowed. She'd gone to the bathroom. No problem, then. He could pretend he was getting a late-night snack or something. He moved closer to the kitchen. Mid-stride, his chest clicked with the distinct sensation that meant magic had activated somewhere.

Lee had gone Liminal.

Without care for how much noise he made, Adam ran for the bathroom. He knocked on the door. Nothing. No light spilled out beneath, and no one called from inside. He flung open the door. Vacant toilet, empty bathroom. She was gone.

Adam breathed in, calming himself.

"She left, didn't she?" a female voice said from behind.

Adam spun to find Risa standing there, her face illuminated by a cool blue glow. A ghost of some sort?

"Did you know about this?" Adam demanded.

"I considered it before I gave her the After Burn." Risa examined her nails.

"After Burn? You gave her a street drug?" Adam's thoughts raced, trying to remember what After Burn did. It was a common drug on the streets, especially for thaumaturgics who had physical decline from their abilities. It reduced pain, it had a buzz to it, not unlike caffeine. It was pretty harmless, as drugs go, except for the unhealthy way people pushed themselves beyond their max when they took it. Some people died, ignoring symptoms that they needed medical care. It was illegal because of the main ingredient, which was a thaumaturgic's blood. Highly variable, and therefore, unstable.

"Where did you even get something like that?" Adam hissed.

"Looking for a supplier?" Risa shot back.

"No! Just...ugh!" He threw his hands up and pushed past her. "Look, Lee isn't in any state to be out there by herself. She's headed for the Jewel Box, and we both know she could face anything there."

"How much is Silas paying you to track her?" Risa tilted her chin up, her dark eyeliner exaggerating the shadows on her face.

Adam stopped. "What?"

"How much is he paying you? It must be a lot, considering how worked up you are. Unless you have ulterior motives with Lee." Risa stepped closer.

Adam put up his hands defensively. "I don't want to fight with you. Not when Lee's in danger. And she is in danger."

"How do you know that? She's a big girl. She can take care of herself. In her shoes, I'd probably do the same thing."

"But you didn't go with her, even though you suspected she might leave?" Adam accused.

Guilt flashed across Risa's face. She scowled. "If she'd asked me, I would have. But the stupid brat doesn't ask for anything from anyone, does she? I'm not about to follow her and get her out of whatever mess she gets herself into. Not this time. Maybe she'll figure out that she can't just expect people to show up for her all the time."

"I get that you've probably been used in your life, that you've given this crew everything and have little to show for it, but taking that out on Lee right now isn't going to change things. You're right that she doesn't rely on anyone. She doesn't want to be close to anyone, not even the only people in the world who care about her. But if you don't help me get to her, and something goes horribly wrong, you're going to be the haunted one."

Risa didn't speak, didn't move. She blinked, and the spectral orb bobbed around her head, bumping into her occasionally.

"What do you want to do?" she finally asked. "Nothing can catch up with her before she hits the Jewel Box. She's across the city by now."

"Do you have anything that can teleport me?" Adam asked.

Risa passed him, moving fast toward the stairs. "Wait there," she called.

Adam watched her go, then opened his phone and hovered his thumb over the call symbol. He might want backup if Risa wasn't going with him. There was no telling what was inside that venue guarding the treasures they paraded out for the public.

But an official call for backup would mean he'd compromised his cover in the crew. Hatcher would move in on Lee, forcing her to become the department guinea pig. And how was that any better than what Bruce had done to her?

But what the department wanted was different. They wanted to help more people like Lee. That's why Adam did this job. For the department to get more funding, so more Liminals could be saved from the Fade.

Adam texted Agent Zarrow. Nothing serious, just a quick, "You awake?"

The agent responded, despite the late hour. "Yeah."

"Standby at the Jewel Box. Stay out of sight. Don't bring anyone else."

Adam shut his phone as Risa exited the stairwell, hefting what looked like a hula hoop barely large enough for a grown person to step through. She thrust it at him, and Adam took it. It was carved wood, something pale like ash.

"Just say *Ravana*, and step through feet first. The symbols will start glowing green, and you'll tell it your destination. You have to be very specific. Location, City, State, Country, Planet, and Time Period. It's glitchy and hard to manage, it can be off by 25 yards and up to two years sometimes."

"Excuse me, did you say years?" Adam asked, holding the hoop away from him. "I'm not sure that's a risk I'm willing to take."

Risa lifted her eyebrows at him. "You want to help Lee? This is the only route I know of that won't take twenty minutes. Don't waver. Don't hesitate. Speak clearly and enunciate. Keep your intention to save Lee in the forefront of your mind. It gives preference to benevolent causes."

"What weird sorcery is this?" Adam muttered. He swallowed, shooting Risa one last glance, then said the activating word she'd given him. "Ravana."

He got his feet through the hoop without tripping and dragged it up his body until it was to his waist. The symbols lit up, glowing a bright yellow-green.

"It seems to work, at least."

"Tell it where you're going," Risa urged. The orb around her head seemed to get excited, zipping about in the air.

Adam cleared his throat. "The Jewel Box, St. Louis, Missouri, United States of America, Earth."

"And the date," Risa reminded.

Adam rattled off the date and the exact time, a bead of sweat trickling down his neck. He tried to keep the location, date, and Lee all in his mind at once. The air fuzzed and blurred, turning green, then yellow, then white. Risa faded from view, and Adam blinked.

The white faded into blue, then grey, then black. He stood in the same place he had before, only Risa was gone and someone was screaming. He wasn't at the hideout anymore. He was somewhere dark, and if his gut was right, that was Lee screaming.

Adam hit the floor running. His eyes barely adjusted to the dark. He gripped the wooden transport device, pumping through the air with it, afraid that if he let go he'd have no way back.

He skidded around a corner, unable to see much more than a tiny silvery glow. A goat in a cage, and Lee crouched beside the cage, cowering at the creature cast in shadow that approached her, snarling.

"Lee!" Adam shouted.

The shadowy creature between him and her turned its

hollow, glowing eyes on Adam, snapping and snarling. When Adam froze, it turned back and advanced towards Lee and the goat, both of which it would no doubt consume in due course.

Adam tried his thaumaturgic Stop motion, putting his arm out and twisting his fist. The creature, dog-like in shape and size, didn't freeze. It wasn't driven by thaumaturgy, then. It was a flesh and blood creature with a spiny ridge-like back and hollow eyes, with webbing between the extraordinarily long claws on each foot.

"Get out of there, Lee!" Adam shouted. Why hadn't the woman gone Liminal yet? Her bloodshot eyes widened with terror. Was the After Burn pill Risa had given her still in her system? Was she coherent?

"Can't," Lee said, her mouth trembling. She licked her lips. "It's this place. My ability doesn't work here."

Adam frowned. Perhaps that was why his Stopping had failed. He pulled out his gun and leveled it at the back of the creature's head. He shot once, twice.

The creature yelped and tugged at its head with its paws instead of crumpling in a pool of its own blood. It whined and fussed, dragging its neck on the ground. Adam gestured towards Lee, who darted along the wall around the dog-like thing.

It saw her and snapped to attention, ignoring the goat's frantic bleating. Saliva dripped from its jaws, and blood dripped down its neck, but not enough. Not nearly enough.

He'd only nicked it. With two bullets, shot straight into its skull, he'd nicked it.

Adam kept his gun up. He aimed and fired as the dog-thing jumped. The sound of his gun cracked off the walls and the creature yelped, falling back as it madly scratched at its head. But when it looked up, there was nothing more than a scrape on its forehead. Its ice-blue eyes had no irises, and the orbs sunk deep into its grey-furred skull.

Lee drew one of her knives, but Adam could feel her quivering through his shoulder where she touched him, and he knew that no throw of her knives would be accurate enough to hit their mark, especially if his gun had no effect.

Adam adjusted his sweaty grip on the relic that had transported him here. He couldn't use it without making himself vulnerable to the beast. And it was coming back around, no longer occupied with the wound on its head. It paced in front of them, occasionally glancing at the goat, which Adam assumed must have been intended to feed the beast.

"Do you think we could smash that crate?" Adam asked, sweat prickling on his brow. The only light came from the beast's eyes and a tiny light in the wall near the floor. The light flashed intermittently, lighting up the beast as it paced closer to Lee and Adam. If they bolted, it would give chase, and Adam doubted they could outrun it.

"I don't have anything to throw. Do you?" Lee asked.

Adam eyed the hoop in his hand. "Uh, yes, but it's our only way out."

"Throw the gun," Lee said.

"What? No. It won't break the cage."

Without warning, the beast lunged. Lee screamed and dove. Adam shot and ducked.

The beast hit the wall and fell on top of Adam. Survival instincts drove him to grab the monster and stand, spinning with the momentum until he let go. The creature crashed into the goat's cage, shattering it. The goat bleated and shrieked in the most horrifying cacophony, limping at a full run into the distant darkness of the hall.

Snarling and foaming, the beast took after it, the strobe-like silvery light following it until it disappeared.

Adam and Lee stared in silence.

Adam finally moved, strapping his gun into his holster. His neck stung, but he couldn't see any blood on his hand when he checked. "We're leaving. Now. Before it comes back."

"No way. We're here. I haven't found the Barat yet," Lee insisted.

Adam pointed in the direction the beast had gone with his empty gun. "I don't know what that thing was, but it's possible there are more. And once it eats that goat, it'll be bored and come back for more."

The goat's bleating stopped in the distance.

"Someone else might find it first," Lee said with a desperate edge to her voice.

"You're going to have to take that risk. Look, come back with me now and I'll help you convince the others to help."

Her gaze found his in the flashing darkness. "You mean that?"

"I do," he replied. He held out the hoop, low enough that she could step into it. Was it just a trick of these walls, or was that the sound of nails clicking on the tile floor? "Hurry."

Lee stepped cautiously forward, eyeing the hoop. "You want to play a game?"

Her response barely made any sense. Why was she joking now?

"Just get in." Adam glanced down the pitch-dark hall. He couldn't see anything, but...

Three forms took shape in the darkness. Large, dog-like forms with bared teeth that glinted in the strange flashing security light.

"Get in!" Adam bellowed.

Lee scrambled into the ring, and he stepped in with her, stepping on her feet, wrapping a single arm around her and crushing her against his body, the salty, somehow sweet smell of her hitting him as he tried to balance them both in the tiny hula-hoop-like device.

He could make out the whites of the dog-beasts' eyes, see the details of the striped spines on the ridges on their backs. He rattled off the first address that came to his mind, the present moment, thinking of how he hoped more than anything else he could just see Millie one last time.

Green light flashed and sizzled, and there was a vague sense of disconnect in Adam's body, and then green turned white, grey, until the pale, blueish light of dawn faded into view. The scene was unnervingly peaceful until Adam and Lee toppled over onto a grassy lawn. They scrambled around trying to get untangled, until Adam pressed on the top of the hoop to release their legs. Lee slid it off their feet and they rolled away from each other.

"Where are we?" Lee asked, blinking in confusion. She glanced around and laughed breathlessly. "This is some classy neighborhood, Finn. You got a girlfriend who lives here or something?" Her voice was pitched too high, and she seemed sweaty, but then, they had just escaped death's clutches.

Adam stared at his house a moment too long, heart pounding. It was late. No one would be awake. But this came far too close to his personal life. He stared at the wooden hoop. "Come on, I'm not using this thing again. Let's grab a bus."

He moved to look away from the front of his home, when a light flicked on upstairs. It was nearly 1 a.m.. Who would be awake?

A muffled scream. Two shadows crossed over the window

as a large figure dragged a smaller figure from one of the upper bedrooms towards the stairs. Adam's adrenaline spiked.

"Something's wrong. Stay here," he told Lee.

"What?" she hissed.

He ran toward the front steps at a crouch. The rest of the street was quiet. His hand rested on the knob, then turned it.

"Mom?" he called up.

Another light flipped on at the top of the stairs. Adam froze.

"Adam? Is that you?" The older woman's voice floated down, and she came into view wearing a robe, a hand in a black sleeve gripping her arm. A man stepped into view, a far-too pleasant smile on his face.

Adam shifted from fear to rage in an instant. "Suarez?"

Suarez spread his free hand out, gesturing with a small gun. "The one and only."

Adam advanced up the stairs, but Suarez waved his gun.

"That's far enough. We can talk from here."

"Are you all right? Is Millie all right?" Adam asked, reading his mom's frightened face.

Her eyes widened, and her chest heaved.

"Millie is still asleep," she said.

Adam narrowed his eyes at Suarez. "Let her go," he growled.

"Sure, sure." Suarez released Adam's mother. "You can go now," he said.

She crossed her arms over her robe and scowled.

Adam slowly pulled his hand away from his gun. He tilted his head. Most criminals didn't give up their leverage so easily. But then, Suarez had never been more than a petty criminal and informant that Adam knew of.

"How did you know where to find this place? Why are

you here?" Adam said, trying to stay in control of the conversation.

Suarez smiled. "I've been following you for weeks. Gotta keep tabs on my favorite customers. I meant to get hold of your phone number from your mother." Suarez turned to Adam's mother and bowed awkwardly. "Lovely woman. Would that we had met under different circumstances. In any case, you arrived, so no phone call needed."

"So...you aren't here to hold my family for ransom?" Adam itched to get Suarez away from his mother all the same.

"Not in so many words, no. They don't have anything to fear from me."

Adam heard the implied 'yet'.

He opened his mouth to reply when the front door cracked and swung open. Lee stumbled inside, cleared her throat, and belched.

Then she *giggled* and looked up, her face brightening when she saw him. "I have to pee," she said.

Adam blinked. What was she doing?

Suarez raised his eyebrows. "Who is this? You bringing a girl home to meet your mama, Finn?"

Adam swallowed. He hadn't known that Suarez knew his name. The situation was quickly spiraling out of control. Not Lee, not Suarez, not in his house. He swore he would never let his family come into danger because of his work. He had to get them both out of there, and fast.

He shot a glance at his mother. "I'll take care of this. Go back to sleep."

"You had better." She said the words in a tone that, in his childhood, meant that he was in trouble. Big trouble.

Adam put a hand on his gun. He leveled his breathing. "We're taking this outside."

"Okey-dokey," Suarez said in a chipper tone, as if he hadn't staged a kidnapping of Adam's own mother. "Wouldn't want to wake the niña."

"What is this place? This your house?" Lee shouted. Adam took her by the arm, shoving her towards the door. "Ow! Not so rough. You know, you don't look mean, but you act it. No wonder Silas hired you."

The door slammed behind the trio.

"What's gotten into you?" he said in a low tone that he hoped sounded dangerous.

"I could've escaped," Lee drawled. Her face was slack, her eyes too shiny. Adam knew that After Burn had side effects, but he'd never heard of these ones. Was it something about Lee's Liminality making her this loopy? The drug interacting oddly with her blood?

Adam snapped his fingers in front of her face. Startled, she looked behind herself. Adam felt the magic sensation in his chest a moment too late, and she blinked from view.

Suarez whistled. "She's a piece of work, man. You sure know how to pick 'em."

"She's stoned, okay. She's not normally like that." Adam ran a hand down his face, realizing how that sounded. He stared at the place where Lee had stood. Hopefully, she'd have the sense to go straight back to the hideout. In her condition, she could get into all sorts of…

Suarez was having a convulsion of sorts, his entire frame shaking with laughter. "S-Sorry, it's jus-just too perfect! Mr. Uptight and Ms. Burnout out on the town. Lucky I already had your mama distracted or she woulda freaked—"

Adam growled and shoved Suarez off the porch.

The portly man showed his hands. "Now then, play nice. I came here to do you a favor."

"A favor? I assumed it was a delusional lack of self-preservation." Adam approached slowly, letting Suarez back up across his lawn. The man chuckled nervously and ran a hand through his hair, his other hand fumbling for his pocket. "This was never part of our arrangement," Adam said. "I should turn you in, let the proper authorities handle you."

Suarez stopped near the hedge separating Adam's house from his neighbor. "I-I think you'll find it in yourself to forgive me eventually." The hispanic Teleporter straightened his back and sniffed. "Seeing as I have critical information that could save your life and that Liminal you've been following. About the Jewel Box."

"How do you know about that?" Adam asked.

"Ah, yes, you see, premonition runs on my mother's side." Suarez cracked a smile.

Adam folded his arms. "You think I could be taken in that easily?" Thaumaturgy had only been around for six years, and Adam had never heard of someone with more than two abilities.

"No, really—I've helped people win bets, find lost things, avoid death, all of it. And my great aunt Lulu was a fortune-teller, so everything I told you is true. Look, I wrote it down here somewhere." Receipts and dollar bills spewed out of the man's pockets as he rummaged through them. He snatched most of them out of the air, turning them over and muttering to himself. Most of them had scrawling on them.

"Come on. Just tell me you have a Seer buddy. Someone with a future-telling ability, right?" Adam asked. Having multiple abilities wasn't unheard of, but Adam had a difficult time believing the bumbling informant in front of him had an ability like premonition.

Suarez muttered to himself as he read through one of the

pieces of paper, then snorted and tossed it. "I don't like to lie when I don't have to. My premonition isn't as strong as tele-portation. And afterward I have these blinding migraines. My longest one lasted four days. The headache, I mean. Nearly killed me. Anyway, this one only set me back a few hours, so I won't ask for much to compensate."

Adam's stare was hard enough to drill holes through Suarez's skull. As it was, Suarez didn't see the stare and continued to rifle through his pockets until a tiny yellow scrap of post-it note surfaced and he whooped quietly in triumph. Everything else got jammed back in his pockets.

"Right here. I got it all down pretty clearly." Adam reached for the paper, but Suarez held it out of reach, wagging his finger. "Uh-uh. Payment first."

"How do I know it's worth paying for? It could be nothing more than drunk ramblings." But Adam knew. He could feel it. There was a clicking in his chest, like a metronome beat being turned up. The paper Suarez waved around held a magical signature, as did many of the others in his pockets.

Adam sighed and pulled out his wallet. He took out two bills. "This is what I've got on me."

Suarez's dark eyes narrowed at the twenties Adam held out. "This information could be life or death for you and that burnout girl. Her crew, too. For that, I'll rip this into little shreds and you can pick up the pieces and hope you don't miss something."

"That's pretty cutthroat for you."

"I'm a desperate man. Several of my recent contracts have fallen through. Fewer fish means more bait." That explained his willingness to break into Adam's house and all but abduct his mother.

Adam sighed. "Well, I'm not about to write a personal

check. We've been working together a while. Can I promise to get you the rest later? Tell you what, write down any amount on a separate piece of paper. Consider it an IOU. You can cash in within a week."

Adam swallowed. The FBI didn't give him endless funds for paying informants. Hopefully Suarez would be judicious, but judging by the man's glittering eyes, he had other things in mind.

"I'll approve the amount, to be sure," Adam added. "Don't try to gouge me or you'll be out of more than just business."

Suarez made a big dramatic show of sighing and rolling his eyes. "Gotta find me some contacts that aren't broke." He produced a pen out of nowhere and scrawled something, then handed the paper to Adam.

Adam's eyes nearly bugged out of his head. "Good luck finding contacts that carry ten grand around with them! I don't think so." He shoved the paper back at Suarez. "I'll take my chances with the paper shreds."

"Fine," Suarez snapped. He crossed the number out and wrote a new one. "That's for this premonition *and* complete silence concerning what I found at this location." He nodded toward the house and smiled a sly, knowing smile.

$7,000. Not a small sum for a tiny piece of paper, but the insurance on Adam's family might be worth that, and more. He'd have to settle it with the department later. Adam nodded and tucked the paper away in his pocket, then held out his hand for Suarez to shake. The man's demeanor flipped from cross to sunny, and his other hand descended with the premonition.

"Now, I don't think I have to say it, but just in case, I'm not responsible for the outcome here," Suarez tapped the paper. With a slight popping sensation resonating in Adam's chest, the man vanished.

Adam crumpled the paper, tempted to toss it to the side and not take a glance. When a Teller gave someone a premonition, it was well-known that they'd better heed it. A premonition came about when something deadly was about to happen, something that could be subverted with the right kind of action.

But how much did he believe Suarez wasn't making this up? Adam had never heard of someone having two thaumaturgic abilities. It could have been a ploy to milk money out of Adam. In which case, he had been taken for a fool. But his spine tingled as he rubbed the paper between his fingers. The buzzing sensation crawled up the back of his neck as he read the words scrawled on the post-it's dirty yellow surface in smeared pencil.

The Mentalist will be there.

CHAPTER 30

Lee's thoughts bubbled and twisted in her head. She couldn't grasp a single one to make it stay at the forefront of her mind. She lay on a park bench in the shadow of a tree, watching starlight peek at her through the leaves. She'd tried to jump another ley line, but her powers had glitched, or she'd gotten dizzy and needed to lie down. The bench had been the closest thing.

She glanced at the playground equipment, then frowned. Since when did this place have four slides and eight swings? The double-image overlapped, and she squinted, then shook her head. Had someone drugged her?

Paranoia swept over her, and she sat up, glancing frantically at her surroundings. How had she gotten here? She remembered going Liminal, but before that, what had happened?

A man walked past the park, hands stuffed in his pockets, then looked over at her. His mouth opened in surprise, and he jogged across the grass toward her.

"Lee! What are you doing here?"

Lee jumped and crouched on the bench, one hand catching a knife handle off her wrist sheath. "You're the one from the house! You tried to kidnap me!"

The man's face creased with confusion. "No, I didn't. I saved you from those dog things and we ended up at the wrong place after. Then you started acting all weird. I can't believe you only jumped a couple blocks away, I figured you would have gone back to the hideout. Did you take more than one of those pills?"

Pills? "You drugged me," she accused.

"You drugged yourself," the man shot back. He rubbed a hand down his face and sighed. In the dim light of dawn, Lee could see the tattoos on his forearm.

"A bunny?" she said incredulously. There was a tiny red rabbit drawn into the sleeve of ink on his arm. Surrounded by black roses and a deck of cards. She snorted. "Like Wonderland much? That's real macho."

"Look, let me take you back to the hideout. I was going to catch a bus."

Lee made a face. "No way. You can get a bus. I'm going Liminal, thank you." She reached internally, ready to phase into the Liminal realm, but mentally slammed into some sort of block.

The tattooed guy held his arm up, raised in a funky position. Why did he seem familiar? "You're doing something. Stop it."

"No. I just found you; I'm not letting you jump all over the city. You'll get yourself killed. Come on." He grabbed her hand and pulled her toward a bench beside a signpost.

Lee's gaze fixed on the tiny red rabbit tattoo. Was she Alice? Alice followed the rabbit. Lee let the man drag her, frowning as her mind danced around the man's name in her mind. She knew it. She knew she knew it, but her mind skipped around too fast for her to follow the thoughts. She just knew she could trust him. Not totally, but right now.

The bus stopped at the curb, hissing and groaning. Lee took the bus steps two at a time after the man with the rabbit tattoo. He sat down, patting the vinyl seat next to him and looking at her with a pair of green eyes that would have been much more handsome if they hadn't looked so worried. Lee flopped down.

The buzzing high was gone. Her back ached slightly, as if strained. She fidgeted until the man covered it with his own.

Damn those green eyes.

"Lee, put the knife away," he said quietly.

Lee glanced at the sharp blade, then across the row. A man stared at her, then slowly shifted out of his seat and went to the back of the bus.

She tucked the knife back into its sheath and looked at her empty hands. When she blinked, she saw his name. *Finn.* And her memories of the past hour crashed over her. She leaned forward on the seat, pressing her forehead into her hands on the cool blue vinyl. A headache crept on, and Lee winced to herself. Had the After Burn worn off?

"I disappointed you, didn't I?" Lee said.

"What?" Finn asked.

"I let everyone down. I took this huge risk for myself, for the crew, and I had to be rescued. I didn't even find it."

Finn shifted next to her. Their arms touched briefly. "Look, you want to get better pretty badly. I can get that. I don't think anyone is mad at you. They probably feel bad they didn't help you."

"How can you say that?" Lee faced him.

Finn struggled to find the right words. "Because I'm... because I'm one of them."

He was, she realized. He'd joined the crew and put it all in, even though he knew times were rough. He'd ridden every wave they'd thrown at him. That Lee had thrown at him. Their drama, their quirky personalities. He hadn't once complained.

"You are," Lee said to him. "You're one of us."

Finn chuckled. "It's only been a few weeks. You don't have to adopt me yet."

Lee cracked a smile. "If you're not careful, Risa will anyway. She's good at mothering people."

"She's worried about you. She helped me get to you in time. With this." He patted a wooden hoop he held on his knees.

Lee glanced out the window. Risa had helped her, too. But Lee didn't want Risa to worry. If Lee didn't succeed at getting the Barat for the Ceteri, she'd be gone, and Risa might even miss her. Lee worried about Sam. She didn't need more people to care about her. She didn't need Finn to care about her.

The rest of the bus ride was quiet. When they got off at the next bus stop, it was a three-block walk to the abandoned warehouse district where the old paper mill sat with blackened windows.

Finn knocked on the door on the first floor.

"Who's there?" Risa asked.

"Finn."

"Is Lee with you?" she demanded.

"I'm here, Risa," Lee piped up.

"Oh, thank the Reaper." Risa threw open the door. Lee flinched, expecting an embrace, but the woman stood as if frozen, eyes scanning over Lee. "I thought we might have lost you for good this time. One way or another."

"Oh, you do care if I die, then?" Lee asked, bitterness dripping from her voice. She cursed herself inside. Why did she push everyone away?

"Someone has to. Idiot girl," Risa said, her eyebrows coming together.

"Can we come in? We're making a scene," Finn said.

Risa stared at Lee for another long moment, then backed up, letting them in. Pain followed Lee up the stairs, and Sam waited at the top, taking her in a crushing hug the moment she appeared.

"Sam!" Lee exclaimed. She wiggled out of his arms, straightening her beanie, and scowled at him.

He beamed, despite her expression. Then his face crumpled. "You shouldn't have gone alone, Lee. You could have taken me, at least." He tapped his ear.

Lee shook his head. "You all chose not to help me. I couldn't wait for you to come around. Not with the Ceteri hiring others for the same job. They're increasing their chances of getting these objects to save their world, while making it harder for me to succeed." She glanced between Risa and Sam. "None of you are mad?"

"Well, Silas still hasn't shown up." Risa walked up with a plate of cookies. Everyone took one.

"You can't do this alone again," Finn said before taking a bite of a cookie. "If you're determined to go in, we're going to do it the right way this time."

"Really?" Lee hardly dared to hope. Her heart thudded and skipped a beat, and her head spun.

Risa shot a look at a clunky watch she pulled from her breast pocket, and she handed the plate of cookies to Sam.

"That pill hasn't worn off yet?" Risa said.

"I think it did. I feel fine. Why do you ask?" Lee grimaced as a wave of pain washed across her back.

"After Burn is measurable and predictable when you make it yourself and know the formula. This one is made with only one thaumaturgic's blood, and I've timed it within five minutes' accuracy," Risa explained. "Your dose should have ended three minutes ago."

"You use it that much?" Finn said in shock.

Risa stared flatly at him, then her face tilted and Lee's ears filled with a rushing sound, like wind blowing past.

And then all the light collapsed, leaving Lee in darkness.

"...The fire devastated the building and caused significant damage to one other building nearby." A radio voice crackled in Lee's hearing, and she sat up groggily, holding her head.

"Here," Risa sat nearby, handing her a coffee.

Lee took a sip and nearly spat. "Decaf?"

"Caffeine and After Burn don't mix. Believe me." Risa offered a plate next.

Lee eyed the grilled cheese with suspicion, her stomach flip-flopping.

"Come on. I know you're hungry. Why is feeding you such a chore?" Risa slid the plate onto Lee's lap and stood.

"Who's got the radio on? That's not wise."

"Finn. He's got some bizarre theory that the fire is in the building the Liminal girls were kept in. That man is full of it, if you ask me." Risa shook her head, and her gears and gadgets gleamed on her costume. More like a uniform, Lee realized as she took it all in. She'd never seen Risa without her steampunk on.

Lee sipped at the coffee. It was warm and sweet, but Risa had put milk in it. What was the point of coffee if you couldn't get an energy hit and it didn't even taste like coffee? She ate the sandwich under Risa's scrutiny.

"You seem to be doing better today. A lot better," Risa noted. "Your back doesn't hurt?"

Lee thought about it, then shook her head. "Not much. There's an ache." She twisted back and forth. Risa reached over and prodded down her spine until Lee cried out and moved away.

"Ow!" Lee said.

"Just a bruise, then. I bet it's huge."

Lee fell silent, chewing her last bite. "Thanks for the sandwich."

Risa was being nice. Maybe too nice.

Lee swallowed. "So, what's the plan now? You all said you'd help last night, and I guess that means we need to do a bit of actual preparation."

"Yeah." Risa stood and walked towards the opening of the cubicle-like room that made up Lee's bedroom. "About that."

"What?" Lee asked, tossing the covers off her lap. Risa's tone made her think something was wrong. They'd changed their minds. They weren't going to do it. This is where they formally threw her out and left her on her own for good.

"We haven't been able to plan much. We're missing our Jewel Box expert." Risa winked and gestured with her head towards the common areas of the hideout.

Lee took it slow getting out of bed. Walking hurt more than she wanted to admit, but she could walk. She wouldn't take that for granted any time soon.

Sam and Finn sat at the table in the kitchen area, laughing. They stopped as Lee walked up, but the smiles didn't fall from their faces. Risa stood at the opposite end of the table from Lee.

"Take it away," Risa said. "This is your gig."

Lee swallowed. She and Shane had wanted to bust the Jewel Box for as long as they'd known each other. They always wondered what mysteries it held inside, why the rumors about it were so prevalent in the local community. Now she had a reason to shake the place down. She'd failed once. She wasn't about to fail a second time.

"All right," she said. "One of the most difficult things about the Jewel Box, as I proved last night, is that we don't know what we're facing. Scanning the building from the Liminal realm, I can see numerous large energy signatures. Some of those could be the obstacles we face."

"Sam—" Lee turned to look at the large man, who nodded. "—could you compile a list of all the rumors about the place? Anything, big or small. I want to know more about those dog things we ran into last night."

"Yeah, Finn said that. You said they fed it a goat, right? That's gotta be a chupacabra." Sam tapped the notebook in front of him excitedly with his pen while he stretched back, making his chair creak. "I'm a step ahead of you, Lee. You've been talking about the Jewel Box for a couple of years, so I've been keeping a running list of all the rumors I've heard about it. I printed it off this morning." He slid a thin stack of papers over to her.

Lee picked the top one up, then another, her jaw dropping. "There must be thousands of things on this list, Sam!" She was grateful for his researching habits, but overwhelmed at the amount of information there was to sift through. She started passing sheets down to Finn and Risa.

Sam bobbed his head. "Yeah. Turns out it's a private

auction point for magical items. Hundreds pass through there in a given month, changing ownership."

"Hold up. I thought you said this was a wedding venue," Finn said, leaning over the table, his eyebrows raised.

"That's the cover. Trade in unregistered magical items is illegal. The government wants to tag every little thing that comes through. Hence why the black market at Kaloyadu exists. Rich people don't want to deal with lowlifes like us, though. So they created their own. It's very exclusive; they have magical detectors all over the place. Most of it gets put away for weddings though, which makes the security on the upper floors more relaxed."

Risa clicked her tongue and sat forward. "They store all their inventory in the basement, then. Anyone who wants a load of magical items auctioned off sends it there, then attends the private auction later, all covered up by Screeners."

"Without a Screener of our own, we're screwed," Sam added. "Unless we go during a wedding. No one can afford that place except celebrities, and they attract a bunch of magic types. The Jewel Box can't have all of its magical equipment going off during the party, so they disarm most of it, disconnect charms, that sort of thing. At least on the upper floors."

"What we want isn't on the upper floors," Lee said. Her heart pounded with excitement. "And I've had a taste of what we'll find below. I don't think I set off any magical alarms, unless they're silent."

"Most are. It's likely you hit their first-tier defenses, the chupacabra pack," Sam said.

"Do we need to bring some goats for distraction?" Lee asked.

"I hope not," Risa exclaimed. "Hard to sneak into a wedding with goats."

"Aren't they considered a traditional wedding present?" Finn said, and Lee couldn't tell if he was joking or not.

"The myths are hard to sort from reality. I'm not certain anyone has killed a chupacabra. Theories include using fire, moving water, acid, sun, salt, hitting them on the head, and bullets."

"Bullets don't work," Finn said with confidence. "Unless you need a special kind?"

Lee nodded vigorously. That much she remembered. The one they'd fought took four shots and barely got nicked. "Its skin is like armor."

"Scratch that, then," Sam muttered, scribbling on his page. He glanced up, looking at Risa. "Can I have another cookie?"

"You ate the rest last night," Risa said.

Sam wilted, then perked up. He scooted his chair out and ambled over to his bedroom.

Lee turned back to the table, smiling in spite of herself. That Sam. Always hungry.

"So," Finn said, drawing out the word. "What are we bringing to fight the chupacabra? And how do we know what lies beyond?"

"Where'd you guys put that backpack? The one we got from the City Museum?" Lee asked.

Risa stood. "Just a sec." She headed down the stairs.

"That's a good hiding place," Finn said. "I couldn't find anything in there if you asked me."

Lee pulled up her chair and sat down, trying not to look at Finn. He'd seen her acting like a loon last night. She didn't remember much of anything after he got her out of the Jewel Box; the After Burn had taken over.

She cleared her throat. "Thanks for coming to get me last night."

"Sure." He shrugged one shoulder, as if he did that sort of thing all the time. He didn't even look up from the papers in his hand.

Lee shook her head and looked back at her own stack. An exclamation from behind made her jump, but it was just Sam.

"Why'd you do it?" Finn asked. Now he looked at her, his piercing green eyes full of questions.

"Wouldn't you risk it all to save your own life?" Lee asked.

"The life of someone else, maybe." He straightened, his face a mask of seriousness.

"I'm not that altruistic," Lee said. That much was true. Shane would still be here, sitting across from her and planning this heist instead of Finn if Lee had an altruistic bone in her body. If she cared more about others than she cared about herself, she would have gotten better at taking other people through the Liminal realm, wouldn't have let fear stop her from trying harder.

She shoved those thoughts away as Sam sat down, spreading an armload of snack packages around the table.

Lee just stared at him.

"I think better when I eat," Sam said.

Risa came clomping up the stairs just then, holding the backpack in her arms. "We all freaked out when you disappeared. When the Ceteri took you, I guess. Silas told me to hide this until we got you back." She reached in and started pulling items out, laying them in front of Lee. Then she sat down.

A flash of guilt went through Lee. Silas had almost died for the museum hit. He should get a cut, at least. But he wasn't here. If he showed up, they could split it equally. Until then, they should at least see if they could use any of the items.

At a glance, it looked like a pile of garbage. A scrap of paper that looked blank. Glasses, a pen, a large ruby, a golden paperweight, a clip-on earring, and a cloth bag holding the hammer. Lee could feel the collective power of the items like a fire warming her chest and face. She picked up the glasses and, without thinking, popped them on her face. Immediately, numbers started scrolling across the lenses. Lee gasped. She recognized them as measurements of the walls, the furniture, even the people sitting at the table.

"Lee, what is it?" Risa asked.

Finn pulled the glasses off Lee's face.

"Hey!" Lee exclaimed, snatching for them. She almost fell out of her chair as a wave of dizziness overcame her. She put a hand to her head and steadied herself. Had that been from the glasses?

"Maybe we ought to think a bit before we try magical objects on each other. Or ourselves," Finn said, turning the glasses over in his hands.

"How else are we supposed to figure out what these things do? We don't have time to go to Kaloyadu and get each item appraised." Lee sat back in her chair, folding her arms.

Finn tightened his lips. "It's about minimizing risk." He put the glasses on. "Woah."

"So it's okay when you do it?" Lee said.

"You seem fine." Finn shrugged.

"What do they do?" Sam asked, pencil ready to take notes.

"Measure everything. Weight, volume, length, depth, all of it. I bet if I tap," Finn moved his finger along the rim and the earpiece. "Yeah, if you tap here, and here"—he showed them on the glasses—"the measurements change. Temperature too, wow." He whistled, then pulled them off.

He blinked, swaying slightly. He looked around the table, gaze landing on Lee. She laughed at his dazed look.

"Dizzy?" she asked.

"You have three heads," Finn confirmed.

Sam scratched notes on his paper. "The brain compensates for the overwhelm of information by attempting to rebalance itself. The magic must draw some function from your own inner ear. Fascinating."

Lee pushed the golden paperweight towards Sam. "Why don't you try one? I never see you test out the haul."

Sam shook his head vigorously and held up both hands. "No way. Nope. I am wearing earplugs to talk with you guys. Anything that overwhelms your senses could tip me into Hulk mode."

Lee picked up the paperweight, considering it.

"Pass me that pen," Risa said, draining her mug of tea. She stole Sam's notebook, ignoring his protests, and made a quick scribble in the upper corner. Nothing spectacular happened, and Risa frowned, writing nonsense. Then she drew a circle, and yelped, dropping the pen.

A hole had burned through the paper and the table, and a quick inspection showed a burn mark in the floor three feet beneath the table.

"Woah," Sam breathed.

Finn pushed the glasses to the center of the table, eyeing the pile by Lee. "It's a bit like Christmas, isn't it," he said. "Finding out what every item does."

"If you say so." Lee rolled the ruby toward him, fingers still playing over the surface of the paperweight. At least, she assumed it was a paperweight. Something like sand shifted inside when she shook it. The brassy surface felt smooth and had no obvious symbols or marks other than the scuffing of years of wear. Lee flipped it over. The bottom had a small symbol etched into the surface.. Lee rubbed at it, feeling the shallow grooves. How to activate its power?

A bright light flared from the paperweight, blinding Lee and everyone at the table, inciting gasps and exclamations, and a curse from Risa.

"Turn it down!" Finn shouted.

"It didn't come with a dimmer," Lee said. She rubbed the same spot on the paperweight and the light faded to nothing, leaving dark spots dancing in Lee's eyes. "Think that might work against the chupacabra?"

"Yeah," Sam said, his voice strained.

"Need a break, big guy?" Risa asked.

"No." He balled his hands into fists, then slid them off the table and into his lap. A vein stood out on his brow.

"Guys," Lee said quietly. They looked at her. "I don't know how much Finn told you. I didn't get very far before he came—pretty much ran into the chupacabra and his dinner first thing. But when I got there, I was able to enter the basement via a ley line. Once inside, however, I couldn't enter the Liminal realm. At all. I don't even know if I would have been able to access the ley line again if I'd needed to leave without Finn."

The room was quiet as that information settled.

"I couldn't use my ability either," Finn said. "Or at least, the chupacabra didn't respond when I attempted. It doesn't work on physical movement, so I can't be sure."

"The hoop worked, though," Risa pointed out. "So magical items like these will be helpful."

"Not all magic is neutralized, then. Just human-based thaumaturgic abilities," Sam said slowly.

"Maybe," Lee said. "Maybe. We don't know for certain any of this is true. I could have been too tired after the past few days."

"But you went Liminal right after we got out of there. You didn't seem to have any problems then," Finn argued.

Risa stood, putting her hands on the surface of the table. "Look, we've done jobs without Lee's abilities before. We're all capable fighters and intelligent human beings with the instincts of thieves. Let's figure out what these things do, form our cover identities, crash that wedding, and wing it. For the score of a lifetime."

"For the score of a lifetime," Lee repeated. Sam and Finn followed suit, Sam lifting a glass of milk. Lee raised her half-drunk decaf, Risa her empty mug, and Finn his glass of water.

Lee's heart thudded as adrenaline rushed through her. This was actually happening. She was going to get into the Jewel Box, this time with the crew. She felt hopeful for the first time in months. But in the back of her mind, she saw the slobbering, snarling chupacabras and shuddered. If the chupacabras were the first line of defense, what could be waiting beyond?

Whatever it was, crashing the celebrity wedding would be the easy part.

CHAPTER 31

Lee bolted awake, a scream escaping her mouth. Risa leapt back, a hand on her heaving chest.

"Glory be, you scared me. Sleeping like the dead one moment and screaming like the restless spirits on Hallow's Eve the next. What's gotten into you?" Risa smoothed the black vest she wore and brushed off her crisp white sleeves.

Lee stared, breathing in and out through her nose to calm the blood pumping through her veins. She blinked.

For once, Risa wasn't wearing her steampunk gear. Instead, a black vest and white blouse hugged her curves, complete with bowtie and dress slacks. Her dark brown hair was pulled back in its typical tight bun. It suited her part as a server with the catering company.

"You sure look the part." Lee rubbed her eyes to get the rest of the sleep out and swung her legs over the side of the bed.

"Yeah, well, it's nothing like your transformation into 'wealthy wedding guest Theresa Ribaldi' is going to be. Have you ever even worn a dress, Lee?"

She had, once, for Shane, at his request. Dresses didn't lend well to burglaring. Lee just shook her head. Her hair fell in tangled curls around her face. She blew on one.

"I didn't realize your hair was curly." Risa reached out and touched one of the bouncy things.

"It's not. More wavy. In a demented, never-to-be-tamed sort of way."

"Well, here's the gown we rented." Risa picked a fancy bag with a hanger off her bed and held it towards Lee, who unzipped the top of the bag. She whistled. Her stomach rolled.

"Did it have to have so much glitter?"

"Hey, you gotta look the part. Glitter is in. Leggings and boots...not so much. Get dressed." Risa tossed the bag at Lee and stepped out of the room. "I'm heating up the curling iron."

Balancing on one leg in the tight space, Lee shoved her way into the sleek, shimmering dress. It fit against her body like a wetsuit. Running her hands along the fabric, zipper still undone in the back, Lee fought the urge to throw her army green canvas jacket over the top. It would clash with the glittering purple monstrosity she wore, but at least her arms would be warm.

"Lee, are you finished yet?" Risa called from the other side of the partition. "We only have thirty minute to do your hair!"

Lee closed her eyes. "I'll just wear my beanie. No one will notice."

Risa let out a shriek and flung herself through the entrance into the makeshift room. She snatched the beanie off Lee's bed and held it high in the air.

"There is no way in this world or the next that this thing is even coming with us."

"How else will anyone recognize my brand of thieving?" Lee teased. But the mirth faded as Risa shoved the beanie into a duffle bag on the floor.

"There. Once we're beneath the venue, you'll want to change your clothes. I'll hide the duffle in the kitchen area and bring it with me when we meet up."

The only entrance to the basement, aside from the ley line Lee had used, was inside the Jewel Box itself. Sam had managed to hack his way to the schematics for the place, and Lee had spent the past two days poring over them. She'd hated waiting, her skin feeling like itchy wool clothes the entire time, but she figured that if any of the others the Ceteri had hired wanted to break into the Jewel Box, they would do it this weekend during the wedding. She just had to get to the Barat first.

Risa zipped up Lee's dress and then led her to the common area of the old factory, where a chair sat in front of a fully-lit vanity, the globe-like lights blinding Lee. Risa curled Lee's hair in perfect ringlets and must have performed a sacrificial ritual to get Lee's hair balanced on her head in an intricate updo. At least, that was what it felt like, with Risa muttering Latin words under her breath and pricking Lee's head with the tiny metal bobby pins. A living voodoo doll. Except Lee knew Risa didn't dabble in dark magic. Probably.

Risa was working to apply the makeup at the speed of light when Finn walked in. He froze at the top of the stairs, which Lee was facing while Risa angled her face to get the perfect blush application.

"Hi," Lee said.

"Don't move," Risa hissed. She smudged Lee's face with her finger.

Finn straightened the lapels of his tux and ran his fingers

along the inner collar of his lavender button-up shirt. "Hey yourself." He cleared his throat, gaze flicking to one side of the room, then back to Lee.

"That color is incredible on you." Lee gestured towards him, and Risa gave an impatient grunt, so Lee sat still as a statue.

"You as well. You too." Finn stuck a hand in his pocket and shook what sounded like keys. "Picked up our ride. Let it be known, Theodore takes his wife out in style."

"I'm almost ready. Right, Risa?" Lee gritted her teeth in an attempt at a smile.

"Yes. Fine. Finished." Risa surrendered her weapons and collapsed as if exhausted. Yeesh. How did some women do this to themselves every day?

Lee stood, tugging down the skirt of her dress so it was a micro-inch closer to her knees. Finn frowned, still looking at her, and she froze. "What is it? Is there a tear in the back or something?" She craned her head to look.

"No, the dress is fine. It's that…" He ran his fingers through his curly brown hair, blowing air from his lips. "I got a tip about the job tonight. I wasn't sure whether to say anything, because the source is less than trustworthy, but I've got a bad feeling about it all."

"Well, spill." Lee crossed her arms. Her breasts puffed up, feeling as if they'd fall out of the top of the neckline. Heavens. Would she be able to move at all tonight? She dropped her arms, holding them awkwardly at her sides.

"The Mentalist will be there. He knows, somehow, about what we're doing."

The hairs on Lee's neck prickled, and her entire body surged with fear. She squashed it, breathing deeply. There was no need to panic. The Mentalist wasn't here, even if Lee's body was acting like the danger was imminent. "And you know that how?"

Risa stood beside her, folding her arms. "Awfully suspicious, newcomer. One might think you were trying to thwart the mission and claim the goods for yourself. Or maybe you're not working alone? What's the name of your old crew again?"

Finn licked his lips. "Okay, okay, no need to get like that. I have a...friend. He gives me information sometimes when I need it. Stuff for heists, you know. Last time we talked, he handed me this." Finn held up a slip of paper. Lee leaned in, but Risa snatched the paper and brought it close to her own face.

"'The Mentalist is coming?' That's it? Is your friend some sort of Seer?"

Lee swallowed. The Mentalist worked with Bruce. Bruce was a Liminal. Had the Ceteri told him about the Barat too? Or had he traced her back to the hideout? She never should have come back. She should have found another place to hide.

Finn cleared his throat. "Teller. Sometimes. He was genuinely concerned for my well-being."

Lee heard the implication behind the last word. *Money.* Why would a grunt-man have a hired informant? She narrowed her eyes. "Did you tell him about the heist beforehand?"

"No, of course not. This is a real problem, Lee. If the Mentalist is there, Bruce could be there. We can't face them again, not after barely escaping them before."

Lee shuddered, and Finn's stare told her he'd noticed.

She gritted her teeth. "Look, their abilities won't work inside the Jewel Box any more than ours will."

"We think. Based on a singular experience. And tonight is

a wedding. Didn't Sam say they dropped a lot of security measures on wedding nights? Perhaps blocking magic is one of them?" Finn straightened his collar, shifting his weight from foot to food.

"It makes more sense to keep that one, given that celebrity weddings are famous for drunk thaumaturgic mishaps," Risa said dryly.

"If I see either of them, I'll stick 'em." Lee lifted the tight edge of her dress slightly, revealing the bottom of the thigh sheath that held her enchanted knife against her inner leg. "Think that'll create a big enough distraction for us to get away with the item?" She grinned, then dropped her skirt.

"You're not taking this seriously," Finn said.

"No." Lee stepped closer, getting into Finn's face. "This is my life on the line. A cure, Finn. Do you have any idea what that means to me? I'm not letting your fear ruin that."

"That's what I'm trying to get you to see—it's your life that you could lose. You seem to have no sense of self-preservation." Finn reached a hand up, then stopped when he touched the gelled surface of his hair.

"Do you want to do this? Or not? No one is going to force you, but if you try to prevent us from leaving, I'll have Sam knock you out and tie you up; don't think I won't." Lee paused, and when Finn didn't respond, she held her hand out. "Keys."

Finn's face hardened, and for a moment Lee thought he would refuse. She held her breath. She didn't actually want to hurt him, but he was being an idiot.

"No. I'll drive." He took the keys out of his pocket and gripped them tightly.

"I want to ride with Finn and Lee," Sam said, emerging from his room. Lee gaped. Sam stood draped in chains and rings, wearing the baggiest purple clothes and sunglasses and massive headphones.

"Yo," he said, making an awkward "hip" gesture.

"You're a DJ at the wedding?" Lee exclaimed. "But Sam, I thought you weren't coming. You never come on heists." There'd been no talk of it. In all of their planning, Sam had spoken as if he'd only be the bug in their ear, as usual.

Risa walked up and fist-bumped Sam. "Looking smooth, kid."

Lee smiled wider than she had in a while, emotion swelling so much in her chest she couldn't speak. To have Sam there meant more than she thought it could.

"I hope you're not mad, Lee. I wanted to surprise you. With Silas gone, I know you need all the help you can get. Plus, if abilities don't work in the Jewel Box anyway, maybe I won't be overwhelmed with everything up here." He circled a finger around his head. "If that's not the case, I've got these noise-cancelling headphones." He tapped them proudly.

"He's technically a backup, but we're arranging for the real DJ, some famous rapper, to get distracted and have Sam take over the set if necessary for distraction. Hopefully, that's not needed and Sam can meet us all at the basement," Risa said, shoving a few final items in the duffle bag. "Ready?"

Lee took a deep breath. "Let's go crash a wedding reception."

CHAPTER 32

The wedding at the Jewel Box was the perfect place for an ambush. Strobing lights, far too crowded, throbbing music. Adam felt for the gun he wore underneath his tux, hoping he wouldn't need to use it here. But if the Mentalist showed up... This was a wedding. Adam needed to smile. Or rather, Theodore, his cover, needed to smile. Even if it did look forced.

The dance floor rocked with a hip-hop sort of country, nothing like the music that played when Adam used to take his girl out dancing.

"It's loud," he shouted to Lee, who rolled her eyes and steamed ahead to the man checking people in at the door.

"Ribaldi," she shouted at him.

He glanced at Adam, then slid his finger down the list and tapped a name. "Theresa, and plus one?"

Lee nodded. "That's us."

The man tossed her a white cowgirl hat. "Compliments of Ray and Karly. Have a good time, you two."

Lee hesitated, then put the hat on her head. Adam stared.

The white, bedazzled hat combined with her glittering knee-length gown sent his head into a tailspin.

"Well, it's no beanie," she joked, lifting the hat as if to take it off.

"It certainly isn't," Adam agreed, still dumbstruck. He swallowed hard. "I think you should wear it."

She raised her eyebrows. "For the job, right?"

"To blend in. Definitely." Adam cleared his throat, then glanced over the crowd. There was Sam at the DJ booth, chatting with the rapper doing the music. The dance floor was packed. Adam realized that Lee was getting away from him and jogged to catch up.

"Don't drink anything. It's spiked," Lee said.

"You frequent celebrity weddings, then?" Adam replied.

Lee shot him a "get real" look. "No. Do you?"

Adam checked his watch. "How much longer do you think it'll be before they cut the cake?" The wedding reception details had included the various events, and the crew had determined that the easiest time to gather would be while everyone else was distracted. Meanwhile, they had to mingle, to be seen without making themselves memorable.

Lee moved further into the wide, open room, the lights from outside the Jewel Box strobing purple and blue through the clear glass ceiling. Light dappled across Lee's shoulders as Adam chased her down again. On an impulse, he grabbed her hand.

"Dance with me," he said.

Lee looked at him in alarm. "Do what, now?"

"Dance with me," he repeated.

Lee gave a hollow laugh. "Oh no," she wagged her finger and started backing away. "You're not going to do this to me."

Adam spread his hands, still holding onto one of hers. "Do

what? We're at a wedding." He drew her in with a snap of his wrist and clasped her against him. "It's all about playing the part. We have to be seen. Lurking around the edges of the room won't get us noticed enough for an alibi."

At that, he spun her across the floor, making nearby couples scatter. He hadn't danced in years, but the country swing steps came back readily.

Lee's eyes widened as he pushed her into the center of the floor and hopped her up against his hip.

"I've never done this before!" she shrieked.

Adam flipped her, and the floor cleared around them. He brought her in close for a few steps. "Just listen to the music and copy my steps. I'll lead," he whispered in her ear.

Lee pursed her lips but nodded, then dropped her gaze to his feet, following the steps he showed her.

"Now a spin," he said as he looped his arm around her and spun her out.

"How does a thug like you know how to dance like this?" Lee asked as he brought her back in.

"You've got to stop thinking of me as your average thug," Adam said, dipping her. She went down smooth and came up laughing and holding her hat, which made his smile widen. A few people around them clapped.

"How should I think of you?" Lee asked, her dark eyebrows baiting him with a suggestive wiggle. She followed the basic steps, her arms moving in time with his in a figure-eight overhead.

Adam considered, spending too long in the repetitive dance move while he thought. "I hope as a friend," he replied, then grabbed her hands and swung her between his legs, pulling her back up swiftly to meet his gaze.

She stared at him, one hand still trapped in his, the other

resting against his chest. She shoved him suddenly, but he kept a tight hold on her hand and spun her out, then in, then out and in again, before dipping her toward the floor with a dramatic swing. She nearly fell that time, not anticipating his moves.

"You gotta loosen up. Maintain light tension." Adam tugged on her hands to demonstrate.

"Are we even on a job anymore?" Lee hissed, sweat glistening on her forehead.

Adam stopped, breathing hard. Damn, it felt good to dance again. But Lee was right; they had a job to do. He had a job to do. And she was a distraction that he couldn't afford.

"I'm hungry," Lee said. She stalked off the dance floor toward the tables of food. Adam followed, picking up a plate half-heartedly. She seemed to trust him more now, but not entirely. So his first objective was complete. As for the second, to get to the Ceteri with Lee, well, that was in the works.

They stood off to the side of the dance floor, eating in silence. Risa passed by to refill eclairs and barely glanced at them.

"Sam seems to be doing well," Lee said after a moment.

"Yeah," Adam replied. "Have you tried going Liminal?"

Lee held out her hand, focusing on it as if something would change, but it remained visible, and Adam's magic-sensing was strangely quiet. He'd grown used to the various strengths of clicks he received throughout the day as indications of large and small uses of thaumaturgy. Now, with his sensor quiet, he felt off-kilter. He had the urge to reach for his gun every time he saw someone approach.

Lee lowered her hand. "Nothing. It's strange, you know?

I've grown so used to it. I wonder, if I could live here, would Liminality still kill me?"

"It stops the use of your magic, not its effects on your body," Adam said, pushing his hands into his pockets and rocking on his heels. He glanced towards the stage, where the happy couple gleamed in white cowboy and cowgirl formal wear, beaming at each other as the DJ announced they would slice the cake.

Servers descended, carrying the cake, a towering five-tier monstrosity decorated in lace and rope and miniature cowboy boots, of all things.

"That's our cue," Adam said.

Lee nodded and walked alongside him as they made their way to the hidden door to the basement. Beyond the kitchens, Lee disappeared into the ladies' restroom where Risa had hidden the bag. She came out wearing the slouchy orange beanie, a black t-shirt and olive-green cargo pants. Her feet were bare.

"That's better," she said, brushing her hands down the front of her clothes. "A girl can breathe in this."

"Want to preen a bit longer, or are you ready to go?" Adam asked, keeping his tone light. She looked just as amazing in the heist gear as she did in the dress.

She scowled, then rushed ahead of him, pulling out her lock pick kit. They passed utility rooms and meeting areas before reaching the end of a stark grey hall. Adam couldn't believe they didn't pass anyone.

He kept watch while Lee picked the locked door, and then it swung wide, revealing a dark stairwell. He couldn't see a light switch anywhere on the wall.

Adam caught movement at the end of the hall and nudged Lee. "Get in."

She skipped down several steps, and he squeezed in beside her, holding the door just before it closed so it wouldn't slam shut. He slid a piece of tape over the door latch, keeping it unlocked for Sam and Risa.

Lee's warmth shifted away from his side as she started down.

"Shouldn't we wait for Risa and Sam?" Adam asked, looking back toward the door. He couldn't hear anything outside, no footsteps, nothing.

"They'll be here in a bit. Come on." Lee's footsteps pattered in the stairwell.

Adam released the door handle and followed. Descending a staircase blind was a new experience. He couldn't see his hands, his feet, anything. The stairs wound on longer than Adam expected. How far down did they go?

He fell into a rhythm and didn't know the staircase had ended until he slammed into Lee.

"Ow!" she whispered. "Shhh!"

He hadn't spoken, but he understood. She was listening. He strained his hearing, listening for any shuffling or walking or a goat bleating. Anything that indicated the place they'd come in the first time was close.

A golden glow emanated from the fanny pack around Lee's waist, illuminating their path and casting long, distorted shadows on the brick walls. Without a word, Adam and Lee walked forward together. Around the first corner, the path split into two.

"A maze," Lee breathed.

Adam glanced at the ceiling. It rose so high he almost couldn't see it. Had they really descended that far, or was it an optical illusion? Adam stretched his arms out, nearly touching the walls on either side. He reached an arm up.

"Eight feet tall, six feet wide," he reported to Lee.

"Couldn't the glasses have told you that?" Lee asked, pointing at Adam. "You did bring them with you."

Adam fumbled for the glasses in his inner breast pocket. He'd forgotten about them. He put them on his face, grinning as the numbers flashed. "I'm not far off. I'm going to climb the wall and see what's up there."

"Careful nothing sees you," Lee warned.

Adam backed up and ran, then jumped and pushed off one wall, bounced to the other wall, and grasped the top of the first wall again. He grabbed the top surface, which was covered in goop.

"Ugh," he said, lifting his hand. He couldn't see much. Lee's light didn't reach up that high. He tried to scrape his hand on the wall, only succeeding partway. He heaved himself up, his suit picking up streaks of the goop.

The maze room was the size and shape of two football fields side by side. The glasses did the calculations for him, telling him the height of the ceiling, and the distance to each wall. Question was, did the Jewel Box vault reside in the center of the maze or at the end? As soon as he thought about the distance to the center, the glasses measured for him. If he could get a bit higher, could he see the path to the center?

He stood, but the monotone color of the brick maze walls made it difficult to discern the path.

"What's he doing up there?" Sam stage-whispered from below. Adam looked down, relieved to see Sam had joined them. He still wore his DJ outfit, except without the heavy chains and jewelry.

Adam jumped down, ignoring the slight pain that radiated through his feet as he hit the floor.

"Where's Risa?" he asked.

Sam shook his head. "I didn't see her. The servers disappeared after they served the cake, and when she wasn't there, I assumed she'd met up with you already. Maybe she got stuck somewhere?"

Risa had the duffle bag, which included the rest of the spelled items. Adam had grabbed the glasses and ruby, Lee had the paperweight and her enchanted knife, and Sam... Adam hadn't seen Sam grab anything. He hoped the man hadn't come unprepared.

Lee tapped her earpiece. "Risa, are you there?" They waited a moment, but Lee shook her head. "No response."

"She might not be able to talk right now," Adam said. "She'll catch up. This maze isn't too large, we could run through it pretty quickly. I think our target is at the center of the maze. If we split up any time there's a branch-off and use the earpieces to communicate, hopefully we won't draw the attention of the chupacabras. They might not even be in the maze."

"Look at you taking charge," Lee said.

Adam couldn't tell if she was offended or not. This was her heist, after all.

Lee continued without looking at him. "These walls look about the same as the ones by the goat cage the other night. Most likely the chupacabras are still sleeping. Maybe they wake up at midnight."

"In that case, we've got an hour. Let's go." Adam cringed as the words left his mouth. Damn his take-charge attitude.

Lee shot him a perplexed look, then took the lead at a fast walking pace. They came across their first split around the next corner, a two-way path.

Adam waited for Lee to direct him.

"I'll take the right with Sam. Adam, you take the left. If you find a dead end, tell everyone and backtrack to catch up."

Adam hated to leave Lee, but orders were orders, and he couldn't think of a reason to send Sam instead of himself down the other path. He'd explore it as quickly as possible and rest knowing that Lee wasn't alone.

A yell startled him. It wasn't Lee, but it was female. A deep, ethereal baying of hounds accompanied it. The chupacabras.

The hunt was on.

Was that Risa he'd heard being chased by the chupacabras? He should go back and help. But he had to get through the maze to help Lee. Adam picked up his pace, running around each corner. He arrived at a dead end.

Lee's voice crackled through the speaker in his ear. "We've hit a split pathway. That yell was Risa, we're circling back to help her."

"No. I hit a dead end. Each of you choose a path, and I'll circle back for Risa." Adam pumped his arms. Lee's confirmation came through his ear, and he gained renewed energy knowing she was moving farther away from the known danger.

But Lee had the paperweight that they'd planned to use against the chupacabras. His gun was useless. What did he have to fight with?

The ruby weighed in his pocket. He hadn't figured out what it did, despite poring over it for hours before the heist.

Adam reached the first junction and took a right, heading back toward the entrance. Risa came into view, sweaty and panting. She had the duffle bag slung over one shoulder as she ran. Adam joined her.

"It's a left ahead," he told her.

"I saw one. The chupacabra. It leapt over the top of my head as I entered the maze," Risa replied breathlessly.

"It was walking on top of the walls?" Adam asked in bewilderment.

"Jumping across. I saw it jump down on the other side." She pointed to the wall at her right, and Adam realized he could hear the dog-like creature breathing heavily.

"Why is it over there? It could easily jump—"

He stopped talking as a chupacabra vaulted over the eight-foot wall and landed in the hall behind them. It snarled, mouth dripping. Another creature darted across a wall ahead of them, then jumped down, blocking their progress. Adam and Risa stood with their backs together.

"Anything in that magic bag that can help us?" Adam asked Risa. He tapped his earpiece. "We're surrounded. Keep going. We'll stall them." He grimaced, knowing full well that the odds were not in their favor as they faced the two hungry beasts.

Risa withdrew two containers from the bag. She handed one to Adam. The clear container held a white, granular substance. Salt.

Next she brought out what looked like a bottle of water with a spray nozzle attached, which Adam assumed was holy water. He popped the lid off his container.

"Let's go," he said, grabbing a fistful of the salt just as the first chupacabra facing him leapt into the air.

Adam flung the salt. It flashed and hissed as it touched the chupacabra's face, and the monster yelped, rubbing at the irritating burns with its clawed feet. Adam chucked another handful, keeping the chupacabra occupied and unable to strike. The salt wouldn't kill the creature, but it would work at holding it at bay. At least until Adam ran out.

Behind him, the chupacabra Risa faced let out a strangled yelp and started whining and cowering.

"That's right. Bad dog," Risa said, working the pump on her spray nozzle. The warmth of her back left Adam's, and he assumed she was moving forward. He started walking backward to keep up.

"We need to get around these guys," he said.

"Got any ideas?" Risa replied in a strained voice.

Adam glanced up at the wall. The moment he jumped, he'd be dead meat. He wasn't a Runner with super speed.

"Got that hammer?" Adam asked.

"Yeah. But no one's been brave enough to test it."

"Hand it over." He reached back over his shoulder. The cool metal of the iron hammer's handle slid into his palm, and ahead of him, a third chupacabra joined the first. His container of salt was frightfully low. He had two handfuls left, and the first chupacabra was wise to him.

It clung to the wall on Adam's left, then darted to the right, zigzagging towards him. The other chupacabra shot straight for him and got a fist of salt in the face. It howled. Adam stopped moving backwards and held the hammer in front of him. The runes glowed purple. If he needed any special words to activate it, he was doomed. All he could do was hope that it was more than a pretty relic.

The chupacabra launched itself, snarling, its eyes bloodthirsty, the spines on its back erect.

Adam swung the hammer. It made contact with the chupacabra and a thunderous boom echoed through the chamber. A sonic shockwave threw the chupacabra back, sending it skidding across the floor. It struck the wall and lay still.

Risa fell as the ground shook, and the other chupacabras

cowered until the shaking stopped. Only Adam's stance remained solid.

He admired the hammer for a split second. He'd have to be careful not to take out a team member with the force of his blows, but at least now he had some hope that they could defeat these blood-sucking beasts.

Adam raised the hammer like a baseball bat. "Come on, you," he encouraged the other chupacabra facing him. It raised its nose and howled, the tips of its spines pulsing red. Then, its eyes lit up. The howl pitched higher than before, and Adam's brain tipped with dizziness.

Risa fumbled with his earpieces from behind, tapping them in a certain rhythm. All sound muted. The pulsing red spines on the creature's back were still nauseating, but not as much as before.

"Thanks," he said loudly. He readjusted his grip on the hammer. Hopefully Lee was having a better time of things than he was.

He blinked. *Three* of the chupacabras advanced on him now. There'd only been one a moment before, but now there were definitely three, all with red spines and arched backs, their tongues dripping with saliva. They converged on Adam and Risa.

"How many you got?" Adam's voice came through the earpiece.

"Two!" Risa replied.

Five chupacabras, and the sixth one that Adam had downed. That accomplishment paled in the face of their new reality. He wished Lee was here with the miniature sun-like device, but wishing would only get him killed.

He couldn't charge; it would leave Risa exposed. So he waited, back against the maze wall.

From behind the two chupacabras near Risa, a brilliant light shone out of the darkness. Lee and Sam raced in, nearly running into the monsters. One monster glanced at the light and the red glow on its back spines turned to yellow, then white, and his hollow eyes glowed like molten orbs. Light shot out of every extremity and each spine on its back, then passed through the monster, disintegrating it.

One of the chupacabras facing Adam combusted as well, its physical form crumbling to the brick-covered floor.

Three remained, eyes covered, tails tucked. Smart creatures. They had somehow known not to look.

"Nice timing," Adam said.

"We figured you could use the help. Good news, we found a door," Lee said.

"Bad news, we still have chupacabra trouble." Risa jutted her chin towards the one that inched toward them despite the light from the golden paperweight in Lee's hand still shining.

Adam charged at the chupacabra, raising the hammer and bringing it down with a thunderous strike. The chupacabra dodged and darted forward, jaws snapping toward Adam. It bowled him over, and he dropped the hammer with a shout.

Lee raised the paperweight, but the chupacabra had its eyes tightly shut and seemed to be unaffected. Adam would be more intrigued if he wasn't rolling out from beneath the creature, narrowly missing having his head crushed in its jaws. It chased after him. Adam had to get it to open its eyes. He punched it once, twice, and landed the third strike as the beast darted in for the kill. His fist struck its nose square on, and the dog-like creature's eyes shot open as it yelped.

The light consumed it in an instant, and Adam breathed in at the wrong moment, getting dog-dust in his throat. He gasped and choked.

Lee rushed over, peering down at him. "You okay?"

"Not injured," he wheezed. "The others?"

Lee pointed. "They jumped over that wall. I think they've had enough for now."

"They might still ambush us later," Adam warned.

"I'm keeping this out," Lee tapped the paperweight. It was too bright. Adam had to squint to look at it. They couldn't keep it on if they wanted to be able to see clearly. The numbers flashing across the lenses of the glasses weren't helping his ability to focus. He took them off, then folded them and slipped them into his breast pocket.

Adam stood. Dust cascaded off him. Well, that was one suit ruined. He dusted off the breast of the coat, then shrugged. He'd never been covered in the cremated remains of a legendary monster before. First time for everything.

"We made it," Sam said. His face shone with sweat, and he seemed a bit out of breath. "We ran all the way here."

"Sam was a champion," Lee said, giving him an encouraging smile. "Come on. We've got to find that door again. Think you remember the way back?"

Sam did. He led them through every turn, only having to double back once before they came to a door in an otherwise dead-end wall.

Lee had her picks out in an instant and started working the lock. It seemed to take longer than it normally would have. A limp curl stuck to her face as she worked.

Adam bounced on his heels and stretched, not wanting his muscles to seize up.

Risa gazed up at the walls around them. "I wish I could reach the spirits of this place. They could tell me what the path ahead looks like."

"I tried getting a look earlier." Adam raised his hands.

They weren't sticky anymore, but to his shock they'd turned a deep shade of indigo.

Sam snorted. "You look like an alien."

"It's not on my face, is it?" Adam asked with alarm, feeling the blue skin. It felt normal.

"Vain much?" Risa asked, folding her arms. "Your face is fine." She turned her attention back to Lee, who eyed the open pick case with a look of concentration.

"I don't have the pick I need," Lee said, frustration lacing her voice. "This lock is unlike anything I've encountered. It keeps changing. Every time I get the tumblers in place, the whole thing moves, like a living puzzle."

"Stand back," Adam said, raising the glowing hammer. Its runes lit up again and it seemed to tug at his hands, as if the hammer was eager to strike again.

"A man with a hammer," Risa said.

"Every job looks like a nail," Sam finished. They fist-bumped each other, grinning.

Lee stepped away, folding her pick case, and Adam grunted, swinging the hammer around and striking the metal door handle.

The door hummed, soaking up the blow from the hammer. The walls and floor of the maze only trembled slightly, all of the hammer's force absorbed into the door. Then it went still. Adam rubbed the back of his neck, staring in disbelief. How had that not worked?

The wood creaked. A crack of light appeared around the edge of the door, and Lee pushed past Adam, grasping the edge of the door and pulling it open to reveal a brightly lit room lined with plants and decorated with statues.

A zen garden at the center of the maze. They entered single-file, all gaping up at the canopy of leaves. There had to be an artificial light source on the ceiling. There had to be a ceiling. Adam couldn't comprehend any other explanation for the singular glow lighting up the place.

Ahead of him, Lee turned with the stone pathway and a gasp tore from her. She froze on the spot, and Adam bumped into her.

Sitting cross-legged near the center of a stone path shaped like a swirl sat the Mentalist, smiling at them with an infuriating calm.

Adam drew out his gun, but he was too slow. Slower than Lee with her knife and her cat-like reflexes as she threw the blade dead-center towards the man's heart.

CHAPTER 33

Lee knew the knife would strike exactly where she'd sent it the moment it left her hand. But as it flew, a blueish-green mist gathered into the form of an ethereal person, who caught the blade in its hand. It straightened from a crouch, its full height nearing ten feet. Lee gazed up at the looming being.

"There is no violence here, save what I am forced to bestow on those who break the rules." The being's voice had a deep alto timbre.

Lee swallowed. "Who are you?"

"I am Rael, guardian of the Garden of Bliss and the Mythic Vaults." The guardian spoke slowly with a voice like pealing wind chimes.

"Are you here to stop us from getting into the vaults?" Lee asked.

"I'm here to ensure that only those with a true need enter the Mythic Vaults, and to guide those who are worthy," the guardian said. She still held Lee's knife tight in one hand. Would Lee be able to get it back?

Lee glanced at the rest of the crew, but they remained

silent. Finn scowled at the Mentalist. The good news was that if they couldn't hurt him, he couldn't hurt them. And his abilities didn't work. She didn't like it, but she would deal if it got her into that vault.

"Where are the vaults?"

The guardian straightened. "They are protected. If you meet the conditions, you may enter."

"What are the conditions?" Lee asked, impatience making her shift her weight from foot to foot as she rubbed her hands against her pants.

"The one among your number with the truest need may enter the vault. Only one of you may enter in a given hour. Withdraw a single item, and you will be allowed to exit. Take more than you have declared and the door will not reopen. Lie to me about your true intent, and I will kill you."

Risa stepped forward, swiping her hands through the air. "Wait, wait, hold on. Is his friend in there?" She pointed at the Mentalist, who stared at them with an infuriatingly calm expression.

"I do not keep track of who leaves, only who enters," the guardian intoned.

Lee narrowed her eyes. Bruce was Liminal. If the Ceteri told him about the item they needed to save their home world, would he be incentivized to come here? Or had he somehow caught wind of her plans to be here and had come to intercept her? Either way, she was in trouble. She had to get the Barat before Bruce did. But what if he already had it?

"Can I have my knife back?" Lee asked.

The guardian shook its giant head, the turquoise hair flowing around its seemingly intangible body. "No weapons within the vault. But I will give it back to you when you return."

Lee turned to her companions, trying to ignore the Mentalist. "I need to get in there. Can you guys handle him?" She jerked her head towards the Mentalist.

"He doesn't have any abilities. He won't be a problem," Finn said. But his forehead creased with worry. "Lee, I don't want you going in there alone against Bruce. Maybe I can—"

"The guardian said only one," Lee insisted.

Risa murmured in agreement. "Use the earpieces," she said. "Tell us what you see. Keep it turned on and we might be able to hear Bruce speaking. We'll help you get out of any sticky situations." She smiled reassuringly.

Sam gave Lee a big thumbs up.

Lee breathed in. "This is a trap. Guaranteed."

"But if what the guardian says is true, Bruce won't have any weapons on him. You still have the Way Mary. Use it to your advantage." Finn gestured to her wrist, where the jade beads sat smooth against Lee's skin.

"Right. Okay. See you soon, then." Lee stepped up to the guardian, squaring her shoulders. "I'm ready."

"State your true need and the item you desire." The guardian said. It drew a sword out of the air, a sword of smoke and glittering particles like dust motes. Lee swallowed. Probably wouldn't feel like smoke and dust if it struck her.

"I need to get the Barat Lapis Lazuli Statue from within the vault. So that...so that my body can be healed."

The guardian considered her. "That is not your true need."

Lee panicked. Healing from her Liminality was the reason she had come. It was everything she had worked for, everything she wanted. But why?

The sword rose in the air, and understanding rushed into Lee. Her future had been stolen from her when she became

Liminal, and again when Shane died. She wanted it back, and she would fight for it.

Lee looked at the guardian. "I want to live. And I want love. These are my true needs."

The guardian halted. It lowered its sword and bowed its head, then melted into the ground. Where it vanished, the ground rumbled and a hole opened, showing stairs leading into the ground.

Lee walked forward with long strides, then descended the staircase, taking one last look at her crew watching her. She adjusted the beanie and ducked out of sight. Immediately, the hole closed up overhead, and a bright, pale light lit up at the base of the stairs.

The vault room held eight massive vault-style doors, each one with a digital code pad.

Energy thrummed through Lee as she crossed the threshold into the hall between the vaults. Her hands and arms tingled with the pins and needles sensation that always accompanied her when she went Liminal.

But she couldn't go Liminal, could she?

Lee reached for the veil between realms, and the buzzing intensified. The red outline flickered around her body, and the bright lights in the vault room dimmed. Ley lines blazed into view, criss-crossing across the vault room in dozens of directions. They were the shortest ley lines Lee had ever seen, and she'd never seen so many concentrated in one place, either. She didn't know much about how the science of the ley lines worked. But maybe it had to do with the concentration of magical items in a single place.

What she did know was that with the ley lines entering and exiting each vault, she could use her Liminality to see what was inside without triggering any alarms or wasting time trying to figure out the codes.

She phased back to Earth's realm and tapped her earpiece. "I'm inside. There's eight vaults. I can go Liminal again. There's so much energy in here, you guys. It's unbelievable. The value of these magical items they must have..." The thought trailed off. She could only take the one she'd mentioned to the guardian. The statue for the Ceteri.

"Roger," Risa replied. "Be careful. Bruce is in there somewhere."

"I don't see him. But he could be inside one of the vaults. I'll keep you updated." Lee left her earpiece activated and went Liminal.

There was a singular node on the floor halfway down the aisle where every ley line intersected. Lee stepped onto the illuminated circle of energy and pointed herself in the direction of the ley line she wanted to ride, letting it tug her into the air. She zipped across faster than she'd ever traveled before, and in an instant she was standing inside the bank vault.

Lee phased out of the Liminal realm and stood in the pitch dark for a moment before realizing she still had the paperweight. She pushed the rune on the bottom, activating it inside the fanny pack. It glowed, but didn't blind her through the slit in the pack.

The vault was packed with crates. Crates of all sizes, stacked neatly with numbers painted on the sides. Other than the numbers, Lee didn't see any other means of identification. The description the Ceteri gave her eliminated the smallest boxes that a foot-tall statue wouldn't fit into, and the largest boxes, which theoretically held larger items. But what if they held multiple smaller items?

Lee considered the crates, then turned back to the ley line. She jumped across the hall to a different vault. It was practically identical to the first. Different layout of boxes, but the same situation. She jumped again, and again, and again, despairing as she prepared to jump to the seventh vault.

Nearly identical crates filled every single one. She would have to pry open each viable crate and look inside for the Barat. In here, that would take days.

Lee landed in the seventh vault and was blinded by a green light that filled the room. She covered her eyes with her arm, but not before she caught sight of the man sitting on a throne made of crates in the center of the room. At his side, a single crate sat open, but Lee couldn't see inside.

"Bruce," she said, hating the surprise in her voice. She'd known she would find him. It had just been a matter of when.

"You found Bruce?" asked Finn through the earpiece.

She stared at the man. He wasn't wearing the lab coat anymore, but a well-cut grey suit and a dark purple shirt beneath. He lounged with his hands in his pockets, staring at her.

"You botched a perfect opportunity to be part of something larger than yourself, you know," Bruce said. "You let me down."

"I'd be sorry, except you didn't have my consent to impregnate me," Lee shot back. What this man had done, what he continued to do, was despicable. She wouldn't stand for women being used to breed more people cursed with this magic that stole life.

Bruce tsked and sat up straighter, uncrossing his legs. "So closed-minded. But hopefully we can change that."

"I'm never consenting to your 'procedure,'" Lee snapped.

"Oh no, we've moved past that. I'm interested in entering

into a different venture with you, my fellow Liminal. The Ceteri contacted you, did they not?"

"How do you know that?"

"Because they contacted me. And they told me they contacted others, and you wouldn't be here, in this fault, looking for this item—" He gestured to the open crate and smirked. "—if they hadn't contacted you. Or at least, the odds are extremely unlikely."

"How did you get in here?" Lee moved closer, craning to see inside the box. She caught a gleam among the styrofoam inside the crate, but the green lighting made it hard to see anything more. Where was the light coming from anyway? Lee realized it just seemed to emanate from the air around Bruce. He must have activated a magical item of some kind, like her paperweight, which still glowed from inside the pack at her waist.

"When you're wealthy, you know people. I knew about these vaults long before the Ceteri contacted me. I've even participated in an auction here. They're by invitation only, you know, and you have to have contributed a hefty sum to the operation of the Jewel Box. So when the Ceteri mentioned the item was here, I immediately called my acquaintance and asked for a favor. It only took a small bribe to also narrow down which vault the statue would be located in."

"Then why not just take it and go?" Lee asked. "You got here well before me. Why wait?"

"I knew you were coming. I had my Mentalist brother trace your signature and listen in on your plans. He was going to collect you for me again, but then I had an idea that I thought would be so much more fun."

Bruce clasped his hands, pointing two fingers out of the fist towards Lee. "Picture this. You and I, searching for the other three items the Ceteri need and taking them in together. We both get what we want, we have an advantage over any others the Ceteri have contacted with both of us pooling all of our resources and intelligence, and we're not fighting each other every step of the way to get it."

Lee had inched forward again while he was talking, getting a much better look at what was in the crate. The feminine statue made of sparkling blue stone with veins of gold and white marbling down one side stared lifelessly up at her from the confines of its box. She glanced back at Bruce, who was watching her.

"You want to work together? Why not work with one of your other girls?" She spat the last word out. He had a room full of captivated Liminals who he could persuade to help. Why not enroll one of them?

"Ah, but you, my dear, are an entirely different creature from them. Out of all of them, none tried to escape. They succumbed to imprisonment, and every single one took the compensation offered. Even Miss Lily, who I hope you're taking good care of since she left."

His tone took on an offended note, and Lee found herself smiling. He was put-out about Lily, was he?

"She's in a safe place. Safer than with you."

"Is she getting proper maternity care? Are you feeding her a balanced diet? What will you do when she goes into labor?" Bruce's voice grew increasingly angry as he spoke, getting louder and tighter as he went.

Lee stared at him, refusing to give him any more information. After a moment, Bruce calmed himself and straightened his tux sleeves with a jerk of each arm.

"Never mind her. This is about you. Working with me. You must see how mutually beneficial this would be."

Lee's stomach clenched. Her fingernails bit into the palms of her hands. She wanted to scream that she would never work with him. *Stay calm and think for once!*

Her earpiece crackled as someone spoke to her, but through her raging thoughts, Lee couldn't discern what the voice said. She only had eyes for Bruce and the open crate at his feet. Could she get to it fast enough?

"I will never work with you," Lee said. And then she skipped into the Liminal realm, darting for the box. She reached for it as she let go of the Liminal realm and became physical again, hoping she'd won a split moment catching Bruce off guard, but Bruce snatched her wrist out of the box before she could grab the Barat.

Lee went Liminal again, but Bruce's hold on her arm held as he phased with her. She twisted her arm around, wrenching his arm. He let go with a grunt of pain, then backed up until the box was at the back of his legs and charged her.

She tried to dodge, but Bruce tackled her. His hands went to her throat and he sat on her stomach. "If you're not with me, you're against me," he hissed, hair flopping onto his face.

Lee scratched at his fingers crushing against her windpipe, then thrust her hand into his gut. He doubled over, relaxing his grip on her throat. She knocked his arm away, and he lost his balance, falling towards her. Lee grabbed his face and smashed her forehead into his nose, then bucked him off and rolled the opposite direction.

She rolled until she reached a ley line node and crossed into another vault. Bruce would follow any moment, if for no other reason than to take out his competition. Jumping twice more exhausted her, and she lay flat on the vault floor, breathing deeply. She needed some luck.

She held up her arm and squeezed the next bead between

her fingers. It activated, and a flood of energy filled her. It felt different from the time she'd used it to escape from the Mentalist and Bruce before. An awareness filled her. Somewhere to her left, back the direction of the vault that held the Barat, she sensed a signature that she knew was Bruce, without any other evidence. And then she heard his thoughts.

She used a ley line.

And accompanying that thought was another sensation, an urgency to follow, to find her, to make sure she didn't live to become even more of a nuisance. She was sensing his intentions, like Sam did.

Lee blinked and lifted the bracelet. Did the Way Mary absorb more than just luck? Was there a chance it drew in different thaumaturgic abilities as well? Lee sat up, then stood and crossed to another ley line. Too late she sensed Bruce drawing closer, and then he appeared on the node where she stood and bowled into her.

Hot rage overwhelmed Lee, and immediately her body mass changed, bulking up, growing taller. Bruce gaped at her as she became a monstrous body-builder version of herself. She roared and swung a fist his way. Bruce dodged and slammed into some crates.

Lee's hand smashed several crates open. Items flew everywhere, the pinpricks of light flashing as they clattered to the ground. Something fragile broke, and the magic wafted out of it and vanished in the air like evaporating water.

"Lee, you have to tell us what's going on," Finn shouted into Lee's ear.

"She's hulked out," Sam shouted. "Listen Lee, I know this is a lot to handle right now, but you have to calm down. Breathe in, breathe out. Count to four each time. I know you can count to four."

The logical thoughts struggled to come, but the breathing Lee could handle. She breathed in for four counts, then out, and repeated the pattern until her body started to shrink. Bruce hadn't moved. Had she knocked him out?

"Talk to me, Lee," Sam said, his breathing quick and heavy on the other end of the line.

"I'm here," Lee gasped. "How do you...do that, Sam?" The hunger hit her in the next moment, and she doubled over as her stomach complained. She didn't have anything to eat, and the next wave of pain forced her to double over. Bruce got to his hands and knees where he'd fallen between the crates.

"How did *you* do that?" Sam replied.

"The Way Mary. It somehow stored your ability." Lee went Liminal and grabbed a ride on the nearest ley line, hopping from vault to vault until she reached the seventh vault again. The Barat gleamed from its styrofoam nest in the box. She considered the box. She couldn't carry anything while traveling in the Liminal realm, except what was attached to her body. Her clothes, the fanny pack...

Bruce's intentions hit her like a wave as he traveled closer to her. Lee knew exactly where he would land coming off the ley line he rode. She was ready for him, pressing another bead on the Way Mary. If the previous one had given her Sam's abilities, would the others have stored abilities from other people she'd been around? Lee felt a surge, different than the awareness of Sam's ability. It added itself onto her body, a clinging coldness accompanied with a sharp sense of several spirits lingering nearby.

"Come here," Lee spoke, her voice changing, lowering in pitch and gaining an echo. She felt resistance from several of the spirits, but with a few more persuading words, they drifted towards her. Lee smiled. She could talk to the dead, like Risa.

She pointed at Bruce and the spirits went to him, swirling about his head.

Bruce swatted in front of his face, then brushed at the back of his head. His arm motions became more agitated, and he shrieked.

Lee bent towards the box again. She'd grab the statue and try to stick it into her shirt or something. She had to get out of here and back to her crew.

Just before she could touch the statue, Bruce beat her to it, pushing her hand away and yanking the statue out of its packing.

"Not so fast," he gloated, holding the statue with both hands. "I am, after all, the one who found it—"

He stopped. His hands vibrated. An electric-like shock passed through him, and his body went as stiff as a board. He fell to the ground with a solid thud.

Finn asked for an update through her earpiece, but Lee couldn't speak. Bruce convulsed, flickering with red light as he must have tried to go Liminal and failed. His skin shriveled like a raisin in the sun until it looked mummified, and then his skeleton crumbled into dust. The statue thunked to the ground on top of Bruce's suitcoat, gleaming innocently in the stream of light emanating from the paperweight at Lee's waist.

Lee swallowed past the lump in her throat.

"Come in, Lee. Lee?" Finn was shouting. He sounded beside himself, but Lee couldn't think of what to say. She crept closer to the pile of dust that was Bruce's remains. Had the statue done that to him? Would it disintegrate her, too, if she touched it?

"Uh, Bruce touched the statue. It, uh, turned him into dust." Lee wiped her sweaty hands on her pants.

"Dust? Did you say dust?" Risa asked.

"Yeah. He's just...gone." Lee said.

"Don't touch it," Finn barked. "It might do the same to you."

"I had thought about that, yes." Lee replied. She knelt beside the gruesome pile and picked up the edges of Bruce's suitcoat. She pulled one arm and one opposite edge up and tied them clumsily. She repeated the action with the other parts of the coat, until she had a bundle.

"I've covered it. I'm going to pick it up," Lee said.

"Don't-"

Lee ignored whatever Finn said and, taking a shaky breath, she grasped the bundle and stood up, squeezing her eyes shut.

Nothing happened.

Lee opened her eyes. The statue's polished surface was muted by a fine coat of dust. Bruce's remains. Lee shuddered. The man had been horrible, but his death was one she wouldn't wish on anyone. Had the Ceteri intended that fate for her? Why not warn her about the statue's properties? Thinking about it made her stomach churn.

"Okay, it worked, I think. I'm not dust yet." She faced the vault door, and her heart plummeted. "Uh, guys, we have a problem."

Unless she dropped the Barat, Lee was trapped inside the vault with no way to get out.

CHAPTER 34

The walls of the vault seemed to close in on Lee. She could take a ley line out of there any moment she wanted, but she'd have to leave the statue behind. After everything she'd been through to get there, she wasn't going to let a closed door stop her.

"Sam, I need your help. How can I open a heavy vault door from the inside?" she asked over her earpiece.

Sam's voice came online. "Got any explosives?"

Lee lifted her gaze to the ceiling. "No, Sam. I don't carry explosives."

"Really? Okay. Well, most modern bank vault doors come with a kill switch that can open the door if someone is trapped inside. But it will likely set off alarms and alert the police."

"Where would I find it?" Lee asked, shifting the bundle from her right arm to her left so she could use her dominant hand more freely. She scanned the wall outside the door.

"Look for a metal box. Like a fuse box," Sam said.

Sweat dripped down Lee's forehead. Man, the vault was warm. And it didn't have much oxygen left. Her head ached.

She had to duck and maneuver around the crates lining the walls. There, in the center of the room behind a tall stack of crates, was the box on the wall she was looking for. She set the Barat on the floor, still tucked in the suit coat, and clambered over the crates. She pushed several off the top of the stack, letting them crash to the floor, then pulled open the box.

Switches of all kinds peppered the electronic board inside.

"They aren't labeled. Do I just start clicking?"

"Is there a red one?" Sam asked.

That seemed oddly specific. Lee spotted a red one. "Yes. Are kill switches always red?" Lee's hand hovered over it.

"No. But red is a good place to start. Press it." He sounded confident, and he was their tech guy, but Lee still hesitated. It could set off an alarm without opening the door. It could spring a trap of some kind.

"Lee, you have to get out of there. Start flipping switches!" Finn said.

"You guys need to leave. Now. You'll be intercepted first if the police respond."

"We're leaving," Finn replied after a moment.

Knowing her crew would get out, Lee snapped into action. She flipped the red switch. Nothing happened, at least not on her end. Frustrated and desperate, Lee flattened her hand and flipped half a dozen switches at once.

The vault door hissed open. A blue light turned on in the vault and a siren started wailing.

"Door's open. I'm out!" Lee yelled into her earpiece. She vaulted off of the boxes, landing in a crouch, then sprang for the black cloth bundle that held the Barat. She ran for the door, shoving it open, then bolted down the hall and up the stairs to the garden.

No siren blared here, and the guardian had vanished. Her

crew, and the Mentalist, appeared to have fled. Lee saw her knife resting on one of the stones on the swirling pathway and grabbed it. She ran for the door at the end of the garden. It had solidified somehow. Lee pounded on it, panicking until she forced herself to take a deep breath. What did she have that she could use to break it down?

She reached into her fanny pack and pulled out a pen. Not just any pen, but the pen that they'd got from the City Museum. The one Risa had scribbled with, making a hole in their kitchen table.

Lee pushed the cap at the end and the nib popped out, ready to draw. She drew a hasty line up the length of the door, across the top, then down the other side, making sure to connect all of her lines. The wood hissed and smoked, then a bright orange line of laser light burned through the door. Lee kicked the rectangle piece she'd traced and it fell to the ground outside the garden.

Lee grinned and closed the pen, tucking it safely back in her pack. Adjusting her grip on the Barat, she ran into the maze. She had to remember the way through in reverse. Left, right, right, left. After a second dead-end she considered climbing to the top, but she remembered Finn's warning about touching the walls and the stuff he got on his hands. No telling what that would do to him.

She passed on the idea and kept running. Was it taking longer than it had before? It didn't look familiar anymore, and looking at the ceiling, Lee realized she was facing an entirely different direction, headed away from the entrance she'd come in. She must have taken a wrong turn.

"Guys, I'm lost," Lee said into the earpiece. In the distance, she could still hear the siren going off.

"I'm coming back," Finn said.

"I'll come too," Sam offered.

Risa sighed. "Guess I'm coming too."

"Not all of you," Lee said. "Just Finn." She couldn't believe the words coming out of her mouth. Why Finn, of all of them?

"Stay where you are," Finn said to Lee.

Lee wasn't sure that was the best advice in a maze like this where who-knew-what could find her before Finn, but she did need a rest. Her belly ached with hunger from her time using Sam's ability through the Way Mary, and the Barat was heavy for a foot-tall statue. She put it on the ground and put her head against her knees. Silence, except for the alarm still going off in the distance. Was the wedding still happening upstairs? Lee couldn't be certain, but there was no reason it wouldn't be. She hadn't been down here that long.

The sound of running footsteps echoed in the maze.

"I just entered," Finn's voice came over the tiny speaker in Lee's ear. She turned her head sideways looking down the hall she assumed he'd come through any minute.

A shadow arched on the wall and she frowned. It didn't look like a person, more like…more like…

A chupacabra.

The creature trotted into view, tongue lolling like a harm-less dog, but the moment it saw Lee it licked its chops and paused, sniffing the air. A dollop of saliva dropped from its mouth to the floor.

Lee scrambled to her feet and picked up the Barat under one arm, double-checking the packaging. She considered her enchanted knife, but it wouldn't do her any good. Not when bullets didn't do anything against the beasts. She still had the paperweight, though. Lee reached for it as the chupacabra broke into a run towards her. She ran backwards a few steps, fumbling with the paperweight. It slipped from her grasp and rolled across the brick floor several feet away.

Lee fell into a crouch. There was nowhere to run, nowhere to hide, and her only weapon was too far to reach before the chupacabra got to her.

The creature yelped. Finn grappled with the thing, its jaws snapping inches from his face. He had his hands against its chest, ignoring the scratching and pawing of its forelegs.

Lee let go of the Barat and scrambled towards the paperweight. She reached it and activated the light, then held it up, walking towards the chupacabra.

It snarled and whined, but didn't look her way.

"Oy, doggy!" Lee yelled, waving her arms.

Finn grunted and dropped back. The chupacabra's spines turned red and it advanced on Finn.

"Hey!" Lee threw the paperweight. It still shone nearly as bright as the sun as it clattered to the ground near the beast. At the sound, the beast turned and its hollow eyes widened. Its body filled with white light and the smell of burning hair and flesh reached Lee's nostrils as the chupacabra disintegrated into a fine dust.

It reminded Lee far too much of what had happened to Bruce. Bile rose in her throat, but she pushed it down, breathing deep through her nose. She picked up the paperweight and deactivated it.

"Thanks," Finn said, accepting her hand as she helped him off the ground.

"I thought you were supposed to be saving me," Lee joked.

"That was the plan. Still is. This way." He jerked his thumb back over his shoulder and started jogging.

"Just a minute," Lee called. She jammed the paperweight

back into her fanny pack and went back for the bundle of cloth and stone. A part of the hasty knot of sleeves had fallen apart, revealing a section of stone. She carefully tied it back together, tightened it extra for good measure, and then she took off after Finn.

She breathed a huge sigh of relief when she saw the stairs leading to the upper floor of the Jewel Box, but halted at the bottom.

"What am I doing with this? I can't walk out of here holding it, dressed like...well, this," Lee looked at Finn.

"That's why Risa left us this," Finn held up the duffle bag, which he'd dragged from the corner of the landing. Lee couldn't help but stare at his stained hands. The deep indigo color glared vibrantly in the staircase lighting.

"Figured out what you got your hands in?"

"Nope. Haven't had a chance to try to wash it off. Hoping it's not toxic." He grimaced, then tossed the bag at her and turned around and covered his eyes. "Hurry and dress."

Lee set her precious package off to the side and shimmied out of her clothes as fast as she could. She tossed the beanie into the duffle and took out the slinky purple dress, then tugged it on. She couldn't get the zipper to go all the way up. Would it be that noticeable?

"Finn," she called, hating that she needed him for this. He turned, and she offered her bare back. "Zipper, please. And don't get any ideas."

"Wouldn't dream of it," he said, and a moment later his fingers fumbled for the tiny zipper pull, then dragged it upward. Lee's neck tingled as he lifted her hair out of the way, then he stepped back. "There. Done."

Lee shook her head, trying to get rid of the not-too-unpleasant sensation that crawled up her neck. "How's my hair?" she asked, attempting to fluff it with her fingers.

"Not worth worrying about. Get your shoes. We can put the Barat in the bag. Why is it wrapped in men's clothing? Is that…?"

"Bruce's? Yeah. And whatever you do, don't unwrap it. You'll get zapped just like that chupacabra back there." Lee jammed her feet into the heels and struggled with the strap for a moment before straightening. "Let's go."

Finn let her lead. She ran up the stairs and out the door at the top landing, glancing around in the hall before coming all the way out.

"If anyone asks, we were making out," she said to Finn in a hushed voice.

"If only," Finn said.

Lee smacked his arm.

"Gotta sell this," he said. "Lean into me and giggle."

"Giggle?" She raised her eyebrows.

"Like those drunk girls. You know." Finn raised his brows right back, and went from roguishly handsome to taking her breath away. Damn those green eyes and that blasted curly hair.

Finn held the duffle back slightly behind him, not totally out of sight, but hopefully out of notice, and leaned in, pecking Lee on the cheek. She nearly slapped him, but checked herself and smiled, then shoved him playfully. He shoved her back, and she laughed, then ran ahead through the door and out into the venue hall.

Everyone danced under the strobing lights. Lee's heart rate had mostly come down. She'd survived. More than that, she'd succeeded. They had the Barat. She just had to get it to the Ceteri and her crew would be set.

But what was that Bruce had said about other items?

Lee dodged two girls who danced into her path and glanced back to make sure Finn was with her. He smiled and caught up, grabbing her hand. Together, they left the party, music and lights leaking into the gardens outside.

She let out a huge sigh, and Finn laughed.

"Relieved?" he asked. They turned off the indicated path and cut through some bushes, headed for the trees on the far side of the property. There were police cars in the valet parking, siren lights going, and they were checking peoples' IDs. An officer glanced up and Lee and Finn dodged behind a statue and stayed there a moment, laughing breathlessly.

There were more sirens, Lee realized. More help on the way. Finn put a hand above her, leaning his weight on the statue. His eyes searched hers.

"Do you ever wish you didn't have to live this way?" he asked.

"What, stealing? All the time. I wouldn't have started, except Silas convinced me my abilities would make me good at it. And I was pretty desperate for something to eat at the time. He said, if I joined his crew, he'd make sure I always had a place."

Lee frowned. Silas had put this crew together. What would become of it with him gone? Then again, once she delivered the statue to the Ceteri, they would set her and the crew up for life. They wouldn't have to do any more heists, no more thieving, no more hiding. Everything they always wanted, given to them.

Then why did Lee feel so sad? She didn't want to think about it, but the thought had already tainted the perfect night. It swarmed around her head, mixing with the other thoughts about what her future - and the future of others in the crew - held.

Finn dropped his arm and peered around the statue. He slid an arm around her waist and cleared his throat. "Shall we, Mrs. Ribaldi?"

Lee bent and unstrapped her high heels, then stood. "Certainly, Mr. Ribaldi."

They escaped the park just as the cops brought out the flashlights and started searching the garden. Public transport took them quickly away, making them another anonymous couple in the throng.

Risa and Sam sat a few rows down from where they stood, to Lee's surprise. Risa winked at Lee, so smoothly Lee thought she might have imagined it.

Finn held the duffle bag towards Lee, and she started to reach for it, but shook her head. She'd be getting back to the hideout first. If anyone was waiting for them there, particularly Silas, she didn't want to have the statue on her. After today, Finn had absolutely earned her trust.

"You take it."

He nodded. "Thanks."

"For what? Making you the bigger target?" She sniffed, then took out her earpiece. The others subtly did the same, tucking them into their pockets.

He just smiled, holding the bag close as the bus pulled to a stop, then made his way down the aisle without glancing back. He could run, make a life for himself with an item like that. But Lee didn't think he would. For a thief, he was as dependable as they came.

Lee got off at the next stop, and she assumed Sam and Risa would get off soon after, each taking their own way to the factory hideout.

It stood, windows black. Lee hesitated, then glanced around, wondering where the others were. No one stood outside the factory, and there was no indication anyone had gone inside. Should she wait for them inside or outside?

The air was cool and still, but there was a flatness to it that made the hair on Lee's arms stand straight up. Her neck prickled, an unnamed fear rising in her.

"Risa?" Lee whispered, wondering if the woman had left one of her spectres watching the hideout. No one answered. Lee walked forward, her stilettos swinging in one hand while the other reached for the enchanted knife strapped to her thigh.

The basement door creaked open at the barest push. So, someone had been there. Whether it was one of her crew members or not remained to be seen. Lee breathed in, breathed out, and slid into the Liminal realm. A bright white light flashed in her mind and nearly sent her to her knees in pain. She stumbled against the doorframe, dropping her shoes, and looked to see what or who had blocked her from phasing. A flashlight flickered on, and a gleaming half-metal, half-flesh face was illuminated in the dark, cluttered room.

Silas.

Lee panted, brushing a strand of hair out of her mouth. "So, you came back?"

"Only to get a few things. I meant what I said, Lee. The others chose you. They also chose the consequences." His lip curled up in the semblance of a smile.

"We don't want you as an enemy, Silas," Lee said. Behind her, the scuff of a shoe shuffled across the pavement. *Please don't be Sam.* Sam didn't need to be here for this. Silas didn't seem to hear it.

He held out his human hand. "Give me the item you stole tonight."

Lee licked her lips, relief flooding through her that she'd trusted Finn with the statue. "I don't have it."

Silas's fingers curled shut. "That's too bad." He raised his mechanical arm and cocked the gun that had taken the place of his hand. "Guess I'll hang around for whoever does."

He fired, and at the same time, a shot fired from behind Lee. She ducked and instinctively phased into the Liminal realm, only to meet a blinding wall of pain again. She pushed against it, thrusting her way through, sensing that the familiar safe haven lay just on the other side of the strange block.

Heaving and panting, Lee crouched. She held her head with both hands, fingers tangled in her hair, and looked around. Silas stood holding his mechanical shoulder, frozen. She glanced behind. The figure was Finn, gun outstretched, a twisted, angry look on his face. He'd shot Silas without hesitating. So much for thinking he was in Silas's pocket this whole time.

Lee walked over to Silas and stood behind him. She touched her knife handle, then took a deep breath, plunging back out of the Liminal realm and whipping out her knife, pressing it against the human side of Silas's throat.

"Are you built with the bleedout prevention upgrades, Silas?" she snapped.

In response, he de-weaponized his arm, turning it into a hand once more.

"You don't want to do this," he said, swallowing. His pulse throbbed against Lee's knife blade.

"Give me one reason I shouldn't," Lee spat.

Silas didn't hesitate. "I've cared for you, I've given you a place to live, taught you everything you know. You owe me."

"I owe you nothing," Lee said.

"Shane wouldn't want this."

Silas was right. Shane hated killing. He'd avoided it as much as possible in every job. Would he want Lee to kill Silas now? After Silas's betrayals and the way he'd used her?

Lee moved her knife away and shoved Silas toward the basement door. "I never want to see you again."

Silas shot her a look, mechanical eye gleaming orange. "You'll regret this before too long. You have no idea of the extent of what I've been protecting you from." He took off at a sprint, moving so fast that his limbs blurred.

Finn ran up, gun trained on Silas until he disappeared around the nearest corner. Sam and Risa came out of their hiding place behind a nearby dumpster.

"That was Silas? What did he want?" Risa asked, eyebrows creased with worry.

Lee wiped sweat from her forehead. Her pulse still pounded from the exertion of moving through whatever had blocked her from the Liminal realm.

Sam looked at her, then squinted in the dark in the direction Silas had gone. "Is he coming back?"

Lee shook her head. "No, he's not. He's never coming back."

I hope.

"Let's get that thing inside."

The list of people who wanted her dead was growing.

EPILOGUE

Adam stepped away from the celebrating crew members to check in with Hatcher. He plugged one ear as the phone rang. What would he tell his boss? He had helped criminals steal a valuable magical item, and he hadn't once called for backup to help him bring Lee into the station. He hadn't even attempted to corner her or neutralize her.

Hatcher's voice came over the line, launching into a conversation before Adam could get a word in edgewise.

"Finley, about that Liminal. The program the Council planned to put her into folded today. Apparently, the man funding it went missing last night. They're scrambling for alternative means to contain her, but I thought I should let you know that it doesn't look good..." Director Hatcher's voice faded as a chill swept through Adam.

Did the disintegration and ultimate demise of Doctor Bruce Tanaka in the vaults beneath the Jewel Box have anything to do with the dissolution of that program? Had the government been part of the private enterprise breeding Liminals?

After meeting Jon Baldwin, the Medical Advisor on the Thaumaturgic Council, Adam believed it.

"Agent?" Hatcher said, voice sharp into the phone. "Did you hear me?"

"I'll report in the morning," Adam said quietly. He hung up and turned around, meeting Lee's eyes. She brimmed with excitement, her curled hair tousled around her bare shoulders, and she stood barefoot in that purple evening gown. She was stunning. And she deserved this moment of happiness after everything she'd been through.

She motioned Adam over to where the rest of the crew stood around the fabric-wrapped Barat statue, but Adam just shook his head, jamming his indigo-stained hands into his pockets, and walked away into the night.

The story continues in Shadowed Minds book 2: Thief of Aether.

ACKNOWLEDGMENTS

It takes a monumental effort to produce a novel, and this one was no different. I had help from so many places in order to write this book.

I'd like to thank my mentor, Rebecca Hamilton, for her incredible courses that have taught me new ways of looking at writing and marketing. Without your advice, I'd still be thinking my problem was my packaging, rather than my writing, and I wouldn't have improved either very much!

A HUGE thank you to all the people who watched my six kids while I wrote, edited, and marketed this book. Heather, Dana, and Brooke, you're the bomb. Thanks for being my village.

To my writing group: Rachel H., Rachel W., Amanda H., and Karma C., you know you keep me sane and humble at the same time. I look up to every one of you, and you're brilliant writers. I NEED YOUR BOOKS. So keep writing, yeah?

And you know I've got to mention my husband. Tyler, you're the stinkin' best even though I know you won't read this acknowledgement unless I show it to you. Thanks for never letting me quit.

Lastly, to the reader who took a chance and bought my book and decided to read the acknowledgements, I appreciate you more than you know! I wrote this story for you. I hope you liked it, and if you did, email or message me because it'll make my day knowing that someone else loves Lee and Adam and the whole gang.

ABOUT THE AUTHOR

Bree Moore lives in Utah with her amazing husband, six children, and two cats. When she's not busy homeschooling or folding laundry, she sneaks off to write more urban fantasy. Bree has a passion for pregnancy and childbirth, which influences her female-led stories. She loves shopping for groceries like other women like shopping for shoes, movies that make her cry, and Celtic music. She likes both her chocolate and her novels dark.

Get a FREE fantasy story when you sign up for her newsletter at www.authorbreemoore.com.
Just click on "GET A FREE BOOK."